WHAT is to decide our role in life after all but our desires, and the degree of fortitude we are willing to exert to gain them.

There's the rub. Endurance, if you like. You must be ready to grasp your chance when it comes round.

It might not come but once.

Also by Joan Smith:

AUNT SOPHIE'S DIAMONDS	50015	$1.75
BABE	50023	$1.75
ESCAPADE	23232	$1.50
LA COMTESSE	23490	$1.50

ENDURE MY HEART

Joan Smith

FAWCETT COVENTRY • NEW YORK

ENDURE MY HEART

Published by Fawcett Coventry Books, a unit of CBS Publications, the Consumer Publishing Division of CBS Inc.

ISBN: 0-449-50051-9

Printed in the United States of America

First Fawcett Coventry printing: June 1980

10   9   8   7   6   5   4   3   2   1

Chapter One

I picture you, Gentle Reader, as being somewhat like myself. My *old* self, that is. You are gentle born, or you would not be able to read well enough to tackle a book. (A fate worse than poverty!) Not so high in society that your taste has been perverted to saucy French novels, nor so frivolous that you favor the gothic nonsense of Mrs. Radcliffe, with her pseudo-haunted castles and Satanic characters. Let me issue you a warning before you turn the first page—I am no swooning heroine, equipped with acute sensibilities and a turn for passivity. But still I am a romantic, as you are, I think, looking for a touch of vicarious gratification for those yearnings that bedevil one as she goes about her chores. I know the feeling well, am kin to you at heart. I have experienced that unsatisfying life of the perpetual onlooker. No more! We were not born for so little. What is to decide our role in life after all but our desires, and the degree of fortitude we are willing to exert to gain them?

There's the rub—fortitude. Endurance, if you like, to give some point to my title. You must be ready to grasp your chance when it comes round. It might not come but once. What a sad thing it would be to miss out on all the excitement only because of lacking fortitude. If you learn one thing from my confessions, let it be that. Take your chance when it comes; recognize it, *grab* it. The rewards you gain will well merit the little inconveniences you will meet along the way. Well, to be fair, let us admit they are large inconveniences, huge, palpable, at times almost overwhelming, but never quite. He (I mean God) is up there, helping us. Absolutely the only embargo I would place on you is that you not break *His* laws. As to those other man-made ones—pooh! Break them if you must, and if you can—but only if you are sure you can get away with it, of course. "For a good cause, wrongdoing is virtuous" is a maxim from the old classic scholars, of whom my brother is a friend. I shall add a maxim from a friend of my own, Miss Sage. Thou shalt not get caught. Always bear it in mind. It would be a sad reflection on my philosophy if you should end up in Bridewell only because you wanted a fuller life, some romance, perhaps a husband. Certainly a husband, in fact. When all is said and done, I expect we would pass up the rest of the adventure fast enough if we could be assured of a good husband.

I nearly ended up in prison myself, for it was necessary for me to bend the man-made laws a little. It happened like this. When my father, who was a gambling magistrate, died, he left my brother Andrew and myself not only parentless, but virtually penniless as well. I say virtually because he had just been paid and had not yet gambled away his quarter salary. It was sufficient to see him decently buried with a nice headstone, a polished granite cross it was, with a pair of doves, to include Mama as well in the symbol. My mother is not even a memory to me, only a name. Andrew has some feeling she was like myself in appearance, but Papa never said so. The fine home in which we had lived all our lives was so heavily encumbered with mortgages that nothing remained after we had paid up the local bills and a rather large debt Papa owed to Squire Porson, my father's most favored gambling partner, but to sell Fern Bank. It was like parting with a piece of ourselves. I would as soon have cut off an arm or a leg, but the property was in Andrew's name, of course, and the wishes of a female were little heeded. He sold it too cheaply too, in my opinion. It was picked up at a great bargain by the Everetts, retired merchants from Kent, who had sold their shop and wished to get far enough from home that they might set up as gentle folks. The wife was the shrewdest haggler that ever set foot in a gentleman's house. Her busy fingers were poking holes in the window frames, pointing out wood rot and termites, her calculating eyes didn't miss a scratch or chip on a single piece of furniture, but missed the rather obvious fact that what was scratched was a Queen Anne bureau-bookcase, or a Kent commode. I had to hint we would be happy to remove this worthless lumber before she came down to any sort of acceptable terms at all.

All that remained to us after the deal was closed was a gig and a farm horse, Babe, to pull it. We took our clothing, and I a strand of pearls, Andrew my father's gold watch, a very fine Gruebet, from France. We also took (it was not stealing, for the library was catalogued omitting them) several tomes in Latin and Greek.

"Now, where are we to put all our worldly goods?" I asked Andrew the night before we had to leave. Andrew is my older brother, twenty-one he was at the time. He is tall, dark-complexioned, shortsighted and bookish. I am short, blond, eagle-eyed and not at all bookish, though I dote on a novel. I am eighteen. It is said locally that I am pretty. My mirror tells me the same, which is a great blessing in a potential heroine.

"Have to take rooms," he answered. Andrew would not much care if he lived in a rabbit warren, so long as he had a good light to read by. He had his nose in Vergil as he spoke. This at the turning point of our lives! But then he was very immature, despite his years at university.

"Rooms! Are Magistrate Anderson's children to take up rented rooms like Miss Plum?" I haven't a thing against Miss Plum but that she is uncommonly common, poor soul. She is called genteel, but a spinster living in a hired room on twenty-five pounds a year is only genteel in deference to her more favored relations, the Blythes, who could well afford to take her in if they would, but they won't.

"Mmmm," Andrew answered, not listening and not caring.

"Andrew, *listen to me!* I refuse to live in furnished rooms next to Miss Plum in a boardinghouse. I shall go out and work first." In fact, I was beginning to think I must go out and work in any case. Andrew was my natural provider, but it was becoming increasingly clear he was not ready even to provide me a partner in conversation.

"Oh, as to that, Mab, Squire Porson is coming to call," he mumbled.

Let me tell you a little about this gentleman. Gentleman—bah! A misnomer if ever there was one. He possesses a gentlemanly income (five thousand a year, they say hereabouts), and the instincts of a weasel. He is what folks call a squarson, to indicate he is a squire so clutch-fisted and so little interested in religion that he acts as his own parson instead of giving the living to a real minister. His double role does not by any means indicate a regard for the church, though he took holy orders in his youth. It was an effort on his late father's part to try to reclaim him. An unsuccessful effort. He is a libertine. When he gambled with my father, he was comparatively well employed. His more usual occupation was ruining the local wenches. Every second parish child you meet on the street has his nose (long and mis-shapen) and his hair (copper red if it were clean, usually mud red in the youthful version).

"I shan't let him in," I told Vergil, who was keeping me from telling Andrew.

"Mmmm."

"You know what he'll have in mind. He'll want me to be his housekeeper or accountant, which is French for mistress." The squarson had been casting lecherous eyes on me since I put up my hair and let down my skirts. Even for a few months before the skirts came down he had been admiring my ankles.

"No such a thing," Andrew muttered.

"Don't be an ass, Andrew. We are not going to live at Holy Hell." Porson's place is called Holly Hill, but is more widely known in the village as Holy Hell, due to his churchly position and his vile nature.

"Must," he said. "Mean to say, wants you to marry him."

Now you may think that if I followed my own advice, I would snatch at this chance for a wealthy husband. Not so. Naturally we must use a *little* discrimination in our adventures. A red-nosed libertine of fifty years was not what I had in mind. "I would as lief marry the chimney sweep. Liefer." Our chimney sweep in Salford is Toby Kiley, who is a knock-in-the-cradle. He was dropped on his head by his mother the day he was born, they say, but actually the whole family is a little retarded, including the mother, who has distressed the village with thirteen of these moonlings or near moonlings. Five of them have red hair, but never mind. They got their brains from their mama, who had not an iota to spare.

I chattered on to myself angrily for a quarter of an hour, at which time Squire Porson was admitted. Looking at Andrew, he jerked his head toward the door. Without so much as saying good evening to either of us, if you please! Andrew, like a demmed puppy, walked out the door, his nose in his book.

I was ready to spit fire before our caller opened his mouth. "I've come to tell ye I mean to make ye my missus," he said, in an uncouth, provincial accent, smiling genially.

I was expected to go down on my knees and thank him for this insolence. "I am not at all interested, thank you," I said.

"Eh, the word was missus, not mistress, lass," he returned, laughing.

8

"I heard you, sir. I am no more interested in the one role than the other."

"With the gold ring and ceremony and all," he went on, as though I were one of his simpleminded by-blows, who could not understand the King's English.

"I am still not interested."

"A diamond ring then, miss," he said, regarding me through narrowed eyes to be sure I was worth the price, as he upped the ante.

"You may take your diamond ring and stick it through your nose, Squire. I wouldn't marry you if I had to live on a bone."

The bold beast laughed merrily and hauled me into his arms, after chasing me around the settee twice, and catching hold of me before I could get safely out the door. He kissed me, with his brandy-soaked lips, and his unshaven face prickling me. He was strong as a bull. I fought to get out of his arms, till I was thoroughly exhausted and no closer to being free than I was at the beginning. Finally I wrenched my head aside and screamed as if my life depended on it. A few of our servants had been kept on by the Everetts and were still on the premises. It was the butler, Hackley, who came galloping to my rescue. Lord only knows where Andrew was in my hour of need. Frolicking in his mind over the ruins of Pompeii, I daresay.

Hackley is built like St. Paul's Cathedral, with enormous shoulders and a rounded head not unlike Wren's dome. He made short shrift of the squarson. He picked him up bodily—and Porson is a large man too—but Hackley got one hand on his collar and another on the seat of his trousers and tossed him bodily out the front door. I followed behind and threw his hat and cane out after him. Then Hackley dusted off his hands and said in a perfectly unperturbed voice, "Tea, Miss Mabel?"

"Thank you, Hackley. Tea in the saloon, if you please," I replied, and kissed him on the cheek. He blushed like a Bath miss, but bowed very formally before going to fetch my tea.

Andrew never did remember to come and take his tea that evening. I had it alone, which provided as good company as if he had been there. There was a certain sense of satisfaction accompanying having delivered Porson to his just desserts, but it solved nothing. My brother and I were still twelve hours from being on the streets, with nowhere to put our

9

books and necklace and watch. I settled down, with my chin in my hands, to read the flames in the grate for some clue to our salvation. Andrew was educated and intelligent, not without some hope of gainful employment in the near future. A tutor's job, for instance, he could fill well enough. But what was to become of me? No employer of a tutor expected said tutor to be accompanied by his sister. There was a dame school in the village where I might make myself useful. Old Dame Aldridge ran it, and she was getting on in years. She had a largish house, lived alone but for a couple of servants. Something might be worked out there.

You will think it remiss of us to have waited so long to solve our housing problem. As things worked out, we had very little time. Our father's death came on very suddenly. Between the funeral calls and arrangements and winding up the estate to find ourselves destitute, we were in no position to be thinking of the future. The very day after we learned we must sell Fern Bank, the real estate agent was at our door with a purchaser. Any persons of *decent* feeling, which the Everetts unfortunately lacked, would have given us a month or two to get settled elsewhere. Nothing would do that witch of a woman but she must have occupancy immediately. I have wondered since whether they were not being run out of whatever town they came from for some crooked dealings. I certainly think they pulled the wool over *our* eyes, rushing us as they did, and both Andrew and myself young and untrained in business matters. I had made some tentative inquiries around the village without turning up a thing. In the back of my mind there rested the thought that an appeal to Porson would give us a lease on the minister's house at a nominal cost, as he had so much of my father's money stashed away. He did not live in the house, of course. My somewhat abrupt treatment of him now made that course impossible. We had an aunt, Mama's sister, living in Devonshire, but such a tediously long distance away that I disliked to go to her. We hardly knew her either, except for letters.

I did not want to leave the neighborhood at all. I had never known any home but Fern Bank, any village but that of Salford, four miles away. I like everything about the Salford area amazingly. It is on the east coast of England. There where Felixstone sticks like a toe into the ocean you will find it on the map, halfway up the arch of the foot, nestled among the cliffs and dunes. The sky of Salford, as with the rest of East Anglia, is a beautiful pearl blue shade seen nowhere else. At least it was not so at London when I was there, choking on the smoke fumes, nor did I see such skies during my one trip to Devonshire. I like the fenland fields,. which foreigners will call marshes still, though they have been drained and cultivated since the seventeenth century. (A foreigner, in these parts, need hail from no farther afield than the next county.) The countryside is not at all flat as you may think. We have beautiful hills and valleys, caught on canvas by some of the best painters of this century. But most of all we have the sea. No one who was reared up here on the coast could be completely happy elsewhere, I am convinced. The regular old East Anglians have an independent spirit surviving still from the days when we were cut off from our neighbors by the marshes. This independent spirit caused me to stick at writing to Mama's sister, Mrs. Harvey, begging for charity.

In the morning, Andrew and I loaded up the gig with our few belongings and went into Salford. We stopped at Miss Aldridge's place, where I dropped a few loud hints as to my dread at taking up lodgings at the boardinghouse with Miss Plum. "You must not think of it, my dear!" she exclaimed at once. "Tell Squire Porson of your plight. He will let you have the rectory. I made sure it was settled long since. Why, I never thought anything else for a moment. Young Andrew can help him out with the church business, and you will keep house for your brother. Your papa was one of the overseers of the poor; the post must go to Andrew surely."

"Sir Elwood Ganner will have something to say to that," I answered. I have little experience in political or business matters. I don't know how it may be elsewhere, but I expect it is not much different from Salford. Here, Sir Elwood Ganner, KBE, runs the town. If you want to get a job or permit for anything, if you want to hire a parish child for a servant or apprentice, if you want a road opened or closed, if you want any improvement made in the town, or in your taxes, you speak to Sir Elwood. He is the parish officer, and a number of other things as well, including the husband of Lady Ann Burack, whose late papa was a gentleman of great importance. This last is more than a coincidence, I expect.

"A new overseer must be chosen. Certainly he will pick Andrew. Go to see him at once. Meanwhile, you must speak to the squarson."

I explained in vague terms that this was impossible. So vague was my explanation that she misunderstood it entirely, and leapt to the conclusion I feared only his advances if harbored under a roof belonging to him.

"He is a shocking flirt to be sure, but would never make improper advances to Magistrate Anderson's daughter."

"To be expected to marry him is worse," I replied.

"Unthinkable!" she laughed. "He is ancient enough to be your papa, child. What a ninny he would look, making up to a slip of a girl. A rare laughingstock; he is much too proud to risk it. Stay right where you are, and I'll send a note off to Holly Hill this minute telling him what you are about. You'll be in the rectory before nuncheon. See if you ain't."

I opened my mouth to object, but thought better of it. He had got the lion's share of my father's considerable income out of him over the past decades. It was no more than just that he pay the small interest of letting us have the use of an empty house. If it could be done, I wouldn't say a word against it. I doubted he would announce to the village he had been turned off by me. Refusing to let us have the house would make him look as mean as he is, which would not please him, for he makes some attempt at a good reputation.

Miss Aldridge was slightly out in her reckoning. We were not into the house till three. We took luncheon with her, and while we we were at table, Porson arrived. I did not go into the parlor to meet him, but let Andrew do it. Within a quarter of an hour, he was gone, and Andrew told us with a great deal of disinterest that he had been appointed church warden, and was to help the squire write up his sermons, keep up the parish register, and perform other such functions. The house, sans any servants or salary, was to be ours.

It seemed a small, mean and crabbed little cottage after the grace and spaciousness of Fern Bank. But then next to the boardinghouse, it was a mansion. In actual fact it was a decent whitewashed house two stories high, with eight habitable rooms. There was a parlor done in oak paneling, rather like my little sewing room at home. But comparisons are pointless. It was a roof over our heads—that was the important thing. The church sits at the east edge of town, the rectory about two dozen steps away from it, toward Salford. On the other side of the church stands the bell tower. The bells have not been played within my memory, but Miss Aldridge thought a few of the old men might still know the method. The church itself was not pretty. Interesting architecturally is the strongest praise over heard in its honor. It is rather low and dark, dating from a very early age. The

12

nave, folks say, is from the fourteenth century, the huge baptismal font at the front fifteenth, the pulpit (dark, oaken and very high), late sixteenth. A hundred or so years later the horsebox pews (the cause for the high pulpit) had been replaced by more modern boxes. There was a strange set of carved stairs at the back of the church that went halfway up to the ceiling, then stopped, leading nowhere at all. Andrew thought they were rood stairs, leading in days gone by to the rood loft, demolished by Edward VI. The most modern item in the church is a sumptuous organ in the gallery, which has not been there but three years. It is a gift from Lord Aiken, an earl who has a summer home nearby. They do say he collected it in payment of a gambling debt and had nowhere else to put it. Inasmuch as there is not a single person in the parish who can play it, and as a gift it was particularly inappropriate, one is inclined to believe this story.

Andrew amused himself with this expensive toy while I set to the chore of bringing our house to order. It had stood vacant for more than ten years, which will give you some idea of the gargantuan task before me. My hands, white as a lily, became red and roughened from the strong soaps required to clean the place up. When Dame Aldridge noticed this, she sent me over a couple of girls to help. I scrimped on household finances to buy a few bits of bright curtain material, while I regretted we had not had the foresight to bring some of our own furnishings from Fern Bank to make us look respectable.

We settled into our new home, becoming familiar with all its nooks and crannies, its drafty windows and creaking doors. We discovered there was an old crypt beneath the church, a thing I had never known before. While investigating the grounds behind for the possibility of growing a vegetable garden, I espied an old slanted door. Curious to see where it led, I tried all the keys till I found the one that fit it. Later I also discovered a door to it from the vestry, hidden under the parish chest.

We had taken the giant step of getting a roof over our heads, but there was very little money to live on, only the pittance paid to Andrew as overseer of the poor. It was my turn to pitch in and raise a wage. There was an old piano in the place. I gave lessons to some of the local girls, but it provided only a mite. Many's the night we went with only bread and cheese for dinner, too proud to beg and too accustomed to better fare to be satisfied. Folks visited us, trying

13

to be sociable, but giving them even tea and cake was a strain on our budget. It got so that I dreaded to hear the door knocker sound. Five times out of ten it would be Mrs. Everett too, complaining about some new fault she had unearthed at Fern Bank, and never offering us a basket of vegetables or fruit or a thing, though she knew very well we were needy.

I asked her quite pointedly on one visit what she was doing with all the fruit from the succession houses. "When my father was alive, we used to distribute many baskets to the poor," I told her.

"Succession houses? I don't know how your poor father ever contrived to grow a thing. Jerome says they will have to be rebuilt before they can be used. He has an architect coming in to see what can be done with them. We have let those puny orange trees and pineapples wilt away and will set up a proper orangery one of these days."

As summer turned to fall, I began taking in a little embroidery, claiming I did it for amusement. It paid for fuel, but still it was clearly not enough to live on. I needed a regular job.

The squire never came next or nigh us. On Friday Andrew took the gig up to Holy Hell to deliver the squire sermons he could scarcely pronounce, and on Sunday they both remained after church juggling the books and discussing church business—i.e., Andrew told him what parishioners stood in want of christening, marrying or burying.

I said "How do you do?" in arctic accent when I met him in the town. He lifted his hat and nodded, without smiling. His pride had been dealt a blow, and I had some misgivings the situation between us would not remain forever so peaceful. In short, he was plotting a revenge, but what form it might take was impossible to tell.

Chapter Two

When my aunt, Mrs. Harvey, finally perceived an inkling of
our circumstances, she was at pains to help us. We declined
an offer to go to her, only to receive within a month another
offer too interesting to disregard. There was a parish living
opening in her neighborhood paying three hundred per an-
num, along with a very nice cottage and a kitchen garden.
She would finance the matter of Andrew's taking holy orders.
It would be madness not to take it. My brother went to inform
Porson of our plans, and came home with a new notion. The
squarson had offered him substantially the same deal. Andrew would take holy orders and take over this parish, where
he was already doing more of the church work than Porson.
I wondered whether I was instrumental in this plan to keep
us here. I was being leered at again in a certain way, which
made me suspect he wanted Andrew out of the rectory so that
I would be alone and undefended. If that was his scheme, he
was thwarted. My ex-governess, Miss Edna Halka, was re-
siding in the boardinghouse inhabited by Miss Plum and
others. She was between positions, and agreed to accompany
me till Andrew returned.

Miss Halka had not been happy at the boardinghouse. She
told me tales of bad food and unaired beds that made me
thank heaven I had avoided it. I soon formed the intention
that Miss Halka would become a permanent part of our
household. That is odd too, for we had not been bosom bows
or anything of the sort when she was my governess. She had
used to nag and pinch at me; she no longer did so. I discovered
that she made a better friend than she had a teacher. I daresay it was our reversal of roles that made us both more comfortable. She was not born to boss, nor I to take orders. Edna—
she asked me to call her Edna—was not physically attractive.
Tall and thin, with brown hair turning to gray at the temples,

15

though she was not much above forty. She seemed eager to get into old age.

Miss Aldridge often came to call. As the fall school term rolled around, she offered me a post at her dame school. She was beset with aches in her joints, and would welcome the luxury of being able to stay at home on a wet or windy day. The rowdier boys had taken advantage of her creeping infirmity to get quite out of hand. There is no point being polite to wretches who bring a badger into the classroom to frighten you, or who keep frogs and mice in their pockets. I instituted a rigorous regime of keeping them in after school when they pulled these stunts on me. It was my being still there at four-thirty one afternoon that first introduced me to my life of crime. I had just released Tommie Jenkins and Bill Marson (the worst of a bad lot) and was locking up the doors. This was in late autumn. They were not much needed at home or I would not have kept them in.

Glancing out the window to gauge how long I had to get home before the rain came down, for of course we get a great deal of rain on the coast, I chanced to see two young fellows fleeing down the road at a great rate, peering over their shoulders in fright. I tapped at the window to get their attention, and noticed it was the Hessler brothers, which told me the pursuer would be the revenue officer, Crites. He is no favorite in our community, Crites. The boys (they were about sixteen and fifteen) saw me and fled to the school. You would need a heart of forged steel not to like the Hesslers, despite their many pranks. They are about the most common sight in the district, their black heads bouncing along the road together, always with a smile for everyone, while their dog—a beautiful collie named Lady—tags at their heels, sniffing at whatever bit of meat or fish they have poached and have slung over their backs in a bag. No, it is not quite fair to use the word "poached," though I haven't a doubt they are into that business as well as their legitimate ones. Jemmie, the elder though he is the smaller, is our local higgler. He is often to be seen in his little red cart pulled by a mule, traveling around to all the farms peddling such urban wares as lace, ribbon, pots and brooms in exchange for any little oversupply of vegetable or fowl that the farmers do not consider worth a trip to market. This is a meager job to provide for a widowed mother and three sisters. It is eked out by the trades of mole catcher, fisherman, warrener, fabricator of snares, traps, fishing rods and flies—anything to turn an honest penny. Young Mark is the junior partner in all these enterprises. I expect he is also Jemmie's partner in the smuggling trade. Their being chased by Crites certainly looked like it. I had some suspicion Jemmie was involved, but was a little surprised to see Mark, not a day over fifteen, had so early entered the profession.

I opened the door and let them in, before Crites should round the bend and see where they had gone. "He's a-coming, miss. Will you hide us?" Jemmie asked.

Indeed he was coming, cantering along on his old gray mare. I waved at him and called, "What's amiss, officer? Are you after smugglers?" with a wink over my shoulder at the lads.

"Two of them, Miss Anderson. Have you seen a sign of them?" he hollered back.

"Two rough-looking fellows just passed by the window a minute ago. They were headed toward the sheepwalk. If you hasten, you'll catch them."

"Thankee kindly," he said, with a tip of his hat, and turned his mount in behind the school to the path where the sheep are taken to the hills, which our foolish geography book describes as the East Anglia Heights, though they are no more than gentle slopes. He would think he had turned the wrong way once he hit the sheepwalk and didn't find them. The sheepwalk is a meandering path that runs more or less parallel to the main road by the sea, half a mile or so behind it.

I closed the door and turned to my two petty criminals. "Well now, Jemmie and Mark, I hope you're proud of yourselves," I said severely. "I'm sure your mother would be mightily pleased to hear you were being chased by Crites."

Mark pulled his forelock and blushed, but Jemmie smiled in a cagey way. "It's yourself we're proud of, miss. I didn't know the gentlemen had a friend in Miss Anderson." The word "gentleman" has no connotation of refinement here on the coast. It is a euphemism for smuggler, lest you are unaware of the term. It was natural they think the magistrate's daughter harbor no love for them, but to tell the truth, Papa liked his nip of brandy as well as anyone, and was never harsh with them when they came before him. There was never a day when there was not a barrel of the best in our cellar at Fern Bank. And half a dozen barrels still there to scandalize Mrs. Everett! I wondered she had not been to chide me for it.

"Only a friend in need, boys. I don't approve of your shenanigans," I scolded, in my best schoolteacher's voice.

"Aye, but a friend in need is a friend indeed, miss, as the old saying goes," Jemmie replied. "We'll not be forgetting your kindness. He nearly caught us hauling a barrel out of the ditch. We had to let him chase us, or he'd have got to routing around and found it."

"You'd best slip away fast before Crites is back," I told them. They scampered out the door, back down the road to retrieve the barrel, while Crites plodded along the sheepwalk. I thought very little about it. Smuggling is a crime according to the laws of the land, of course, but here at Salford it is the largest employer, and has gained a certain respectability, as any well-paying employer will do. Work was scarce, and if a husband was to have bread and meat on his table to feed the family, he resorted to smuggling.

Little real harm was done by it, in my eyes at least. People were taxed to death, and what was done with the money but pay off the debts of that expensive raft of royal dukes and their mistresses? We were generous in the extreme with our war heroes too. Wellington set up for life, but what of his "scum of the earth" soldiers, as he was kind enough to describe the men who saved England from Napoleon's heel. They came home, mutilated, to grub for a bare existence, if they came home at all. No, no, there is no question in my view. Smuggling is an honorable profession. Call me an anarchist if you like, but I maintain I am a *Christian* anarchist, and would rather be that than a heathen royalist.

I always had a sneaking admiration for the gentlemen. Andrew and I used to play at it when we were children. Hidden in the middle of our spinney at Fern Bank there is a tumbledown shack called the poachers' shack. No doubt it was well named, but in our games, it was where the gentlemen (me) hid the brandy, and the revenue officer (Andrew) got his comeuppance. I enjoyed the game, and can well imagine the real thing must be thrilling. What a break in the dull life of a laborer, to slip over to France on a moonless night, or hide in readiness at home to receive the countraband. Had I been a man, I would certainly have joined them. But I was only a woman, so I winked at their activities and lent a hand when I could.

Then too, Officer Crites was not at all popular. The man he replaced, Officer Daggar, had been much better liked, due to his willingness to take a bribe upon occasion. Crites was a martinet. He'd have turned in his own mother. In fact, he did turn in his fiancée's brother, which lost him a fiancée and made him a host of enemies.

My infraction of the law did not trouble my conscience unduly, though of course I knew abetting the gentlemen was a crime. I would have forgotten it by the next day if it had not been for the reward my new friends chose to bestow on me. Next morning as I went out to school, there was a shiny golden guinea sitting on the doorstep. We had had no callers the night before. No one but myself had been through that door since late yesterday afternoon. It was a payment for services rendered. Helping them caused not a twinge, but taking money for it did. I determined to purchase new books for the school with it, and did so.

Two weeks passed, bringing us to the cold, rainy, windy, disagreeable month of November. As it was a Friday and I looked forward to getting an early start on my weekend, I kept no one in that night. The animal sessions at school were well under control. Miss Aldridge had a wicked cold, and I had taken the school alone that whole week, which made the weekend loom with more pleasure even than usual, since I did not exactly like teaching for a living. There was a timid tap at the door as I put on my pelisse. I went to answer it, thinking some student had forgotten his lunch basket or books.

There stood Jemmie Hessler with his cap in his hands and a very worried frown on his youthful face. Lady sniffed and yelped at a brown bag that was slung over his shoulder. "G'day, miss," he said, shuffling his feet. I peered down the road, but he was not followed. "Could I come in for a minute?" he asked.

We went in and sat at two little desks that buckled both of our knees, making me realize the taller of my students must spend acutely uncomfortable hours here, for I was not tall myself, and Jemmie was a small, compact, wiry fellow about my own height. "What is it, Jem?" I urged him on, curious but still eager to be home.

"It's the stuff, miss," he said. "Crites has tumbled to it we're keeping it at the warehouse behind the lumber, and there's a load in tonight. We've nought to do with it till it goes out Sunday night. We've got a tranter coming to carry it south Sunday night, but there's two days for Crites to sniff around and find it."

"How about the stable loft at the inn?" I asked. During

19

Daggar's entire reign the stable loft at the inn had been used. It had been no secret you could go there any hour of the day or night with your bottle and buy any amount you wanted.

"That's the second place he'll look."

"Are there no haystacks or potato graves you can use?"

"He's on to all the old regular stunts, miss, the fuelhouses and chimmers, ricks and rainwater butts. We don't want to divide the load up, for the tranter won't make a dozen stops nowadays, with Crites prowling like a ghost."

I looked at him, bewildered. "But what is it you want *me* to do, Jem?"

He swallowed twice and blurted it out. "We was wondering if you'd let us keep it here."

I stared as though he were an apparition from Hades. "Here, at the *school* you mean? No, no, I couldn't consider it. It is too dangerous."

"It's not dangerous at all. It's the last place in the world he'd look."

"Oh, but if he *should* look!"

"With the cold winter coming on, and warm clothes to be bought and all, it seems a pity..." He said no more, but looked at me with the eyes of a starving puppy. Lady, sitting at his feet, cast a similar glance at me, gently accusing.

"It smells. The children would notice it at once on Monday morning," I said brusquely. But I thought of my schoolchildren, walking home in their threadbare garments, with that winter wind getting colder by the day.

"The smell's no stranger to most of 'em. They'd never notice it."

"No, I don't like this. Let me think." I suggested a couple of other spots, all of which were vetoed for one reason or another. "If I were ever caught, I'd lose my job."

"You'll not get caught, miss," he promised cockily.

"I have the only key, except Miss Aldridge's. If you are seen with it, it will be known where you got it."

"Nay, miss. It'll only be known you dropped your key, and the wicked gentlemen picked it up and used it. We'd never be incriminating you, and you've the word of the gentlemen on that."

"No," I said, making up my mind hastily. "I'll not give you the key, but I sometimes forget to close the back window in the teacher's pantry. And mind you leave it open as well to get rid of the stench by Monday morning."

He grabbed my hand, then released it hastily with a beet-like blush, while Lady barked her approval. "You're a right one, miss," he said, beaming broadly.

"I am a fool," I replied. "And will be a very cold fool Monday morning with the window open all night. Never mind, go on with you. I'll open the window before I leave. Can I give you a ride home, Jem? No—we'd better not be seen together," I decided. Already my mind was turning devious on me.

"You're awake on all suits, miss. We'll be frowning daggers at each other anytime we meet, but we thank ye kindly."

He went off home on foot, and I let him get well away before I left the school myself. Being an accessory before the fact was a larger, more serious crime than merely letting on I had not seen the boys, and it bothered my conscience more. All weekend I worried about it. Worried whether they would get caught, whether they would remember to leave the window open to kill the smell, wondered whether I could trust them. But their word was as good as a bond, and on that score I was fairly easy. It was a weighty business for me.

It was weightily recompensed. On Monday morning I went early to my school to air it out if the gentlemen had neglected to do so. They had not neglected. There was no smell but the cheery, warm odor of hickory logs burning in the stove. They had been here before me, closed the windows and lit my fire for me. When I went to my desk to take out my attendance ledger, five golden guineas were placed neatly beneath it. I felt criminal indeed as I scooped them up and put them in the bottom of my reticule, carefully knotted into a handkerchief.

Never did money burn such a hole in anyone's pocket as those five guineas burned my reticule. What was I to do with them? One guinea can be spent up and the traces covered, but to buy five guineas' worth of new supplies for the school would be remarked upon. I put them in the bottom drawer of my bureau, hidden beneath my petticoats, and said nothing.

Andrew returned after having taken holy orders, a full-fledged minister now, but alas no more interested in the world than he had been when he left. I hesitated to intimate to him my wish that Edna remain with us, for while he scarcely notices the time of day, he does notice a strange body in the room, and dislikes it. He is one of those unsociable persons who is never so happy as when guests leave, and he can stop feeling guilty at not having paid the least attention to them while they were there. It turned out I had forgotten something that had apparently been on my brother's mind since the moment he left. It was the organ, sitting new, shiny and unplayed in the gallery of the church.

"Well, as you have Miss Halka to bear you company, Mab, I think I shall just run up to the loft and see how the organ is liking the nasty cold weather."

I don't know how the organ liked it, but it did not deter Andrew from spending his every spare second in the loft. Eerie squeals and squeaks resounded from the walls of the church, sounding at times like an infant howling, at other times like caterwauling. Another time the tones were lower, like a foghorn or an angry boar. Then he decided he needed lessons, and for three consecutive evenings he sat beside me at the piano in our living room, learning the most basic rudiments of reading music. The nature of his organ work changed after that, the trick now being for Edna and myself to try to figure out what "tune" he was playing. But it was all well worthwhile, for it was a perfect excuse for Edna to go on living with us. Andrew suggested it himself, after a couple of hints.

Two weeks later, Millie Hessler, a sweet little six-year-old sister of Jemmie and Mark, toddled up to me before leaving school. Dame Aldridge was back, so that there was little privacy. "Jemmie says to tell you it's going to be a hot night, and you should leave the window open," she said, with a smile of pure innocence that sent a shiver down my spine. They needed the school again!

"What's that you say, Millie?" Dame Aldridge asked, coming up behind us.

Before the child should utter her senseless-sounding message again, I patted her head and said, "Very well, dear. I understand."

"He said to be sure you don't forget," she added, then mercifully walked away.

"What's all this about?" my employer asked.

"Mrs. Hessler wants me to stop off on the way home. Mark wants to study more arithmetic on his own, and I offered to give him a book."

"Hmph," she said. "He'll be wanting to figure out how much profit he's made on his smuggling, the bounder. We should encourage the ex-students, to be sure, but you don't want to have much to do with that lot, Mabel. They are not our sort."

Miss Aldridge had her own gig. I remained behind a little in case she should take the idea of going to the Hesslers' with me. I required privacy with Jem. He was at home, and looked astonished to see me. "You shouldn't have come, miss!" he exclaimed.

"Jemmie, this won't do. Dame Aldridge is back at school now. If she notices the fire on Monday morning and sees the money..."

"We'll slip back at six Monday morning and close the window, and not light the fire. The place will be aired out by then, and as to the money, you can take it now."

"No, I don't want any money."

"Don't be daft, miss. Why should you not? Lord Aiken takes his share."

I could not have been more surprised had he said Lord Liverpool, the Prime Minister. Lord Aiken was an earl, an extremely wealthy and influential gentleman who associated with ministers and bishops. "Very well, I will," I said, and was handed my golden guineas.

I suppose rationalization is the proper word for the thinking I did on my way home. Talking myself into doing what was not right. But where was the harm in it? Do unto others as you would have them do unto you—that was the golden rule, and I could not see that I was bending it. Still, I decided to talk it over with Andrew, who is an incurably honest man. It would be done by indirection, of course, not revealing why I had developed this sudden and unlikely interest in theology.

"Andrew, what do you think of the gentlemen?" I asked over dinner, as we gnawed our way through a leg of rubber beef. With Andrew and myself both working, we had lost our heads and hired a woman to cook and clean, and she was no great shakes with a bar of soap, but she needed the job.

"Society has become badly depraved," he told me.

"I meant the smugglers, Andrew."

"Ah, *those* gentlemen. Why, they are criminals." My heart sank. I too was a criminal then.

"Yes, the foolish laws have made criminals of honest men," he rambled on, giving me a rush of hope.

"It is a foolish law, is it not?" I urged him on.

"It is a criminal law, if I may be permitted to indulge in a paradoxical statement." I permitted him to indulge in as many as he wanted, if I understood his meaning. We discussed the matter with enthusiasm all through the elastic beef and concrete sponge cake our cook had served up. Andrew will occasionally unbend to orate on an abstraction, but when I tried to take him a buttonhole lower to actual cases, he began turning his views around to conclude, "Of course, everyone ought to obey the laws of the land, or we would have chaos."

"Even the *bad* laws?" I asked.

"Laws are not generally bad. They are made to protect society."

"Yes, but suppose, for instance, the law decreed that one man should kill another..."

"It does so decree. We execute criminals, yet the commandment states Thou shalt not kill. There are extenuating circumstances, however. When a man puts himself beyond the law, then he must be punished."

"Oh, but surely God's law must come first."

"God's law is sometimes contradictory. An eye for an eye, and a tooth for a tooth. Then surely by extrapolation, a life for a life."

"Men are executed for no less than stealing a little something. That is not an eye for an eye, but a life for a loaf."

Andrew considered this, while I considered that I had got badly off the point. I returned to it. I wanted his approbation. He was older, better educated and to be perfectly frank, more upright than myself. Round and round we went, but the best I could get out of him was that in certain undesignated circumstances, a man might be right to break a law. I dared not make the circumstances in which I was interested too explicit, so I had to be satisfied with this sort of possible exculpation.

Andrew never took port. The minute dinner was over, he disappeared out the side door, which meant he was flying to the rafters again to wrestle with the organ. Had he not gone there, he would have immersed himself in Latin in his study. The trouble was, Andrew did not really live in the world to any significant extent. With him it was all abstraction and hypothesis. The physical facts, ignored by him, were that poor people were trying to make a living in a way that hurt no one so far as I could see, so I took counsel with my own soul, and permitted myself to break the bad law.

Chapter Three

I quite simply adored being a smuggler. It lent a spice to that long, dull, hard winter that had been sorely lacking before. A young lady ought to have been finding her excitement in suitors; I had none. You'd be surprised how quickly your wealthy friends drop you once it is learned you are poor. Any mother with an eligible son was at pains to direct his attention elsewhere. Much I cared! There was not a really handsome or dashing gentleman on the whole coast, or that part of the coast which I frequented in any case. I began to think in terms of spending a summer perhaps with my aunt, to see what sort of male specimens they grow in Devonshire. Already by April I had saved eighty guineas for the trip, for it was a busy winter. Winter is the prime time for smuggling. A little of it goes on year round, and moon round too here at Salford, but winter with a new moon is the ideal time. "The dark" the gentlemen call that short period of the lunar month when the moon is no more than a sliver in the sky. The nights are long, and the weather nippy enough that the revenueman is likely to stop in at the tavern to warm his toes, while our good friend the tapster pours him a tipple on the house, to slow him down.

I learned all the little tricks of the trade. Knew to the last wrinkle the families that would tolerate having a couple of kegs concealed in their applelofts, ricks and stables. Took a keener interest in every hollow tree along my route, the culverts, faggot ricks, hedgerows and rainwater butts. To prevent being caught, a cesspool might be used, but the stuff was not recoverable after that step. Jem suggested I buy a share in a load, to increase my profit. The gentlemen were each entitled to do this—take a barrel home and decant it for small local trade, but of course in my position it was impossible. The bulk of the load went straight to London on the wagons of Will Phillips, the tranter. Will has six wagons and does all the hauling for the area. He moves households, grain, fish, farm produce or just about anything that is too large to go on the coach. The gentlemen kept three of his wagons fairly busy. He would usuaally put a layer of something else on top of the barrels for the purpose of concealment.

I was only a silent partner in the business, my secret known to none but Jemmie and his family. Jemmie, though he was as sharp as a needle, was only a boy, and certainly not the chief of the operation. Naturally I wondered who the boss could be. I asked him more than once, my own guess being Lord Aiken, but in this I was mistaken.

"Lord no, we only used Aiken's place once in an emergency. He caught us dead to rights, but took his share and kept mum. He wasn't interested in getting into it regular," Jem told me.

"Do you bring it in at his place? He has a nice quiet stretch of beach there, and he is often away too."

"Nay, he cautioned us not to."

"Do you bring it in at the Eyrie?" was my next question. I found myself becoming quite engrossed, and wishing to know more about it.

"They do say it was used by the Sizewell Gap Gang in the old days, but we've never tackled the Eyrie."

The Eyrie is a highly romanticized ruin. Driving past it on the road, you could take it for a little fairy castle, sitting atop one of the highest points of the cliffs. A closer inspection will show you that what looked like weathered stone is in fact waterlogged shingles. The building is rapidly tumbling into decay, but its reputation is in no way marred by these details. It is associated by legend with smuggling, but its height so much above sea level inclines one to think this is mere romanticism, unless the smugglers were seagulls.

This meeting took place at school at the end of April. Jem often made an excuse to drop by, bringing some item supposedly forgotten by Millie, which he gave to me. He knew I would be found out in the yard at recess, for with Dame Aldridge getting old and gouty, she never went out herself. I could not discover from him who the chief was, but he did ask me if I'd like to watch a load being landed. "On the sly, like," he added with a knowing wink. I was extremely curious, and made an arrangement to sneak out with him next time a lugger was coming in. Two days later Millie told me Jemmie was going to a party that night at the cove.

"Did he ask you to tell me?" I inquired politely.

"Yes, miss, but he said there's nothing but men going, and if a woman was to go, she must wear trousers or she'd not be let in."

"That sounds a highly irregular party," I answered, smiling.

"'Tis that," she agreed. "And it doesn't start till midnight. Jemmie said to tell you so, but I told him you wouldn't be interested at all."

"You tell your brother I expect a written invitation," I told her, hoping to give him the hint I wanted a confirmation in writing.

"He said to tell you they never write anything about the parties, lest strangers get hold of it," she replied, smiling sweetly, but with a face not so innocent as it had been last year. "He means Crites," she added in a confidential tone, then bounced away. She knew the whole, the minx. And what a crafty helper she was at seven years. Knew enough to come to me with her message when I was well away from Miss Aldridge. I shook my head ruefully.

The party was a great success. I wore an old pair of Andrew's dark trousers, his jacket and boots, with my curls stuffed up under his hat. I could have swum in his clothing. I rode Babe down the road in the direction of the cove. Exhilaration kept me from being frightened. Jem was waiting for me just at the edge of the village. He handed me a mask and donned one himself.

"Just in case," he explained briefly. I put on my disguise.

"You'd best tether your nag to a tree," he suggested. "You never take a white animal poaching or smuggling, miss. And if you're wise, you don't take one that's known to the whole village either."

"What about Lady?" I queried, for his dog was at his heels.

"Oh, she's wearing her disguise as well," he answered. Glancing back, I had difficulty spotting her. "She has a mud bath an hour before we go, to hide her white fur," he explained.

"If she were ever caught, your secret would be out."

"My Lady wouldn't be stopped, except by a bullet," was his answer.

There was a fingernail of moon hanging low in the sky; the breeze was chilly. Till we were actually at the sea's edge, the sails of the ship could not be seen, nor did she show any lights. We stayed apart from the men, concealed in the shad-

27

ows. The ship was not large; she had four-cornered sails set fore and aft.

"Is it safe to work so openly? What of Crites?" I whispered.

"He's on the other side of town. We were burnt off there earlier."

"What do you mean?"

"We settle always on three sites beforehand. If Crites is around, we give a signal with the torch from a spot where he can't see us, and the lugger goes along to the next spot, letting on it don't plan to stop at all. Crites is still at Harbour Bay. We have a few of the lads there keeping him amused by leaping about the rocks a bit."

"Won't he see the lugger stop?" was my next question.

"She won't be pulling in tonight. The stuff is put on a smaller pair of boats—lowered overboard on the far side from the shore. Our lads know their job. Crites will be busy enough chasing them over the rocks that he'll not see the little boats coming in. Mind we must move hasty, for he won't be too long in tumbling to our ruse."

Move hastily they did. Not even a donkey to help them! Each man had two barrels slung over his shoulders, one resting on his back and one on his chest. It must have been a fearful burden, yet they moved quickly along the shore, to disappear into the night.

"They'll never make it all the way to the school, Jem."

"Nay, only beyond the roadway into the fields, where the mules are waiting. We use the cart trails; they're more private, like."

We went along to the schoolhouse to watch the rest of the operation, I hiding behind the corner like a truant while Jem went forward to speak to them. How strange it looked, to see my prim classroom full of kegs of brandy, with the desks all shoved off to one side, piled on top of each other, with the chairs on top of that. I trembled to think what might happen if Crites should come in, but the lads kept him busy, I assumed, for he never came near us. Jem offered to "breach a barrel" for me to try the brew, after the men had left. "We always breach one to test her," he informed me.

He produced an awl and hammer, pushed up a metal hoop to make his hole in the barrel there, where it could be concealed from the purchaser. "You never want to use a gimlet, miss, for the sawdust might get in and give the show away. You take the tub betwixt your knees so, and give the heads a squeeze," he said, doing just as he explained. The brandy flowed freely as from a tap, to be caught in my teacup, then with his finger he stopped the hole and handed the cup to me. It was powerfully strong stuff. My eyes watered with it, but it had a satisfying warm aftertaste. I could feel it burn down to my stomach.

I handed the cup to Jem. "She's a fair brew," he allowed. Then he asked for water, and with his finger still in the hole, he tipped the barrel on its side with the hole up, produced a funnel, and poured water into the barrel till it was full again. "She gets to swishing on you if you leave her not quite full," he explained. "I don't know the swishing harms the stuff, but it do make a noise, like. Phillips don't like it." How careful they were at every step. The hole was plugged with a wooden peg, the ring lowered over it, and we were off.

I was escorted back to Babe. "I hope you enjoyed the party, miss," Jem said.

"Thank you for a delightful evening." A sense of heady exhilaration hung about me as I rode on home alone. The more I came to know these gentlemen, the more I admired them. What a daring business it was, and how profitable, I thought, as I put my five guineas into my drawer.

Monday morning I feared the jig was up. Crites came right to the school and asked for me. My heart was in my throat when Miss Aldridge called me out to our little office to speak with him. "Miss Anderson, Officer Crites has spoken to me, and he now wishes to question you," she informed me, with a haughty, rebuking look at the revenueman. I assumed a pose of polite interest and asked him if I could be of help.

"I hope you may," he answered, smiling genially, which did little to improve his face. Crites, among a host of other unattractive traits, has teeth like a rabbit. In full smile he is not a pretty sight. "I have been led a merry chase by the gentlemen the past winter, and have come to the conclusion they are using this school for hiding their contraband," he told me.

If he suspected at all, then the school was no longer of use. Best to go along with him, and divert suspicion from my own culpability. "Now isn't that odd! Do you know, I thought I noticed an odd smell in the room this morning. I made sure one of the children had not left a partially eaten apple in his desk, but it was not so. I asked them all to have a look, for an apple will smell like the very deuce in a closed room. You don't think they'd have the gall to put it in the school surely, Officer!"

"Ho, as to gall, miss, it wouldn't surprise me if they stashed it in the church. Miss Aldridge claimed to know nothing of the matter, and I daresay she is innocent herself, but that is not to say the wool isn't being pulled over her eyes. Say not a word, ma'am. I'll catch them next dark, see if I don't."

"I'm sure you will, Officer. They ought to be arrested, every man jack of them."

"No need to mention a word to Miss Aldridge. It will only upset her, poor old malkin. The fewer who know of our suspicions, the better. I'd appreciate it if you'd tell me if you see anything of that pair of wastrels belonging to the Widow Hessler lurking around the school. They've got some way of getting in, stands to reason. You haven't noticed a lock broken or such like?"

"No, nor a window either," I could answer without blushing.

He chatted on a few moments, but when he began to get personal, I excused myself and returned to my classroom. Crites tucked his teeth under his lower lip in a way he has developed to try to hide them, and departed. I had to be in touch with Jem at once, and said to Millie that she was to tell her brother the revenueman had been at the school that day.

"I seen him," she answered, with a wise face.

"*Saw* him, dear."

"That's what I said. I'll tell Jem."

Grammar was irrelevant at such a moment. Next day Millie "forgot" to bring her lunch, and Jem dropped it off during his higgling rounds. I told him the story. "I'll speak to Miss Thyme," he answered. "Thankee, miss."

"Who is Miss Thyme?"

"Oh, 'tis an alias, like. You mind in the good old days the ringleader called himself Miss Marjoram, and we call our chief Miss Thyme. It is said, you know, that gentlemen are most easily led by a lady."

I was highly curious to know who Miss Thyme might be, but knew well enough the futility of asking. I was sorry my part in the business was over. With the school *hors de combat*, however, my use was at an end. I mentioned this to Jem. "Buck up, miss. You never do know what the Lord has got in store for you, do you?"

The Good Lord had nothing of any interest in store for me for the next few days, but He had not forgotten me entirely. On Friday I went home to find Mrs. Hessler sitting in my saloon with Andrew. "Mrs. Hessler has been telling me of her problems," Andrew said. I darted a guilty look to the woman, who looked at me with a warning stare.

"I was just telling the reverend the troubles I'm having with my lads, dear," she inserted quickly. "Jem has taken to drink, the devil. Come home foxed t'other night, and I'm asking your brother to remember him in his prayers." It was about the only help she was likely to get from Andrew. "Your brother's been telling me how long the evil of drink has been with us," she rattled on. "That Bacchus sounds a rare rascal."

"Can I give you a cup of tea before you leave, Mrs. Hessler?" I asked.

"That would be dandy," she smiled. When Andrew arose to leave us, I said not a word to detain him. "They need your help," she said in a very blunt way, as soon as we were alone.

"They can't use the school. Crites will be there. It is madness to think of it."

"I know, Miss Anderson, but you must come up with something for them. What are they to do with the stuff?"

"What does Miss Thyme suggest?"

"He suggests we talk to you," she answered.

Here was my chance to discover at last who Miss Thyme was. "Tell Miss Thyme if my help is wanted, I shall be at home alone this evening. Andrew has a meeting of the Parish Council, and Miss Halka goes to play whist with friends."

"Well, but he can't come while the meeting's on," she countered, frowning at me.

My mind hastily darted over the members of the Parish Council, unable to credit that any of them would be involved in the free trade. She obviously thought I knew who the chief was, had figured it out in some manner myself. To my relief, she spoke on. "After the meeting is over leaves it pretty late. Why don't you run along to the Parish Office now and see him before it closes?"

"I'll do that," I managed to reply, with my ears singing and my senses all reeling. Then I drank up my tea in a hurry to get there before Sir Elwood Ganner, KBE, had turned the key in the door and gone home to his mansion and his wife, Lady Ann. Yes, Sir Elwood Ganner, the parish officer, the paragon of the town, the father-in-law to our Member of Parliament—the biggest toad in the puddle—was Miss Thyme. I had never for a moment suspected him. He was always rushing around, dipping a toe in every bit of good that was done locally, and receiving praise and citations for it. His

KBE, to be sure, was felt to be a reward for his long years devoted to helping others. All the while he had been helping himself as well.

He was bald-headed, perfectly bald with a very shiny pink scalp, which would be speckled with brown marks later in the season. He had been a frequent visitor at Fern Bank when my father was alive, putting in a good word for some miscreant about to appear in the dock. His gentlemen, very likely, whose services he required. Ah, the world was changing focus before my eyes. White becoming black, black white—or maybe it was all gray.

"You are surprised, Miss Anderson," he began, with a glint of amusement in his very blue eyes. "But I was not always an elderly and respectable gentleman, you must know. I was once young, poor and ambitious, like yourself."

"That must have been a good many years ago, Sir Elwood."

"Aye, so it was. More years that I like to think. Over forty years ago I started in the business. Now it is time I retire, and pass the reins to my successor. I've only hung on so long waiting for the right man—er, person—to come along. I had some hopes your brother...but Andrew is very bookish when all is said and done."

"I can't do it. If it ever came out, Andrew would be ruined."

"It won't come out. I've run the gang forever, with never a soul knowing but the Hesslers. Old Jim used to be my accomplice, and his son was so bright I took him on when Jim died, despite his youth. If he were a little older, he'd be my replacement. You need not stay in it so long as I did myself. Build yourself up a dowry, and retire as soon as Jemmie is a little more mature. I gave only my brains to the outfit. I took no active part, and naturally as a lady you would not be active in the physical end of it. Give them a hand. They're stouthearted lads, but not so bright and wide-awake to the business end of it as is required. You will be dealing with London merchants and French exporters—dealing in large sums of money. They want sharp managing, the lads. There's a tidy profit in it for you. I make a hundred guineas a trip. Better than five, eh?"

My heart was beating like a hammer. It seemed too large, too dangerous an undertaking. I wanted to say no, and run out the door, but something kept me in my seat. The hundred guineas a trip had something to do with it, but it was not just greed. He spoke of the "enterprise" having to be abandoned. "It will put a lot of families on the parish dole," he said. "The fishermen are idle from Christmas till March or April, giving extra hands just when you need them. Summer, being a light season for the free trade, is a good time for you to get your toes wet. Don't think the civil authorities will give you a hard time—I—*they* won't. They know well enough it is only the smuggling that gives us the lowest poor rate in the country. They are not eager to have to support the poor out of the mill rate. As to cash to finance it, you must have some monies saved."

"Not nearly enough."

"I'll lend you the rest. You must pay them when they land. And never double-cross them, Miss Thyme." He smiled as he gave me his name. "You can repay me over the next few months. I shall be happy to lend a hand when I can. It will not look exceptionable if the rector's sister drops in on me from time to time, eh? I have a list of London agents here, and some other information you will need."

He went to a file cabinet and drew out, from his parish records, one innocent-looking folder that contained all manner of criminal information. My own name was there, with the rest, on the bookkeeping sheet. He called me only Miss A, but what a thing to have written down.

I stayed with him an hour, and went home the chief of the smuggling gang at Salford, with five hundred pounds in my pocket. It was announced in the Salford *Sun* next day that Sir Elwood Ganner was being raised to the rank of baronet for his unceasing efforts to better the conditions of the poor of Salford. That was why he wanted out of smuggling, of course. He was aiming to be Lord Something or Other before many more years were out, and did not wish to have the skeleton of Miss Thyme in his cupboard. I doubted very much if I would ever be so grandly rewarded for my own efforts on behalf of the townsfolk, but I never had any hankering after rank, so that did not vex me.

Chapter Four

My first duty as Miss Thyme was to discover a new hiding place for the load coming in. Coming in that very night, in approximately six hours! I was distracted over dinner. Any brother but Andrew would have noticed it, but with the Parish Council meeting on his mind, he was content to eat with very little conversation. Edna inquired, after dinner, what ailed me, as I had eaten so little. I had been arguing with myself the pros and cons of making Edna privy to my secret. I felt it would be well to have an accomplice under my own roof. Indeed, close as we two were these days, it would be no easy matter to hide my career from her. Like most of the ladies in the village, she looked up to Sir Elwood as a tin god. If I told her, I would let her know the whole; that I was replacing Sir Elwood. Well, to make this uninteresting episode brief, I *did* tell her. She was first incredulous, then disagreeable, and after I adopted a bout of sulks, she came round to accepting it. She maintained, however, the right to dislike it very much, and tell me so at every possible opportunity, always forecasting disclosure and disaster. I don't say she is not a moral person, but it was clear her main concern was not that I acted wrongly, but that I might get caught. The name Sir Elwood Ganner had often to be spoken, to remind her what high company I kept in adopting this profession.

She finally went to prepare herself for the card party and let me get down to some heavy thinking. I had to get five hundred pounds to Jemmie to pay off the French importers, but more importantly, I had to come up with a hiding place for approximately one hundred barrels of brandy. Jemmie was soon tapping at the door.

"Is it all set, miss?" he asked.

I took him into Andrew's study, lest another caller come and see this unlikely guest in my saloon. I gave him the money, but was hesitant to tell him what spot I had selected for concealment. I had not told Edna yet the full depths of my depravity. She was initially so upset that she did not know there was a load coming in this very night at all. "Well?" he asked, waiting.

"Bring it here," I told him. The church was at the east edge of town—it would not be necessary for the barrels actually to go through Salford. It was perhaps a daring idea, but its very daringness made it unlikely of discovery. Who would think to look in a church for smuggled brandy?

"There's a service Sunday morning!" he pointed out. "The tranter don't pick it up till Sunday night."

"I don't mean to put it in the church proper. There is a crypt underneath, a burial vault with enough room to hold the barrels. The men must move very quietly, mind. Not a sound, or Andrew will awaken and discover them. I'll be at the back door and let them in, and be there again Sunday midnight to open up for them."

"Don't show yourself, miss," Jem cautioned, worrying about me. "Just leave the door on the latch and go back in the house."

"That's not a bad idea. I'll have a look from the bell tower too, to see if anything is stirring that shouldn't be. Not that I'll see much in the dark. They must leave the mules in the woods beyond the road and each carry his two barrels on his back to the crypt door. I'll try to think of a better place for next time, but for this once, we'll use the church. Crites, we know, will be at the school, so he won't be pestering us. He doesn't mean to scout the shore at all tonight, but catch us out at the school."

Jem's freckled face broke out into a smile. "Aye, you're a wise one, miss. Thyme is the wrong name for you. It's Miss Sage you are, and no doubt."

As our scheme came off without a hitch, I was dignified with the title Miss Sage. Do you know, it is amazing how you can become accustomed to anything after a while. I knew many a nervous hour the first few weeks, but with time I settled down to my old routine and hardly thought of the business but on Friday. The crypt proved so successful a place of concealment that we continued using it for the whole spring and summer. Fewer loads were made in the warmer weather, but with such smooth work as we were making of it, we did not discontinue as most gangs were in the habit of doing. Our supply was so steady too that we became quite a favored crew in London. I paid Sir Elwood Ganner, Bart., off his five hundred pounds. He cautioned me that certain official folks in London were becoming irate at my success, but I thought it was only professional jealousy that I was performing better than he had done himself. With the chief official of the town in my pocket, and with a fool of a revenueman half in love with me, I foresaw no immediate difficulties in my path.

Edna poured an unending stream of mournful prognostications over my head, but I felt strong, clever, unbeatable. I almost regretted the ease of it. It would be more exciting if we had a smarter foe than Crites to deal with. It never occurred to him anyone would be horrid enough to hide brandy in a church. He returned several times to the school, then reverted to the inn, the warehouse and the old places of hiding. I spoke to him most civilly when we met, even let him take the idea I admired him. "Did you not catch the smugglers at the school, Officer?" I asked him one day.

"No, I was mistaken about the school, Miss Anderson. It must have been an apple you smelled after all. They never did show up."

"They have heard you are on to them, Officer, and didn't dare go back when they knew they must have *you* to conten with."

The rabbit teeth jutted forth in pleasure. I am convinced men are conceited enough to believe anything. He actually believed he was feared by the smugglers, and admired by me. I hardly knew which joke was funnier. "They'll not be using your school if they know what's good for them," he boasted.

Andrew came down with a bad cold, which troubled his sleep. I expect it was the hours spent in that drafty gallery playing the organ that caused it. The result was that he complained one Monday morning of hearing noises at his back window, which is, unfortunately, above the crypt. It was necessary to use the school again for a spell after this. I wanted to have a key made up for Jemmie, and it was this that led to my trip to London, for I would not have it made locally. This was not the only reason, of course, nor even the main one. The piles of gold heaping under my petticoats had something to do with it. I wanted a chance to spend some of it, and put some in the bank. I don't mean to say I never spent a shilling previous to this. I gave some to charity in nefarious ways. Sukey Millar, whose mama is a grass widow with three children, went home more days than one with a guinea hidden in her coat pocket, and never suspected its source, nor ever questioned it either. Its final use was visible in a better coat on the children's backs, and better lunch in their baskets. I was practically the sole support of Mrs. Kiley (mother to a parcel of red-haired adulterine children, you may recall). As the sister of the rector it was not unexpected I should befriend her. It was a thankless task, for she had no management, but as often as I could attend to it, she had food in her cupboards at least. Indigent callers to the rectory were given a couple of shillings by Andrew, and a couple of pounds, "saved from the household money" I told them, from myself.

This may be an ineffective way of performing charity, but it is a highly satisfying one. Money put into an institution will be dissipated in no visible way, but to give cash to a poor man and see him walk down the street and turn into a shop gives a warm feeling in the heart. With a job myself now and Andrew's position, that we had a little money to spare was not remarkable. I also fixed up the rectory in a way to please me. Andrew did not have to be accounted to for anything, as he never noticed if a new chair was in the saloon or a new lamp on the table. He was perfectly oblivious to his surroundings, which was very convenient.

But of course if I were to vanish for two days, he would notice it, so I had to invent a pretext for a trip to London. "I am going to pay Cousin Dora a short visit," I told him.

"Dora, which one is she?" he asked. Mama's sister in Devonshire had three married daughters, one of them living in some unfashionable suburb of London.

"The one married to a solicitor," I answered quite at random.

"That's nice. Don't invite her here," he replied.

"No, I shan't, Andrew. Can I get you anything in London?"

He could think of nothing in all of London to tempt him. I had a great deal of business to attend to. Getting the key made was only a trifling part of it. I wished to meet our agents firsthand and try to get a higher price from them for our brandy. The price had not been raised in three years, I had noticed from Miss Thyme's records, and prices were rising everywhere else.

It was a Mr. Pettigrew I first locked horns with. A very genteel establishment he had, right on Bond Street amid the fine shops serving the gentry. Edna would have it I was come to the wrong address, for what Mr. Pettigrew purported to sell was snuff and all the paraphernalia that goes with it, but then he could hardly have contraband goods sitting on his shelves, and with such a shop as this, he would be in touch with all sorts of gentlemen. In fact, Edna and myself were the only ladies in his shop, but we were not long in the shop proper once my name was mentioned. We were whisked off into a private office at the back where we got down to hard bargaining. The man took the misguided notion that as I was a female, he could bullock me into a lower price. I arose at once from my chair. "I have come to negotiate a *higher* price, sir. If you are unable to pay it, I shall not waste your time and my own, but go to my other agents."

The upshot of the meeting was that I got the price I wanted under the condition that I sell my total haul to Mr. Pettigrew. This was agreeable to me, and joyful news to Will Phillips, who would now have to make only one stop to deliver. In a fit of gallantry, he gave me a sweet little box which he said was a lady's snuff box. I had no idea of ramming snuff up my nose, but used it for holding face powder. The ladies in London were using something called "pearl powder" which lent a delica⸱ ⸱⸱⸱⸱nous glow to the cheeks.

This t⸱⸱ ⸱vas a pleasure jaunt to reward myself for all my work and worry, as well as a business one. I cannot think of any pastime more enjoyable than spending money on items one does not actually need. It was sheer luxury to roam the shops, picking up silk stockings, fancy feathers, scented soaps—all the delicacies a woman desires but can neither afford nor find in a small town like Salford. I felt quite a pampered pet when I unwrapped my treasures back at our hotel. We stayed at the Reddelstone. A good, respectable spot, but I think I would aim higher next time.

With a little judicious arm-twisting, I got Edna to accept material for a new gown and bought her a very pretty fringed shawl. I treated myself to similar items. In the evening, we hired a carriage and went to an opera at the Haymarket, where we were the recipients of a good number of stares from the gentlemen, which we were obliged to pretend we did not see, of course. One wayward male accosted us at the intermission to let on he mistook me for his cousin, while at least a half dozen of his cohorts stood off in a corner laughing, to see how he would be received. I told him that to my knowledge, I did not number any popinjays among my relations, after which he did not pester us again.

I was very sorry we had to leave so soon. We were glancing at the newspapers as we had breakfast on the day of our departure, to kill time till the coach left. What I read there nearly made me choke on my coffee. "Edna—look!" I shrieked, pushing the paper under her nose.

"A new officer appointed to the Board of Trade—what is that to us?" she asked.

"Read the rest. Read what he says."

She read, and I shall tell you what it was that caused me to shriek in horror. The new officer appointed was a Colonel Sir Stamford Wicklow, retired from the Army since Waterloo, with a leg wound sustained while in active duty under Wellington. Nothing to cause a shriek there, but an interview with the president of the Board of Trade went on to state Wicklow had been appointed to look into a loss of revenue due to smuggling. He went on to pinpoint the east coast as the prime spot for this smuggling, and further to finger Salford as the one spot where the stuff was flowing in as regularly as the tide. So it was too, since Miss Sage had taken over. There was a long threnody on the many thousands of pounds lost yearly due to this business, and a statement that it would be brought to a stop.

"Isn't that all we need, and I have just made a very good contract with Mr. Pettigrew," I lamented.

"You know how these commissions work," Edna assured me. "He'll send Crites a letter, Crites will send back a report and that will be an end to it."

"I hope you may be right. All the same, I shall keep a sharp eye out for a stranger in town, especially a stranger who strikes up a friendship with Officer Crites."

"He'll never come to town himself," she thought. "An officer and a gentleman—devil a bit of it. At best he'll send some petty clerk down with a pen and pad to try for a few names."

"They mean to put a stop to us. Hundreds of thousands of pounds—what our Prince Regent couldn't do with the money. Build another onion dome on his pavilion, or throw up another row of porphyry columns at Carlton House."

"What do you know about Carlton House?" she asked me. About the latest renovations to the ever-changing pavilion she knew as much as myself, as we had read an article on it together recently.

"I overheard some ladies talking about it last night at the opera. They say it is a party every night he is in residence, with music and feasting and dancing. Wouldn't it be lovely to go, just once?"

She regarded me severely. "Never you mind about such carrying-on. Carlton House indeed!"

It was time to go. I thought of the article as we jostled home on the coach, and thought there was much to be said for Edna's view of the matter. It was hardly likely we would have an officer from the Board of Trade take up residence in Salford. My mind wandered off to other matters. Next time we came up to London, we would take the mail. It was more expensive, but a much faster, more comfortable conveyance. It was always tended first at any coaching house it stopped at, and the passengers looked more respectable than the crew we shared our carriage with. I doubted the odor of onions and unwashed bodies would be as high on the mail either.

It seems nothing ever happens in town for years on end, then as soon as you leave for a day or two, great events occur. The big news when we got home was that Mrs. Owens from the local drapery store had suddenly taken ill. Her husband had spirited her off to Bath to recuperate, but of more interest than this, her cousin was coming to take over the store during their absence. Lest this not strike you as world-shaking information, let me go on to state he was a young bachelor. You must surely agree that the introduction into our limited society of an unattached male of marriageable age is worth noting. In common with all the other women in town, I made an excuse to get a look at Mr. Williams. I had to wait till after school to do it, as it was now September, and the doors of the dame school were open once more. I had a good excuse into the shop. Andrew was a member of the Parish Council, and had been assigned the duty of purchasing calico for the charity cases. Any duty of this practical nature was promptly dumped into my lap—a point considered when they stuck Andrew with these jobs, of course.

My first impression of Mr. Williams was good. He stood alone in the store, the women having all come and gone long before I entered at four-thirty, after school. He stood leaning his hands on the counter, with his eyes riveted on a book. I could see he was young, good-looking, with wide shoulders, unfortunately covered in a blue coat that pretended to fashion, but was of a poor cut and quality. With it he wore a very gaudy waistcoat and shirt points too high for true elegance. Many such dandies were to be seen on the streets of London, clerks and merchants who spent their wages on their backs, to try to impress the girls. The whole getup was garish, in poor taste, but the head on top of all this tawdry clothing was well shaped. The hair too, wheat-colored hair, was nicely barbered, not curling in cunning disarray like the dandies, but neatly brushed back. Looking at the profile, I could not but admire the straight nose and strong chin. Really he looked a remarkably handsome fellow. He would provide one of the merchant's girls a beau before many days were out. He looked up as I approached, a questioning look. His face was alert, intelligent, the eyes a deep, stormy gray.

"Can I be of help to ye, ma'am?" he asked, surveying me with polite deference. What a pity it was to hear common speech utter from that face. Peacocks enchant better with their mouths closed.

"I would like to see your calico, sir."

"I've a very fine white calico in. Is it for sheets you're wanting it, miss?"

I had sunk from ma'am to miss in two speeches, and wondered why this change had occurred. If the ma'am had been a mark of respect for his betters, it was odd he had changed it so quickly, so I took it as a compliment to my youth, caused by his ill breeding. "No, sir, I want your cheapest quality, the brown calico."

"Ah, it's dust rags you're after. There's a bit of unbleached out back that's got summat soiled..."

"I require fifty yards," I told him.

"What on earth for?" he asked, staring rudely.

"That is hardly your concern, but as you ask, it is for distribution to the parish poor."

"Ah, ye'd be Miss Anderson then," he informed me, walking toward me at a halting gait. He seemed to have twisted his ankle. I concluded that even if his speech were common, his mind was uncommonly sharp, to have discovered my name and business within the space of one day in the shop.

"That's right."

"I'm Williams," he told me, smiling. A greasy smile it was, which did not match his face. "Here's what ye'd be after," he said, pointing to the brown calico.

It distressed me to have to buy that horrid cheap stuff for the poor. I would have liked to get a better quality, or even let them have a voucher equal in value to the price to buy what they wished. But the rules were strict—not without reason. Mrs. Kiley, for instance, would buy ribbon if she had a choice. The rules stated one sheet length of unbleached calico for a small family, two if the family were large. "It's two shillings and sixpence an ell," he said.

"Mr. Owens always gave us a discount; he left off the odd pence, as we buy in quantity."

"Did he then? I didn't notice it in the books," he replied, regarding me with the innately suspicious eye of the shop-keeper, convinced you are out to gyp him. Pettigrew had the same look. The book he had been perusing with such interest when I entered was the bookkeeping ledger, and here I had taken him for a reading man.

"If you look under the record of the Parish Council, I believe you will find the price always paid to be two shillings," I replied haughtily.

"I'll just have a look," he answered, and limped back to the counter. He was as well as telling me he didn't believe me. "Aye, so it is, two shillings the ell," he said, nodding his head judiciously.

"You may deliver it to the rectory, and bill the Parish Council," I said, still on my high ropes. So much so, in fact, that I had given him the wrong spot for delivery. It woul be more convenient to have it taken directly to the church.

"I certainly will do that, ma'am," he answered, "as soon as ye've signed for it." I was back to ma'am, in deference to my fit of pique. I stood by to sign the voucher he was scribbling up. I rather expected to see him surreptitiously counting up the price on his fingers as Mrs. Owens does, but he jotted down the right sum pretty quickly. Two times fifty is hardly an impossible sum, however. "It's a grand little place, Salford," he said, looking up between strokes of the pen.

"Where are you from, Mr. Williams?" I condescended to inquire.

"I get around a good bit," was his answer.

"Where is your home, I meant?"

"Devonshire," he answered.

"I have an aunt from Devonshire. Whereabouts in Devonshire is your home?"

"It's just a wee place. Ye'd never have heard of it. I left when I was a lad. I've been living in London since."

"How nice. You will find Salford quiet after the city."

"Not too quiet, I hope," he said, and smiled up at me in

Chapter Five

The week passed quietly and uneventfully. There was a shipment due on Friday evening; I was trying to decide whether to have it taken to the school for a change. Even when one has a very good hiding place, it is a good idea to make a change occasionally—just in case. Yes, Crites had given up on the school, so I would revert to it. The week was a busy one for Mr. Williams. He was seen to visit not only the Trebars, but two other young females that week. A dull scald it must have been for him all the same, with nowhere better to go than the parlors of a yeoman farmer and the local harness maker. He was not a gentleman, but he might have looked a little higher than that. He regularly took his noonday meal at the tavern with whatever company he could find, bachelors like himself, or travelers. I believe he had very little time to spare for Mr. Milton. The shop, Edna informed me, was busier than it had ever been, with all the girls nipping in to buy up one button or spool of thread at a time, to allow as many visits as possible. I did not go back. Even when I ran out of blue wool for Andrew's slippers, I had Edna pick it up for me sooner than satisfy Mr. Williams by returning. He asked her to convey his compliments to me, the brass box.

I was always nervous the day of a shipment. As evening wore on, I became very unsettled. It was the routine worked out early in the business that Jem would come to me after the brandy was safely stored, to let me know. I made a point to be lurking about the front dooor, or if Andrew were still up and about, which he was not usually, Jem knew by the lights that he was to slip a note under the back door. Andrew chose that night to be up. He had been practicing a new piece on the organ, and was pestering Edna and myself with details of his feat, without regard to the hour. At twelve-thirty I slipped down to the kitchen to await my note. I was there when it came under the door, accompanied by a light tap. As

Jem did not usually tap, I feared there was something amiss. I went out to talk to him, in case Andrew should decide to follow after me. It was an eerie night. Not yet so very cold, but with a high wind that soughed through branches in a plaintive way. It stirred some feeling of dissatisfaction in me, that wind.

"What is it?" I asked. "Is something wrong?"

"I don't know that it is, miss, but I thought I'd best mention it to you all the same."

"Yes, what is it?"

"The window was open when we got to the school. Since you gave me the key, I thought we were to keep it closed. Did you forget and leave it open?"

"No, I did not." I had got the key to be rid of this telltale sign of the open window, in case Crites should tumble to it, or in case some wide-awake vagrant might notice it, and go in to steal what was lying about.

"It was wide open when we got there."

"It's impossible. Are you *sure?* Maybe one of our men was there before you."

"Nay, I was the scout myself, and it was open."

"There was nothing else amiss? No one interrupted you? You didn't see any sign of Crites?"

"We fooled him proper tonight. The stuff came down from Ipswich, instead of up water from the ocean. We weren't burned off at all."

"What can it mean?"

He hunched his houlders. "I've let the lads go on home, as I didn't want th. all hanging about. With nothing better to pass the time, th y might take to roistering."

"We must move the stuff."

"Tonight?"

"Yes, tonight. I don't like the looks of this." I did not worry Jem about the special agent, but it was in my own thoughts that there might be a better brain than Crites working against us now.

"The lads are all gone off home."

"Get them back. They'll be paid double for double work. Have them bring it here, to the crypt."

"It'll take *hours* to round them all up, miss."

"That's all right. I don't want it done at once. If there is anyone snooping around, let him get good and tired and go home. We'll make the move toward dawn, Jem."

"Seems a bit unnecessary, like," he thought.

46

"Better safe than sorry." Jem was not satisfied with this platitude. Of course he was tired after a hard day, poor boy, and wanted to go home to bed. I decided to divulge to him my fears regarding the special investigating agent.

"Gorblimey, it's a good thing you read the papers. We've never heard a word of this. I'll round up the lads and bring the load here."

I felt a pang of pity, to see the poor boy dart from the yard, Lady a shadow at his heels, and to know he had a sleepless night before him. My own was hardly more restful. I had a great deal of thinking to do. The agent had arrived, and was already beginning to become a nuisance. He had discovered somehow that we used the school—Crites of course would have mentioned it. But why had he not arrested the men and taken the cargo on the spot? This puzzled me for nearly half an hour, till I realized the new agent was more ambitious than Crites had ever been. He did not mean to content himself with my carriers. He was after the chief—he was after *me*, and had very nearly caught me. Had he followed Jem to the rectory? The barrels arrived at the crypt door at four-thirty in the morning. I watched from the kitchen window, unseen, terrified that at any moment a shout or a shot would ring out. None did, nor did any subsequent hammering at the door come to signal my arrest. My care had paid off. The agent, if he had been lurking at the school, had given up and gone away, thus missing out on the second move. But he was dangerous. Thank God the men wore masks. Even if they had been seen, they could not be identified.

I blush to consider all the hours I sat puzzling over who the investigator could be, suspecting first the traveling salesman who had been selling brooms and brushes on Monday, the cousin of the Trebars, who stayed from Tuesday to Thursday, even the colonel visiting at Squire Porson's place, trying to remember if I had seen any of them in conversation with Crites. The answer had been staring me in the face, and I should have been shaken for not seeing it sooner. It was Mr. Williams. He even had the lame leg, from being wounded at Waterloo. He was Colonel Sir Stamford Wicklow, with his military haircut. But how had he got himself into Owens' store? The government could arrange anything—had worked some deal with the Owenses—a lucrative deal you may be sure. Owens' business would not be worth a Birmingham farthing when this came out. Not a smuggling family in town

47

(and that was the majority of the families) would go next or nigh them.

All Williams' courting of the local wenches was similarly explained. He was sniffing around for news, trying to work his way into confidence with the men via the girls, calling at any house that would give him sitting space. I had to get a warning out to my men at once that Williams be told nothing.

I gave up any pretense of sleep, and went downstairs to make myself a pot of tea to help me work out my arrangements. There is nothing like a pot of tea; it is the greatest panacea there ever was. It can wake you up, put you to sleep, settle your nerves or steel them to do your unpleasant duty. It performed all those functions for me that night, in a little different sequence than I have mentioned. Of prime importance was that Williams not suspect I was on to him, which made it poor policy to tell the men directly. They were a close lot, but if even one let anything slip, the secret would be out. They would be warned that old bogeyman, the government, was taking special steps to trap us, but Wicklow would not be pinpointed. Next item was to find a new hiding place, for the school was now useless, and I had no desire to implicate myself or Andrew by using the crypt.

The cautious, the *intelligent* thing to do would be to discontinue deliveries for a while, but if we stopped taking shipment, others would soon take up the slack. I had just been at some pains to arrange a good price in London providing we delivered regularly. Interrupting the supply so early in the game was a poor business tactic. It was autumn too, with the winter, the best season, coming on. I might as well confess the whole while I am about it.

On top of all these rational reasons, there was a quite irrational one as well. The game had been becoming almost dull. Crites was too easy to fool. I welcomed taking on a more challenging foe. I would not be brought to a standstill by Colonel Sir Stamford Wicklow, with his greasy grin and double-dealing. I would continue to accept every load I could get my hands on, and devise a way of doing it without his knowledge. I had the advantage of having pierced his disguise early in the game. This might be turned to good account as he seemed intent on flirting with anything that wore a skirt. I would try his own trick, and see what I could discover by making up to the opposite sex.

But first I must make arrangements for storing the next

shipment—that was more important. I remembered Jemmie telling me Lord Aiken's place had been used once in an emergency. I must discover whether Crites had ever caught on to this ploy. The weekend was always a good time for making contact with Jem. I led the church choir, and he was one of my singers—a very good tenor voice he had. We had a small musical group comprised of flute, violin and cello all sitting up in the gallery (everyone of them smugglers). Andrew would have liked to rout them out and play the organ instead, but his presence was necessary below. This Sunday there would be the added contact of my handing out the calico as well, in the church porch. Sunday was time enough to talk to Jem, but on Saturday I would go into the drapery shop and give Mr. Williams' nose a tweak.

After considering my tactics for a while, I decided the best ruse was to pretend to be smitten with him, like all the other girls. Bachelors were in such short supply around Salford that all the girls and even half the ladies were running mad for Mr. Williams. Still, as he was posing as a draper, he could not seriously expect any real romance with me. I must be at some pains to conceal that I possessed a brain, and rather regretted having boasted of my imaginary love of Shakespeare. It was unlikely my visit would reveal a single fact of any importance; a clever investigator would not let fall his plans, but still I looked forward to it as a game. I was curious to get a sharper look at him, to try to find a flaw in his accent or manners, now that I was on to him. I suppose it was no more than a wish to weigh up the enemy.

Saturday was always a busy day in the shops of Salford. On this Saturday, you had to fight to get a foot into Owens'. Around noon hour the crowd thinned out, and I went in to see what luck Sir Stamford was having with the wenches. Those saucy, ill-bred Turner twins were making faces at him in a disgustingly forward manner. They were his only two customers. One of them held a tiny bag that could not possibly contain more than a yard of ribbon. He looked up when I entered, then excused himself to the twins. This first move confirmed in my mind he was Wicklow. Mr. Owens or anyone of his class would not have automatically excused himself so prettily.

"G'day, Miss Anderson," he said, with a good imitation of the provincial accent. "A lovely day, isn't it? What can I do for ye?"

"I came to inquire if the calico has been delivered. I expected to see it at the rectory some days ago." I knew full well it sat on the table in the church porch, but I had directed him to deliver it to myself.

"I had it taken over to the church," he answered. "I understand that's where it's measured up and handed out."

"Yes, it is, but I *did* particularly ask you to deliver it to the rectory."

"I'll have it sent right over to ye. Why, I'll take it myself, ma'am, as I am about to go for my luncheon."

"That won't be necessary, Mr. Williams, but next time, perhaps you would be kind enough to follow my orders." I then peeped over his shoulder to the giggling Turner twins. "Mr. Williams is free now, girls," I told them. "Sorry to have disturbed your little cose," I apologized to him. "So nice to see you are finding some congenial friends in town." I hastened out the door before he could think of a retort, but not before a certain pugnacious jut had taken over his jaw.

The delivery boy came to the door of the rectory within ten minutes to hand me the bale of calico. When you are a working lady, the weekend is not long enough to attend to the dozens of little personal chores that accumulate. There are your laces and collars to see laundered and ironed (by your own hand, as these rare treasures are not trusted to just anyone), broken shoelaces to be replaced, sewing and mending, the hair to be cut, coiffed or rearranged, and so on. If you happen to be a teacher, there is a pile of badly written work to be looked over and corrected as well. I had wrung a dispensation out of Andrew to do the schoolwork on Sunday. I consider him quite a Solomon in all religious matters, and as he considers *me* the judge in anything of a practical nature, we all three—Andrew, God and I—go on quite happily.

On Sunday morning I was in the gallery with my choir boys and musical group. I had arranged for them to come early that we might greet the congregation with music on their way in, and hopefully rid them of the habit of gossiping quite loudly before the service started. I kept a sharp eye below me, particularly on the Owens box, to see if Wicklow planned to attend. When I saw a dozen bonnets turn around, I suspected he had arrived, as he had. He carried no hymnbook, but arose and sang with the others at the appropriate times. Once early on in the service he turned around and looked up to the gallery, and again on his way out he craned his neck quite openly up, staring at us.

We in the gallery sang the congregation out the door as

well as in, after which we nipped smartly down the staircase to receive compliments on our performance. I was usually the last to get away, as I had the job of rounding up the music and storing it in the cupboard. As I finished up this chore, I heard a heavy tread on the stairs. I turned to see Wicklow coming toward me, hat in hand, greasy smile in place.

"Good morning, ma'am," he said, bowing politely. He had switched from the local g'day, using Sunday manners.

"Good morning, Mr. Williams. Did you wish to see me?"

"Aye, I did. That was grand music ye provided. I enjoyed it very much."

"Thank you. It was kind of you to come and tell me so."

"Not at all. A good performance ought to be congratulated."

He deserved congratulations on a pretty good performance himself, but I could not bestow the earned praise. "You must excuse me. I have to go down to the porch. This is calico Sunday," I reminded him.

"Ah yes, ye got the calico all right?"

"Yes." Oh, and had forgotten to have it returned to the porch for distribution! I hastened to the stairs as though the place were on fire.

"I was hoping to speak to ye a minute," he called after me.

"Later," I said over my shoulder, then caught Billie Marson by the elbow to go and fetch the material back to the porch, lest Mr. Williams should begin to wonder at my having had it removed.

There is a certain etiquette involved in the giving out of calico, which is as follows. Those *not* receiving stand around to see which of their neighbors are, but do it with all possible finesse, only flickering their eyes to the door as each recipient comes out with her length carried as inconspicuously as possible under her arm, or stuck into a reticule if she has one large enough. Those who are ashamed of receiving aid have a son or daughter stand by their side to dash off home with it, while the mother returns to the yard to chat with the non-receivers, as though she is unaware this is calico Sunday at all. When you see a small handful of women remaining behind long after all the others are gone, you know they are the handful who would want and could well use a length, but are too proud to go on the parish record. They will saunter into the porch, looking over their shoulders, and mention having dropped a glove or left a book behind. If an overseer has been at my shoulder, this is his time to depart.

51

"Oh, Miss Anderson," they will say in surprise. "You are here! But it is calico Sunday, of course. It quite slipped my mind. What quality is it?" They come and feel it, and if the woman has the good fortune to be alone with me, she will then proceed. "All this left over? There must be six ells at least. What will be done with it?"

"I haven't a notion, Mrs. Samson," is my line. "Would you care to take a piece?"

"Oh, I am not on charity!" she will exclaim, offended.

"Seems a shame to waste it. But it may find a use before long."

"If you are *looking* for something to do with it..."

The scissors are already snipping off a length, soon the hands (Mrs. Samson's) are folding it into a parcel of the smallest possible dimensions and stuffing it into a recticule of the largest possible, carried on purpose on this day. Then Mrs. Samson goes to pick up the glove she carefully forgot behind, while Mrs. Carr comes to comment with surprise that several yards are left over, and what will be done with it?

The process was speeded up today as Mr. Williams, not on to our routine and the privacy desired, stood at the doorway waiting to speak to me. I cut the overlength up and folded it myself to give to the unentitled poor with only a nod and a smile as they went to get their glove. "Left over," I said, as they each snatched it up eagerly.

"Ye certainly keep yourself busy, Miss Anderson," Wicklow said as the last woman departed, her calico miraculously disappeared into some fold of her pelisse or pocket. The recticule was not bulging as it ought.

"Be not solitary, be not idle. *You* follow the first rule, I the second."

"I follow both when I can."

"What is it you wish to see me about?" I had an idea he meant to ask me to walk or drive out with him. It had been discovered during the week that besides a handsome mount, Mr. Williams also possessed a whisky, a one-horse open carriage. I prepared my refusal with an inward smile.

"About the choir," he surprised me by replying.

"You have already complimented me on the choir."

"Aye, so I have. It's so fine I've a mind to join, if ye'll have me."

I hastily considered this. It would be inconvenient to have him in the gallery, where I often managed a quiet word with Jemmie, as I had done this morning, discovering Crites knew nothing of the one landing at Lord Aiken's place, so that we could use it for the next delivery. "How is your voice?" I asked, to give myself time to think. There were advantages to his joining. I could not be forever running into the shop like the Turner twins, and if I were to get at his brain at all, this would be an opportunity.

"It's considered fair," he replied. "Good and loud at least."

"If you like, Mr. Williams, why do you not come to the practice next Wednesday evening, here in the gallery."

"I'll do that, miss."

Let it be understood from henceforth that when I was "miss," Mr. Williams was smiling and flirting with me; when I was "ma'am," he was more formal. It will save a deal of repetition. "I hope it will not cut too severely into your socializing," I said, with a little bit of encouragement.

"It's a sociable town surely. Everyone very friendly. *Almost* everyone, that is to say," he added with an arch look.

"You must refer to the men, sir, for I'm sure *all* the girls have been very friendly indeed."

"Yes, the *girls* have, but the *ladies* are not so kind. I hope to sing myself into charity, ye see."

"Let us see how prettily you sing, sir, before we speak of charity."

"Ye are active with the charity work in town, I see."

"As the rector's sister, many small duties come in my way."

"It's an awkward way the business is arranged, to give the calico so publicly, is it not?"

This was a bone of contention between myself and the Parish Council, but no better way had occurred to me. A visit to the doors of the poor, or they to the rectory at calico time, would be equally well noted.

"If you have a better idea, I would be happy to hear it."

"The best idea is to obviate the need of charity entirely." That high-flown "obviate" had slipped out unnoticed by him. "Is there a great deal of poverty in the town?"

"You would not be inclined to think so from the hordes who pass their days in the drapery shop, but there is plenty of poverty."

"I wonder how the poor people keep body and soul together. There is quite a bit of unemployment around, but I suppose here on the coast the men are into a spot of free trading."

"Very likely," I answered innocently, while my heart beat

53

faster. He was angling for information. I must take care that he learn nothing from me.

"How is it done, do ye know?"

That he was asking me so openly was a relief. He would not do so if he suspected for an instant I was in any way involved. "It comes in on ships, I believe, Mr. Williams," I answered, feigning surprise at his obtuseness. "Brandy comes from France—it must come in on ships."

"To be sure, but I meant once it is landed, what is done with it?"

"It is sold."

He nodded, and finding me singularly uninformative, changed his tactics once more to dalliance. "Nice day for a drive, miss," he said leadingly.

"A lovely day. My brother and I plan to drive up to Felixstone to visit friends."

"Do ye usually drive out with your brother?" he asked.

"Why no, I more often drive out with my companion, Miss Halka," I replied, arising to indicate the meeting was over.

He frowned in open displeasure at the putting off, as he held the door wide for me to exit. There were no less than three groups of common girls *still* hanging about outside the church, three quarters of an hour after the service was ended. They were waiting for a chance to try their charms with Williams.

"If you dislike driving alone, Mr. Williams, I cannot think you will have any difficulty filling your gig," I told him, looking at the girls.

"Ye are very kind, ma'am, but I do not stand in need of any charity."

As I took a peek from the window of the rectory, I noticed he had taken Mary Slack up in his whisky to carry her home, leaving all the others behind to agree how forward Mary Slack was become. And so she was too. I believe she *asked* him for a ride. She spoke to him first, and he nodded his head as though in agreement. From such a distance, with the cut of his coat concealed, Williams gave a very good impression. I could not but wonder how he looked and behaved when he was being Sir Stamford Wicklow.

Chapter Six

Monday after school I drove the gig and Babe down to Aiken's place to see just where the brandy would be brought in, and of equal importance, where it would be stored till Phillips picked it up Sunday night to take it off to London. Lord Aiken had a sailboat, a great white schooner it was, beautiful. It bobbed at anchor at his dock, the spars sailing straight up into our beautiful blue hazy skies. I was curious to learn whether His Lordship was in residence. This was only a summer home for him. In September it was probable he would be in London. I invented a sudden thirst to have an excuse to seek out his housekeeper, Mrs. Hilbury, for a glass of water.

She was extremely helpful, not only in giving me wine in lieu of water, but in informing me His Lordship was in London, with no intention of returning here in the near future. He planned to go on to his country seat in Oxford when he left the city. Before leaving, I asked casually, "Would it be all right if I went down to have a look at Lord Aiken's sailboat? It calls to mind the old days..." I finished with a wistful sigh, to make her believe I was recalling my golden youth, when I had been a little rich lady, being taken out for sails on His Lordship's boat.

"Go right ahead, Miss Anderson," she replied immediately. "The lads are in the boathouse this minute getting the rollers ready to put it up for the winter, as Lord Aiken doesn't plan to use it before spring."

Away I went, to scout out the dock and boathouse, to see if the latter might hold the brandy for a couple of days. A glance told me the impracticability of this scheme, with the ship to take up the better part of the covered space. I rambled in the warm autumn sun over the grounds in a pointless way, my eyes darting hither and thither. At the stables, I took a peek in, and knew I had found my spot. The only nag in the

55

stable was the gig horse that Mrs. Hilbury herself occasionally drove into Salford. Aiken had removed all his mounts and carriage horses, leaving large spaces, with plentiful piles of hay that could give concealment. With only a very small staff in the house, privacy was secured. The stables were well set away from the house too, to prevent even the least sound from being heard.

I allowed myself one quick glance in the window of Mr. Owens' drapery shop as I passed by, grinning inwardly at how well I had outwitted Williams-Wicklow. He stood at the door, carrying on with Mary Slack in a bantering way. The girl had no more sense than to be chasing after him before the whole town. No doubt the evening would find him in Slack's parlor, trying to pick the brains of her brother Joe, one of my best boys. As close as an oyster, Joe. Indeed, the boys and men were all chosen for their closeness. Williams was wasting his time playing up to Mary Slack.

On Wednesday he came to the church gallery for the choir rehearsal. We were just beginning to practice the hymns for Christmas—we would introduce them at Advent and continue singing them through New Year's. He had a good voice, almost overpowering I felt, though he was modest enough to sing more softly when everyone turned and stared at him. He was either familiar with the songs or could read music. It was such usual fare as Coventry Carol we sang—nothing esoteric at all.

On rehearsal night, Miss Halka always sent Andrew to accompany me home. She was solicitous to keep up every appearance of respectability, due to both my fallen fortune and my criminal activities. On this evening, Williams hung back behind the others. "Could I see ye home, miss?" he asked, when privacy allowed.

"How thoughtful of you, but my brother always takes me home."

"Ye'd not want to be walking the whole ten yards alone," he answered, smiling.

"Especially not when the neighborhood has lately fallen heir to the most gazetted flirt that ever left London" I answered playfully, casting a bold smile on him.

"Upon my word ye are hard on me!"

"Very true, but *someone* must make you realize the whole of feminine Salford does not sit at your feet, Mr. Williams."

"No, at the door of the drapery shop," he answered, then laughed, delighted with his easy conquest. "I don't see any sign of your brother," he continued. "Will ye not let me escort ye to your door?"

Looking over the gallery railing, I noticed Andrew coming from the vestry, telling me he had come in the back way to the church. He looked up and nodded. I reached for my pelisse, which I always removed to allow free movement of my arms during rehearsal. Wicklow automatically came forward to help me, again revealing his origins, for I am sorry to say there was not a man in the little musical group or choir who had ever bothered to perform this office for me.

"That's a very nice organ you have there," he said next. "It looks new. How does it come no one plays it?"

"Ignorance, Mr. Williams. We are all ignorant of the art, though Andrew is trying desperately to learn. He speaks of holding a concert one evening. Christmas may be a good season for it."

"I play a little," he mentioned, going to the keyboard to have a look at the stops. He was still there, pulling knobs and preparing to be seated, when Andrew clattered up the stairs, stumbling at every second step. He needed new spectacles, but would not get the lenses changed till he dropped this pair and stepped on them. This usually occurred every few months.

"Good evening, Mr. Williams," Andrew said, peering through the gloom of the poorly lit gallery. I wondered how Mr. Williams had so rapidly made Andrew's acquaintance. Andrew seldom went anywhere.

"Good evening, sir," he answered.

"I see no introduction is necessary. When did you two meet?"

"We met here last Tuesday," Williams replied. "I stopped by at my noon hour to admire the church, and your brother was kind enough to point out a few features to me. The font is very impressive. I have never seen one so huge."

"Fifteenth century," Andrew said. "They immersed the infant for baptism at that time."

"That pair of rood stairs below would indicate the church is very old," Williams remarked. "I wonder if there isn't a crypt beneath it."

"As a matter of fact, there is," Andrew informed him. I was sure the revenue officer would request a view of it, but before he could do so, Andrew was pointing out the organ, his pride and joy.

"It's called a baroque organ," Andrew told him. "It has a

beautiful tone, clear and light." This came as news to me; I would have called its tone squealing or thundering.

"A Praetorius, if I'm not mistaken," Williams mentioned. He could hardly have said any words to make himself more interesting to Andrew. Behind those glinting spectacles, the blue eyes smiled, making Andrew look about twelve years old. "You know a little something about organs, do you, Mr. Williams? Do you play at all?"

"A little," he confessed.

"I dabble a bit myself." About eight hours a day he dabbled, but still he was not proficient. Dabble was as good a word as any.

"I see you have two manuals," Williams said, sliding onto the seat.

"Thirty flue stops," Andrew added. "One of the largest made."

"No swell pedal of course in the Praetorius," Williams commiserated, in just the proper tone.

"Oh, it's plenty loud enough for this small church."

"True, and you can achieve a good tonal contrast by alternating between the two manuals," Williams pointed out.

Andrew perked up his ears, like a hound after a hare, at this bit of news. Tonal contrast was not one of Andrew's familiar speeches regarding the organ. They began pushing and pulling knobs, and uttering such words as diapason and stopped diapason and accouple. It was like trying to understand Greek. I could see a fanatical gleam in Williams' eye that told me the knob pulling would go on for some time. I fastened up my pelisse and went the ten yards home, alone and unmolested.

It was a full hour before Andrew returned, and when he came, Williams was with him, still cropping out with diapasons and *badinerie* and *fonds*. Andrew had discovered a fellow fanatic.

"The best luck, Mab. Mr. Williams is an excellent organist. He has taught me a dozen tricks in ten minutes."

"In sixty minutes, Andrew, if you have been there ever since I left."

Williams smiled apologetically. "I see you got home safely, Miss Anderson," he said sheepishly.

"I fought off the marauders all by myself. What tricks have you been teaching my brother?"

"A dandy new combination of stops—sixteen, eight and four flutes, and he explained about coupling the keyboards,"

58

Andrew exclaimed, smiling widely. "But I don't quite understand what you meant about dynamic range, Mr. Williams. I say, what is your *real* name?"

Mr. Williams' eyes flew open a fraction wider, as I bit back a smile, for Andrew meant by this only what was his given name. "I'm Andrew—Andrew Anderson. I daresay you're William Williams."

"No, Stanley," Williams corrected, the eyes settling down with relief.

"You really must come over when you have a moment free and give me another lesson. I think I have nearly got the idea of the footwork—the root and the alternate, you know, as you were explaining to me, only I'm not sure how you figure out what the alternate is."

"I would be happy to come. I am eager to get my hands on the organ. I used to play at home, and miss it. I'm pretty rusty, I fear."

"I wish I had such rust," Andrew said.

"Would you care for a cup of tea, Andrew, or a glass of wine?" Miss Halka asked.

"Tea, I think, if that's all right with you, Williams?" my brother answered.

Mr. Williams nodded in a little perplexity and took a seat. Andrew would happily have talked organ the whole visit, but Mr. Williams was more conscious of his social duty. He began diverting the talk, bit by bit, to other matters. I first thought this was to include Miss Halka and myself, but his true purpose was not long in dawning on me. He was trying to see if Andrew knew anything about the smuggling. He broached the matter again by talking about charity and the poor of the parish, but soon his true subject was out.

"Is smuggling much of a problem?" he asked, in a conversational tone, not changing his voice or posture.

"The real problem is the necessity for it," Andrew replied, with a certain little ecclesiastical shake of the head he had picked up since coming into office. "It is not right that so many people be forced to earn bread for their families' mouths by that means."

"It is unfortunate, but still smuggling is illegal, and the folks could find some other way to earn their bread. Fishing, for instance, ought to provide good income here on the coast."

"*Good* income? No, Williams, it provides a very poor income, unless a man can afford to outfit a fishing vessel for himself, and they are too poor to buy a rowboat, most of them.

What chance has a downright poor fellow to make a living, fishing with a rod or net? Commercial fishing requires a large investment. Some of them are hired on as hands on the larger ships, of course, and eke out a living in that way. They're paid a shilling a day. They make six shillings and nine as a carrier of brandy in one night, I hear. That's about a week's wages on a fishing smack."

I could see Mr. Williams come to attention at the mention of the specific sum paid smugglers. Actually, the price mentioned was out of date. I had raised the rate when I got a better price from Pettigrew. "I expect the larger, ocean going fishing vessels pay more," was what he said.

"What a life for a family man! Gone from his family for months on end. I almost think smuggling is preferable," Andrew said.

"I am surprised to hear a man of the cloth speak for breaking the law."

"Oh no, you misunderstand me," Andrew corrected him at once. "The law ought certainly to be changed."

"Until it *is* changed, it ought to be obeyed," Williams decreed.

"I don't know that it is required of a man to uphold a bad law," Andrew decided, sinking rather rapidly into disinterest.

"If every man decides for himself which laws he likes, w would soon be reduced to chaos," Williams challenged him

"I speak only of bad laws. As a man of the church, I am more interested that my people obey God's law, and I can find nowhere in the Ten Commandments that a man ought not to smuggle."

"Thou shalt not steal," Williams reminded him.

"The government should not steal from the people, especially the poor people. Mab is just back from London, and indeed I have to go there myself from time to time, and we cannot justify such extravagance as is seen there among the wealthy, most noticeably the royal family and the aristocracy. Clothe the naked, feed the hungry, comfort the afflicted—those are the laws with which I am concerned."

I smiled my gratification at Andrew. Inside that distracted exterior, he had been pondering the problem I had presented to him some time ago. Williams was now regarding him with downright suspicion. I rushed in to divert his thoughts.

"All this smuggling has nothing to do with us. Naturally Andrew, the local minister, has nothing to do with it."

"Who does run the local outfit?" Williams asked blandly, as though he were inquiring for the name of a good tailor.

"No one knows, Mr. Williams," I told him. "It is kept a great secret, because of being against the law, you know."

"I see," he answered, trying to stifle all his annoyance with my poor answer. "Still I should think that between a schoolteacher and a minister, you would have *some* idea."

Edna had been sitting perfectly rigid in her chair since the conversaiton had turned to smuggling. She looked as though she had been turned to a pillar of salt. It was fortunate that Williams was not paying any attention to her, but he now turned in her direction, as though to judge whether she might not have some sources of information as well as the minister and the teacher. I spoke up quickly, to prevent his seeing her chagrin. "Officer Crites is the one who can tell you all about it. He is well informed on the matter."

"He makes no arrests; I wonder if he isn't one of them."

This was so far off the mark I had to laugh, and then I had to explain my laugh away. "You misjudge him. He tries very hard. A year or so ago he thought they were storing it right in the school. Imagine the gall! But in the end he decided it was only an apple gone bad that caused the odor."

"Bad apples do not smell like brandy."

"It was a horrid smell anyway," I answered innocently.

"Say, Williams, I _have_ just _had_ an idea," Andrew interpted, smiling in a way that said "organ." "If I dropped over ⌐ the shop tomorrow with my book, maybe you could find a minute to explain to me about that root and alternate you spoke of."

"He might possibly be able to spare you *one* minute," I said, with a coquettish glance at the Lothario.

He met the look, pleased that I was flirting with him. "I would be happy to help you," he said.

There was nothing unusual in the words, but he had slipped into an accent during the visit that was not far removed from a gentleman's, and seemed to become aware of it at about this time. He arose immediately to begin a series of leave-takings, throwing in every low-class idiom he had picked up from the shop. "Ye'll be thinking I've no manners at all, overstaying my welcome, as ye might say. And yourself having to be at your school bright and early too, Miss Anderson. I'll be off home then, and thank ye kindly for the cup of tea, Miss Halka."

He was gone, with the burst of rusticity unnoticed by Andrew, who took up his book of organ techniques and went to his room, without saying goodnight to either of us, but mumbling something about roots and alternates.

"Do you know, Edna, I think for a minute there Mr. Williams began to suspect Andrew."

"I nearly died of fright. Won't it be a great nuisance if he decides to set up spying on us?"

"Good God, and Jem stopping off at our door as often as you please. I must find some good excuse to account for it. The Hesslers have enough evidence of their smuggling wealth that he will know perfectly well they are in on it."

"Oh, but the higgler stops at plenty of homes, what with buying and selling and doing errands as well."

"We have never dealt with the higgler—rather a pity. It would look odd if we should switch our custom to him now, after having our milk and eggs from the Browns for a year. Edna," I exclaimed suddenly, "our wits are gone begging. Jemmie buys as well as sells. He shall buy those pretty bookmarks you embroider, and sell them to his other customers on his regular rounds."

"I have already given them to anyone who reads books."

"Something else then—you must take up the manufacture of some small item—glass beads perhaps."

"I wouldn't have an idea how to make them."

"No, no—buy them and string them into necklaces for sale to the farmers' daughters. That will give Jem a good excuse to come to us as often as he must."

"There are no beads for sale in town. It's a pity we hadn't bought a box when we were in London."

"I'll post an order off for them this very night."

I did so before I set my head on its pillow, and Miss Halka was soon in business as a fabricator of necklaces, and making a tidy profit out of it too.

Chapter Seven

I had thought Crites would often be stopping off at the drapery shop, as he would serve as Williams' contact in the neighborhood, but I never once saw him anywhere near it. An event occurred which led me to believe Crites had no notion of Wicklow's true identity. It occurred on a Friday as I wended my weary way home from school in my gig. It happened that Dame Aldridge sat with me, her own horse having stretched a tendon. Crites hailed us up along the way, riding his old underbred gray mare. It was generally understood that when Crites raised his right hand to you, it was only a salutation, but when the left hand was held straight out before him, the oncoming person was to stop, as though his arm were a toll gate. Today he raised his left arm. I always experienced an unpleasant twinge of guilt and even fear when I saw Crites, though my main preoccupation these days regarding smuggling centered on Williams, the more dangerous opponent.

I drew in and smiled prettily at him, while his own teeth extended out to return the pleasantry. "A stiff breeze," I mentioned. Stiff enough to worry me actually, but it did not seem to be rising, and it was not yet unmanageable.

"Can you spare me a minute, ladies?" he asked. We nodded our acquiescence. "It is about Mr. Williams I want to speak to you," he went on, causing my interest to increase sharply. "Very strange the way he landed in on us, and no one having heard a word in advance from Mr. Owens that he was taking his wife to Bath."

"It was odd surely," Miss Aldridge agreed. "I was in the shop myself not two days before she left, and nothing was said of it. She had not complained to anyone that I heard of, but was her usual hale and hardy self."

"A very strange affair," Crites said, nodding his head. "I didn't think old Owens was in league with the gentlemen, but I'm beginning to wonder if he isn't"

"What do you mean?" Miss Aldridge asked. I was happy to sit back and listen quietly.

"What I'm getting at is, Owens might have called in Williams to give him a hand bringing the stuff in. There is a better mind behind the operation these days, I am convinced." I mentally congratulated myself on this unintended compliment. "Owens is getting on in years. He might have invited his cousin to come and lend him a hand, and thought to make it look innocent by claiming he had to go off to Bath for a spell, but when he comes back, Williams will stay on. Mr. Williams has joined your choir, Miss Anderson, and I see your brother has been into the shop the past two mornings. As you've scraped an acquaintance with the fellow, I was wondering if he ever said ought to make you suspicious of him at all."

Andrew was well known to live in a dream world. What Crites actually meant was that he knew Williams had visited us last Wednesday, and what was my opinion of him.

"It is odd you should ask, Officer Crites," I exclaimed with the greatest enthusiasm. "He spoke of smuggling for full fifteen minutes."

"Did he indeed?" Crites asked with the satisfied air of a man having his suspicions confirmed. "It seems he speaks of the matter often when he is courting the local girls."

"I shouldn't think he would harp on it if he is Miss Sage," Miss Aldridge mentioned. The name Miss Sage had seeped into the conscious of the townspeople, by what means I know not.

"That's true," I had to agree. "Also, when he spoke of smuggling the other night, he spoke hard against it."

"He would, wouldn't he?" Crites asked knowingly.

I saw his meaning at once but let him go on to explain it.

"He is pretty bent on setting himself up as a foe of the smuggling business to such worthwhile persons as yourself, Miss Anderson. When he visits with the Slacks and Turners and the more common people, he has not a word to say against it. No doubt he has heard that you have been kind enough to help me in the past, and wishes to establish to you that he is innocent."

"The bounder!" I declared, with an admiring glance at Crites. I know I need not tell you this admiration was simulated. The little laugh that escaped my lips was sheer delight. What fun to have the old revenueman wasting his time chasing and pestering the new! A neat turn on Wicklow, who thought he did not require any help. "He didn't fool *you*, Officer Crites."

Crites blushed modestly. "Nothing is proven, but as you ladies have helped me in the past, I would welcome hearing anything you pick up around town. It is good to know the upholders of the law have *some* friends they can count on. Most of the people in Salford wish me at Coventry, as I well know. However, I would not want to harass an innocent man, and would appreciate your saying nothing of what we have discussed here. I shall keep an eye on him. He behaves in a strange way, I can tell you."

I was much of a mind to have this dangerous statement expanded on. Crites was happy to oblige me. "He never stays in his apartments over the store for a minute at night. He is always out prowling."

"He is a womanizer," Miss Aldridge stated categorically.

"He is in that line, no denying, but he usually leaves the girls' houses early on. He doesn't go home."

"Where does he go?" I asked.

"Strange places," was the intriguing reply. "Spends many a night riding up and down the shore road, poking his nose into any barn or hole along the way. I've lost hours of sleep following him. I think he is looking for likely spots to conceal the brandy, but I check out each and every one of them, and have found nothing thus far. I'll keep after him. If he is up to what I think he is up to, he'll be caught. We'll conquer yet, ladies." With a gallant lift of the cap, he nodded and rode on down the road.

"It wouldn't surprise me a bit," Miss Aldridge stated, then turned at once to gossip of the schoolroom.

I began to see that if Williams was as busy as Crites indicated, he should have an eye kept on him by the smugglers as well as the revenueman. He would be the most watched gentleman ever to have set foot in Salford. Andrew retired early that Friday evening, giving me good privacy to speak to Jem about his coming to sell Edna's beads, as well as setting a guard on Williams at night. We agreed on Mark Hessler for the job. Jem was too busy, and if we were to keep it within our own tight little circle, it must be one or the other of them. Williams' early night courting was no secret—the thing to be done was to wait outside the girl's house and follow him afterward.

I should imagine Mark slept very well during the daytime with such busy nights as he had. It was incredible to me that

65

Williams could be smiling each morning in the shop, when he spent several hours of the night skulking about the shadows, to see which men left their homes, and where they went. That was what he was trying to discover. Mark found he wasted more time chasing poachers than anything else. It was Williams' own fault, for if he had consulted with Crites as he should have done, he would have had at least an idea of where to begin. We had to use all our wits to confound him all the same. If nothing else, he was a hard worker. It was mainly on Friday nights that he annoyed us. Once we knew for sure what he was doing, Mark ceased to tail him on any nights but Friday. His duty on that special night of the week—Mark's duty, I mean—was to find out who Wicklow was spying on, and if it were one of our men, to get into the house unseen and warn the man not to come to work. He was paid full wages as if he had carried his load. I wanted no trouble from my men at this critical stage.

Aiken's place worked out very well. Williams did not consider the home of a nobleman, and one besides that was an inconvenient two miles' walk from the village, as a spot to be watched very closely. We used it all through the autumn. Throughout that same autumn, Williams came on Wednesday evenings to the choir practice, usually walking home with Andrew and myself afterward. Our little à suivie flirtation continued apace. Andrew had taken Wicklow down to show him the vault beneath the church, a detail which I learned quite by accident. The two of them were working up an organ recital for Christmas, to be given in the church as a concert, with Andrew practicing half a dozen simple tunes, the brunt of the music to be played by Williams. He was very musical—a nice lively style he had, which sounded better on the pianoforte in our saloon than on the organ, which required a more decorous pace.

He quite often slipped without noticing it into his own speech patterns, and used phrases too that spoke clearly of a good education. One Sunday after services he walked me to the door, talking of Andrew's sermon, and chanced to say (the sermon was about "no room at the inn" as Christmas drew near), "I feel personally culpable when he speaks of charity, for I had to deny credit to the Morriseys just yesterday at the shop. But then I am only the caretaker. I have no authority. Owens' orders were to restrict credit to one month's wages."

This may not sound a remarkable speech, but the wording

of it, the accent, was so clearly genteel that I was surprised he had let himself slip so deeply into a respectable utterance. What I replied was not about the high-flown speech, but something else entirely. "When do the Owenses plan to return? The visit was spoken of as for six weeks, was it not?"

"It has been extended. Mrs. Owens is not responding so quickly as they hoped."

"You hear from them often, do you?"

"Every week."

"When do you think they will be back?" This, of course, was a matter of deep interest to me, to know how long Williams would be around our necks.

"Not before spring, I believe," was his answer. Had he mentioned an earlier date, I would have worried he knew something, but this long visit assured me he was as ignorant as on the day he came. "I am in no hurry for their return," he added, with one of his flirting smiles. There was no "miss" to accompany the speech. I had somehow become "Mab" during those occasions when he was in our house—not by my invitation either. In the shop he continued to call me "Miss Anderson." I never called him a thing but Mr. Williams.

"I hope they are not back before Christmas at any rate, as the whole town is on tiptoes to hear your recital."

"It will be my first public performance. It is only the anticipation of your party afterward that steels me to go through with it at all."

We had planned a small do after at the rectory for a few of our close friends. The inclusion of Mr. Williams in this party was felt to be not out of place, as he was the star performer of the show. "It is not to be a large party. No dancing, you know, due to Andrew's position."

"A very select party, nevertheless. It was kind of you to include me. You may have noticed I am making some efforts to brush up my speech and appearance, that I not disgrace you." I had noticed he wore a jacket of a better cut the past few weeks. Not the work of Weston or anything of the sort, but he had got the wadding out of his shoulders, and looked less merchant-like. The disclaimer regarding leaving off his accent was long overdue. I believe he must have noticed my eyes widening several times, for he often gave a conscious start after he had committed some particularly elegant utterance.

"It is not necessary for you to don any airs or graces on our behalf, Mr. Williams."

"Still, a man dislikes to appear underbred in front of a pretty lady." The look that accompanied these words nearly knocked me speechless. It was not the cunning, greasy smile he wore when he was trying to con us. It was not flirtatious or insincere, if I am any judge of sincerity. It was sort of bashful, questioning, youthful. It held very much the look of a man thinking of falling in love. My heart beat faster at it. A totally new field of possibilities opened before me, and Mr. Williams was at pains to see that they did so. As a merchant, he knew he must be considered beneath me; he therefore began mentioning a more elevated future for himself.

"Actually I should take every opportunity to better my conversation, for I hope that soon—when Owens gets back, I mean—I may get a position in London."

"What sort of a position?"

"I have a friend, a patron that is, from home who is active in Parliament. Lord Hadley is his name; he thinks he may find a spot for me. With hard work at improving myself, he thinks I might stand for Parliament back home."

"I thought you left Devonshire when you were very young."

"So I did, but I often go back to visit. My father was overseer for Lord Hadley. We have kept up contact with him. He gave me some education, and plans to do something for me in the way of a career. I hope to be better employed soon than standing behind a counter."

"That will be nice for you," I answered, refusing to meet his gray eyes, which regarded me closely, still questioning, hopeful.

It would be futile to deny I found Mr. Williams attractive— or Sir Stamford Wicklow, I ought to say. In his guise of Williams, he was less so. When a young, single lady regularly sees a very handsome gentleman whom she knows to be of birth and breeding, when added to that the gentleman is at pains to please her, some little attraction will inevitably spring up. Throw in an interesting limp won in some heroic battle, and you have a man that is well nigh irresistible. The attraction, on my own side, was in no way diminished by the battle of wits going on between us, but this was the first indication I had that Wicklow felt any *real* affection for me. Thus far we had both been playacting, which added a dash of spice to life. I was now faced with a new dimension. He liked me; with some encouragement, I felt he could be brought to love me.

What a dilemma to find yourself in! A perfectly eligible gentleman falling in love with you, and eligible gentlemen as scarce as hens' teeth here in Salford. How fine to be able to attach him! But it was impossible. Only to think, had I *not* been Miss Sage, I might be instead Lady Mabel Wicklow before many months. But an officer of the law would not be likely to offer marriage to a criminal, and a criminal besides whom it was his chief aim in life to bring to justice. Then too, how was I to keep him at a distance, keep him from falling in love with me? He was now on such a basis of amity with Andrew that he came often to the house.

"It would raise my position in society considerably," he pointed out. "Not that I mean to say I could aspire to marry a—a proper lady" he added, with some of the humbleness and insincerity of Mr. Williams.

I was glad he added that touch of insincerity. I was sorely tempted to break down on the spot and confess my crime, but that brought me to my senses. He was the enemy, and I must not go letting myself fall in love and spoil everything. Nor must I allow him to become any fonder of me.

"You will break the heart of every improper lady in the neighborhood if you do, Mr. Williams," I answered in a joking way, pretending to read nothing personal in his speeches.

He regarded me so intently I was half afraid he was going to crop out into a confession of his own. I really think for half a minute he wanted to do it, but soon he laughed, a cocky Williams laugh, and answered, "Ye must know, ma'am, those females have no hearts. It's only ladies like yourself that are so encumbered."

"*I* am not so encumbered, sir. I lost my heart aeons ago."

"May I know the lucky gentleman? One does not hear in the town that you are attached." There was a lively curiosity in the question.

"In my position, you must know, I have assigned my heart in advance to the first gentleman of fortune who comes along. My father left Andrew and myself destitute, and I am bent on recouping our fortunes by making a grand match."

"You shouldn't have any trouble." Again I was bothered by that soft, sincere smile that I did not want to see. "No trouble at all, Miss Anderson" The words were as gentle, as insinuating as a caress. Indeed I felt as flustered as if I had been kissed.

I wondered just how rich a gentleman I was whistling down the wind. There was something anticipatory in his smile, something that made me think he was looking into the future, to the day he had caught Miss Sage, and come back to Salford wearing his true identity, to claim me. "A lack of fortune produces some little trouble," I pointed out, half distracted.

"I know that better than most," he answered swiftly. So swiftly, and with such feeling, that I was drawn to the conclusion that whatever else Sir Stamford was, he was not wealthy. If I confess it did not detract from his suitability in my eyes, you will have a fair idea of how far I had slipped into insanity. "But if a gentleman has any brains and determination to make his way in the world, a lack of fortune need not stand in the way of his marrying where he pleases," he hastened on to inform me.

I was allowed to misunderstand his meaning, as he spoke of "a gentleman," which he was not yet acknowledged to be. We were at the door of the rectory. I did not dally a moment, as I occasionally did, but began discouraging him by going inside at once. Peeking through the window from behind the lace curtains, I was happy to see (well, anyway I saw) his heart was not entirely crushed by my abrupt departure. He drove Miss Trebar home.

Chapter Eight

As Williams had twice mentioned Devonshire, I assumed it was his own home territory. With an aunt from the same place, I decided to inquire of her if she had ever heard of Sir Stamford Wicklow, saying that someone had mentioned knowing him, and I thought she might be acquainted with him. I waited two weeks for my reply; when finally she answered, she wrote not one letter but two, on two consecutive days. They were well worth the wait. Mr. Williams had proved impossible to set down in the interval, and my conscience was nagging at me. He by no means deserted the shore road or his late-night pursuits, but the early evenings he frequently spent at the rectory, using the excuse of organ practicing to drop in. He would play for an hour after dinner, then spend two in the saloon with Andrew, Edna and myself, or whatever combination was free, for Andrew was busy practicing his six tunes for the concert. I know what you are thinking, and I was *not* always free! Several times I stayed abovestairs on purpose to discourage him from dangling after me, but he usually stayed till I at least made an appearance, and it looked so very odd for me to stay away entirely. I could not even claim illness, as I was at work every day.

One evening I had a batch of papers with me, correcting them at a side table while he chatted to Andrew, but after fifteen minutes and about the same number of peeps in my direction, he arose and offered to help me.

"All this grammar stuff is fresh in my head, as I have been working at correcting my own grammar," he mentioned, drawing up a chair beside me. "Let me give you a hand, so that you can finish up quickly and join us."

"Your own grammar does not need correcting, Mr. Williams. I recall the first time I met you, you were reading John Milton. With such elevated literature, you must be perfectly aware of proper speech."

"I remember our first meeting very well, miss! You gave me a lesson in behavior I did not forget in a hurry."

"I come to think it is time for another! But let us proceed with these students' lessons first."

"Just what is it you are doing?" he asked, picking one up at random and perusing it. "Correcting the spelling and so on?"

"Everything—spelling, punctuation, the sense of it."

"Ah—I never could speak in semi-colons," he admitted, "but I am an expert at sentences and question marks."

"We do not aspire to semi-colons, Mr. Williams."

He picked up another paper and read it through, silently, without making any corrections, then picked up another. It too was set aside without using his pencil. "You are either a very undemanding marker, or have got hold of some other papers than the set I am working on. Don't tell me there isn't a correction to be made on either of these two."

"What is this the students are writing?" he asked, frowning pensively.

"You suspect me of being a Jacobin, I suppose? The assignment was to write what they would do if they had ten pounds. It is interesting, is it not?"

"It is heartbreaking. Listen to this one. Spelled abominably, and *highly* ungrammatical, but the content! 'I would buy my mammie a new dress a bright red one coz she likes pretty things and has no nice clothes I would buy pa a pipe coz he broke his and I would buy a bone for Fritz with real meat on it.' Doesn't that wrench your heart?"

"Unselfish—not a thing for himself."

"It's a girl—Mary Morrisey. That would be the family I had to refuse credit."

"They are very poor. I believe Mrs. Morrisey is in an interesting condition again. They have pulled Sally out of school, in any case, and that usually augurs an increase in the family."

"The other paper, the first, the fellow said he would buy glass for his window to keep out the wind but still be able to see the sky. He can't see the sky through the oilskin. Are the people really that poor? I did not get the impression when I was at the Slacks' or the Turners' they were *destitute*."

"Some are less poor than others," I answered, not liking to mention the word smuggling.

"Morrisey and Slack both go out on the fishing boats. Both make a shilling a day according to Andrew."

"There are other ways of making a little extra money."

"Smuggling, you mean?"

"Possibly. I believe Mrs. Turner takes in washing as well. Fine washing for the gentry—linen tablecloths and such things that want careful pressing."

He sat on, lifting up another paper and reading, still without making a mark with the pencil. "I begin to see why they do it," he said at last in a very reluctant voice. "My God, I thought *my* family was poor till I read this."

"With a patron so generous as Lord Hadley seems to be, I cannot think you have experienced real poverty at all, Mr. Williams."

"I have not often gone to bed hungry, but I know what it is to be looked at askance by the richer boys at school, who wore finer jackets. I come to think my problem was pride, not poverty."

"It is very hard for these people, and some of them have quite large families of youngsters too. Have you brothers and sisters?"

"No. Still, the law is the law, and smuggling, especially of brandy, is no solution. The government ought certainly to institute some make-work program here at Salford, though. Something must be done."

"Oh pooh—about *that* law—smuggling—we are not so strict here."

"If they break one, they'll have no respect for any of them."

"I never hear you speak against poaching. That is also illegal. Do you feel so strongly about it as well?"

"It is less harmful than smuggling, in my opinion, but ought also to be discouraged."

"You speak like a soldier, all discipline and obedience."

"You may imagine how impossible it would be to lead an army if commands were not obeyed."

"You have the instincts of an officer, have you?" I asked lightly, as though I had no idea he had been one.

"And am working to acquire the instincts of a gentleman. I believe I am sinking myself in a paradox here."

"It is not to be wondered at. I often find myself spouting gibberish after too long an exposure to the writings of the students. But alas, I must show the instincts of a schoolteacher, and set a red pencil to these paragraphs, however heart-wrenching they may be."

He too set himself to the task, sometimes frowning over one, which I made sure to read later myself, and sometimes pointing out that the instruction in mathematics was sadly neglected if a boy thought he could buy a carriage and team of four for ten pounds, and still have money left over for a castle on the side.

"Ten pounds is as high over their heads as ten thousand. Had I said ten pennies, they would have had a clearer idea."

When the chore was finally done, we arose to join Edna and Andrew before the fire in the grate.

On another occasion, Edna was in the kitchen, working with Cook, trying to impart to her the secret of a light pastry. Under Edna's tutelage, Cook was coming on. She occasionally served a piece of meat that did not bounce, and was slowly being weaned away from the notion that potatoes to be eaten at six need to be put on to boil at four. With our Christmas party approaching, the lessons increased. Andrew was called to his office to discuss parish business, leaving Williams and myself alone. Being a gentleman, he realized this was not quite the thing and began shifting in his chair, disliking to leave as he had just arrived, and disliking to stay lest I thought it bad manners on his part. "Perhaps I should return later," he suggested uncertainly.

"If you cannot behave yourself, Mr. Williams, by all means do so," I replied, smiling at his dilemma.

"Oh, I trust myself," he answered quickly.

"It is *my* forward behavior that puts you on edge, is it?" I teased him.

"No, Mab, your reputation. A concern for it, I mean. I would not want anyone gossiping about your entertaining a man alone."

"Especially a man notorious for his way with women."

"I no longer flirt with the girls," he told me blandly. This was not quite accurate, but certainly he had curbed his Don Juanish activities.

"In that case I must be safe with you, must I not?"

"You may feel safe from *flirting*. As to more serious intentions, you will know better than I whether you stand in any danger from me."

I felt an uncomfortably warm flood at the serious look that accompanied his speech. Here was I being told he wished to court me, and I had determined I would not lead him on. I could not meet his eyes. I looked to my lap, where my fingers clutched at my skirt.

"Mab, you know I..." he began, all in a rush.

Edna was at the door to save me. "We've just baked up a

74

batch of these cream buns. Won't you try them for us, Mr. Williams, and see if you think they would do for the party?"

He was all smiles and easy conversation again, complimenting her on the cream buns, and partaking of two—a heroic feat, considering the consistency of the pastry. He stayed for some time, chatting to both of us as though it were an ordinary visit, but still the little dab of lovemaking had taken place, and I had not turned aside his ardor as I should have. I felt perfectly wretched when I went to my bed that night. Wretched at misleading him, worse that I could not accept his advances as I wanted to. My aunt's first reply to my letter, when it arrived the next morning, threw me into consternation. She was not personally acquainted with the Wicklows, but the reputation the family wore in those parts was unsavory. The father an out-and-out drunkard who had all but lost his estate, and the son a ne'er-do-well who had been turned from his ancestral door at an early age for some unspecified misconduct. I was saddened at the news, but being infatuated, had soon twisted it around so that all the discredit was heaped on the father. The son, I knew, had made his own way in the world. A man of Wicklow's age, still in the twenties, to have been a Colonel—obviously he had straightened out remarkably. Certainly there was no fear of the son's turning dissolute from drink, for he drank very little. That would be in reaction to the father's bad example, of course. A young man who had seen his inheritance dwindle close to zero because of drink would naturally be against it. And equally against the persons who brought the most pernicious of all drinks into the country. Here was a new dimension to my problem. If Wicklow considered his job in the light of a moral crusade, there was no hope left. I thought the situation could not be worse, till I received her second letter the very next day.

The first page of it cheered me enormously. She had been a little misinformed regarding young Wicklow. The papa, to be sure, was no better than he should be, but he was dead, and the son busy re-establishing himself to fortune and respectability. The fortune was still uncertain, but the respectability was well in hand. He was in the process of becoming a son-in-law to a neighbor and friend of my aunt, Lord Hadley. This was to come about through the person of Lady Lucy, the lord's daughter, who, it was generally understood, was promised to Sir Stamford. There were a dozen questions as well as to how I knew him, and why I had inquired after him,

75

but this was routine stuff. The interest of the letter for *me* was that so far from being attracted to me, Sir Stamford was using me as he used all the other girls. He was promised to Lady Lucy, a great heiress, no doubt—he with his fine talk of a man not caring whether a lady had a fortune.

It solved my immediate problem. I could flirt with him to my heart's content without a fear of bruising his feelings. Lead him down any primrose path I chose, without a single qualm of conscience, as he was doing the same to me. Lord Hadley's "good offices," his efforts on Wicklow's behalf—how clear it all was now. Naturally he would want his daughter's husband to do him credit. My fingers shook with anger as I quickly finished up the letter. The Hadleys were going to London for Christmas, to remain till mid-January. Collecting a trousseau, very likely.

I wondered that Mr. Williams-Wicklow should remain behind for the concert, with his fiancée so close by. Never mind, I would keep him entertained with the flirtation of his life, if that was his game, to wile away the country hours with the local belles. Some prize Lady Lucy was catching for herself. One could almost pity her. Almost.

I wasted no time in getting on with the game. I stopped in at Owens' on Tuesday after school and spent a coquettish half hour selecting ribbons for my recital party, outstaying even Meggie Turner, the most determined shopper ever to have appeared anywhere.

"It is a pretty shade of blue I want, Mr. Williams," I told him, running a look over his wares.

"Cornflower blue, to match your eyes, Mab?" he asked. I need not say we had got rid of Meggie Turner by this stage. Williams, while a villain of the worst sort, had some residual instincts of a gentleman, and would not compromise me by such a speech before one of the Turners.

I batted my lashes at him like a common trollop and smiled hard enough to bring out my dimple, which is a stubborn thing that does not show except when I indulge in laughter. Actually a smile does not do it. He was adept enough at appreciation of a lady's appearance that he noticed it at once. "When did you grow that *charming* dimple?" he asked.

"I sleep on an acorn every night, Mr. Williams. You must recall I am bent on finding myself a wealthy parti, and wish to be in best form when I meet him. A lady without a dimple must settle for a solicitor. I am after a magistrate, like my papa."

"From using my eyes in business the past months, I have become a good assessor of value. I calculate that dimple to be worthy of better than a magistrate." He touched the spot, and looked at me with the eyes of a lover. We were behind the drapery racks, so that the street was denied a view of this dalliance. We were neither of us so lost to appearance as to be doing all this in the full glare of Tommie Barr, who had his nose flattened against the pane out front.

"Now isn't it a shame I hadn't a pair of them, and I might aspire even to a baronet," I answered mischievously. The "Sir" that precedes his name indicates a baronetcy, if I failed to mention it earlier. He was not just a knight.

I understood very well that little secret smile that crept into his eyes, but must show no understanding. I proceeded to business. "Well now, are these faded sky-blue ribbons the best you have to offer? Mr. Owens was used to do better. He kept special ribbons for me, a little deeper shade of blue."

"What color is your gown to be?" he asked.

I rather wished my new gown to be a surprise for him. You must realize without being told it was my intention to make him *really* fall in love with me, to show him a lesson. The gown was one step in my conquest. I had picked up the material in London on my visit and had made it up myself. It was grand beyond anything I normally wore—blue velvet in fact, and with it I had a white lace collar, whose price nearly equaled the velvet's. The ribbons were no more than an excuse into the shop. I had no notion of wearing them. "Blue," I answered.

"You want blue ribbons with a blue gown?" he asked.

Angry at my mistake, I took it out on him. "You are turning modiste, Mr. Williams! If your career is to take a downward trend, would it not be more proper for your talents to be directed at tailoring?"

"Not modiste, connoisseur," he replied unfazed.

"The ribbons are for my coiffure," I retaliated, giving back French for French.

"Ah, the hair! I have something much prettier. Let me show you the new combs I ordered last week. I had you in mind when I bought them. They are above the touch of most of the women in the village. Cost three shillings a pair, I'm afraid."

"Bring them on. I begrudge no expense in garnishing myself, Mr. Williams. By all means let us see these extravagant combs."

77

I did not go to the counter with him, but made him return behind the racks for more teasing, which he did at a lively pace, I might add. "Here we are," he said, opening a box that held a pair of very pretty combs, with little rows of pearls along the tops.

"They would look lovely on a *brunette*. I cannot believe a connoisseur selected these with *my* hair in mind. Come now, confess it was Lucy you were thinking of when you bought them." It was no coincidence that I managed to pull a Lucy out of the air to roast him with. There was a Lucy in our town, a very common girl, Lucy Henderson, who was not one of his flirts at all, nor a brunette either actually, though her hair was a shade darker than my own.

He looked at me, startled into silence for a moment, while a guilty pink rose from his collar. "Lucy?" he asked.

I let him stew a minute, while I gave him a bold, knowing smile. "Lucy Henderson, of course! Who did you think I meant? Why, I think I have caught you out in a new *affaire*, Mr. Williams. For shame."

"No! No, I—I didn't recognize the name at all. I don't believe I know Lucy Henderson." He fumbled with the combs, pulling one out to set it in my hair, then stepped back to regard the effect judiciously. "You're right. The pearls were a poor choice. I suppose I only bought them because I like to see pearls on a lady."

A vision of my pearl necklace from Mama hopped into my head. I had not planned to wear it with the lace collar, but I would do so now. "No doubt you will have the pleasure of seeing the combs on a lady ere long. Stick them in the window, sir. Your salesmanship is sadly lacking."

"Yes, that is apt to happen, when one becomes diverted from business," he answered, turning it into a compliment by his tone and the admiring glance he bestowed on me.

"With the Christmas season coming on, there will be someone willing to pay three shillings to primp herself up."

I began pulling on my gloves preparatory to leaving. He reached out and took my right hand, which was still bare, and held it a moment. He did not say anything, or do anything more than look at me in a way an engaged man should not have looked at any woman other than his fiancée. Something more might have happened had the door not opened at just that moment to admit Mrs. Dustan, in quest of a packet of pins.

78

Chapter Nine

Our deliveries were usually on a Friday, but with our revenuemen both to be accounted for so handily on the Thursday
with the organ recital, I arranged through Jemmie to have
the brandy landed on Thursday, and very nearly came a
cropper. The first part of our evening was a great success.
Andrew got through his six Christmas tunes without many
errors, and Mr. Williams performed beautifully. For an hour
the strains of Bach and Haydn swelled through the church.
The reason we heard Haydn being performed on the organ,
not the instrument for which he composed, was a direct compliment to myself. Williams had arranged a piece of his *Cre-
ation* oratorio especially for the organ, as I had once expressed
admiration for it. It seemed odd not to be up in the gallery.
Afterward the select of the parish came to us at the rectory.
There were no Turners or Slacks or Hendersons in this ex-
alted gathering. We had decided, in the interest of providing
a good number of young girls, to call Miss Trebar a lady for
the evening, but she was as low as we went. I would have
left her out had I been sure Miss Simpson planned to attend
from Felixstone, but that latter young lady did not trouble
her head to reply to my invitation. She did come, however.
She was the daughter of a wealthy independent farmer from
that area, a pretty girl with reddish curls, famous for her
tiny waist, which any gentleman could span with his two
hands. I believe most of the local fellows had confirmed this
fact for themselves. A flirt, in other words.

It was not to be supposed she would pass up Mr. Williams.
She may have been misled into thinking him better than a
merchant when she saw him at the rectory, but even after
his secret was made known to her by a solicitous Miss Trebar,
she did not lessen her pursuit in the least. He sat on the sofa,
pinned between them, and not looking too unhappy either,
till Squire Porson entered the door.

It had never occurred to me Andrew would invite Porson. Had I bothered to think of it, I suppose I must have known he could not well do otherwise. In any case, Porson stepped in, wearing a hideous brown jacket with a shiny yellow waist-coat and canary-yellow inexpressibles. With that crest of red hair, he looked very much like a bloated bird of some sort, whose name eludes me, but I have often seen the bird perched in the apple tree in spring, before the leaves are fully out. Some kind of an oriole I think it is. His brown eyes toured the room. As soon as he spotted me, he was off in hot pursuit. Never did I put in such a night. He made it clear to the whole assembly that he was dangling after me. "Ye've done a grand job of fixing up the little rectory, lass," he praised in a boom-ing voice.

"Thank you, sir," I answered frigidly.

"Aye, a grand job. Any time ye want to try your hand at a bigger place ye know the offer's still open. Ye know where I mean," he added waggishly, while every old cat in the room craned her neck forward to watch us. I realized by his speech that he was three sheets over. In the normal way, he would not have revealed having been turned off.

"I am quite content here, Squire," I replied, with a little tact as I came to realize his condition. A drunken lecher was all we needed!

"A fine lot of blunt ye've spent fixing up. That velvet settle didn't come with the place, nor them rich window hangings. No sir, there's been money spent here, plenty of it." His sharp eyes looked around, picking out every new item I had added with my dishonest earnings.

All this was said in a carrying voice, and it was all news to the villagers. With the rectory having stood vacant for so long, no one had any memory of its exact condition. "I can't think Andrew's three hundred gave ye so much class. And a new gown ye're wearing too—very fancy," he added with a meaningful look. More than meaningful—menacing. He *knew!* Knew or at least suspected. Ganner must have told him. My eyes flew to Elwood Ganner, Bart. He looked quickly away, indicating guilt. This was a complication unseen by me. Jemmie I knew I could trust, but for Porson to know! I was at his mercy, and I would sooner have been at the mercy of a fanged tiger.

"You forget *I* work as well, Squire," I answered, with a smile intended to conciliate.

"I don't forget it, lass. It fair breaks my heart to see ye

trudging home from that demmed school. What ye want is a good man." He patted his yellow vest as he spoke. Here is the man you need, he implied.

There was more of the same, but I kept away from him as much as I could. Never was a hostess so solicitous of her guests. I whirled dizzily from chair to chair, pressing drinks and hors d'oeuvres on everyone. As soon as Porson took a step toward me, I was off on a new tack. All this with Williams observing me from between his jailers on the sofa, and the local women wrinkling their brows and discussing behind their fingers whether Andrew and I had not got a little more out of Papa's estate than we had claimed. As I shoved the nuts and olives to Miss Simpson, Mrs. Everett came up to me, hinting ever so broadly that the chair beneath the window had used to stand beneath the window at Fern Bank, from which spot it had been illegally removed after the sale. Such was my state of agitation that I could think of no good setdown for her, and only denied it flatly.

"How odd. I wonder what can have happened to the one that used to be there then, for there is not a sign of it in the whole house."

I was goaded to suggest that the termites must have consumed it. This sent her back to her seat in a high state of dudgeon. "What a pretty Wedgwood plate, Mab. You never mean this came with the rectory?" Mrs. Trebar asked with a suspicious eye.

Lady Ann, Ganner's spouse, exhibited her breeding by asking not a single horrid question, but only complimenting me on a delightful evening. It was a perfectly ghastly evening for me. At one point Porson followed me right out of the room as I dashed to the kitchen to refill the nut dishes, and to see if Cook had culinary matters under control, a thing by no means certain. "Eh, I hope I didn't offend ye, lass," he said, slipping an arm around my waist. Both hands full, I could not well evade him, but wriggled free, only to be grabbed by his left arm coming at me from the other direction. Williams came bolting up from behind us. That must have looked mighty odd to the company too, for *him* to be on such terms that he felt free to visit the kitchen.

"Let me do that for you, Mab," he said, taking the two empty dishes. Porson let his hands fall away, and I darted down the stairs as though the hounds of hell were after me, without the dishes, while Williams, bearing the empty dishes, led Porson back to the saloon. When I returned, Williams had got him in a corner and was keeping him entertained. By salacious stories, I am sure, for the air was rent with the most lecherous laughter ever heard to echo in a minister's house. I noticed Mrs. Everett raise her brows and whisper to her companion, with a "what can you expect when you entertain merchants" look on her merchant's face, till Sir Elwood strolled over and joined them. He likes a joke as well as anyone, and is not too particular as to the color of it, I hear. When the majority of the gentlemen, even including Andrew, had drifted off to the joke corner, and the ladies were reduced to discussing their ailments and gowns with each other, I decided it was time to serve the meal.

What a relief, for the end of this ghastly night to be at last in sight. I dashed to the kitchen to see all was in order, and heard a tap at the backhouse door. The girls I had hired for the occasion were chattering so loudly among themselves that the sound was not overheard, but it filled me with apprehension. Jemmie had orders not to bother contacting me this evening. With Crites and Williams in the saloon, I felt the cargo must be safe. Crites was there by virtue of the most shameless hinting ever undertaken. He did everything but ask me if he could come, and as Miss Trebar was invited, I decided to allow one male commoner in as well. I was rather curious to see if I could detect any secret looks or whispers between him and Williams, wondering if they had come to terms, but there was nothing like that.

That Jemmie had come clearly spelled disaster. "Cream!" I exclaimed, and went to the door. None of the girls noticed that it was to the backyard I went for this commodity.

It was dark and chilly in the yard without any pelisse. A frost-laden fog hovered in the distance, toward the sea, rising like steam from the ocean. Jemmie looked worried. "Aiken is home!" he said. "Came down for Christmas without telling anyone, and has the stable full of cattle and two grooms. What's to do, miss?"

"Oh Lord, that's all I need!" The crypt was useless tonight, with the two revenuemen sitting smack above it. "The school. Use the school. Christmas holidays—it won't be used for a few days."

"That's what I figured. I've got the lads heading down that way, but I thought I'd better check with you. Come on, Lady!" Lady, lured by the aromas from the kitchen, was sniffing at the back door.

I nipped smartly back inside, with my heart quaking so

I feared an attack. But it was not really a disaster, only a nuisance. The disaster did not come till I entered my saloon. Miss Aldridge was its cause. I sat beside her to try to calm myself, and the first words she uttered were, "I was just thinking, Mabel, the holidays are a good time to give the school a cleaning. I've spoken to Mrs. Wallace, and she's letting me have two of her girls to go over tomorrow and scrub the floors and tidy the place up."

"Not tomorrow!" I exclaimed, in a voice too loud. She looked at me oddly. "Oh, surely not the very day before Christmas, Miss Aldridge."

"It will give the girls a little extra pocket money. They can well use it at this time. It is all arranged, but I do not expect *you* to be there, my dear, as I know you have the Christmas baskets to see to. I shall go myself." She smiled benignly, while I pinched my fingers, and ordered myself not to faint dead away on the spot, as I wanted to.

The only other calamities that could befall me were for Porson to announce me a smuggler, and Williams to clap me into irons. Thank God, neither of them occurred. The evening ground down to a halt at about 1 A.M.. I could not be at all easy to see Williams escort Porson out the door, talking amiably and even mentioning having a run up to Holly Hill for some shooting one of these days. "Lovely party, Miss Anderson," Williams said politely. Not another word. Not a compliment on my velvet gown and lace collar, or even the pearls.

"Aye, a right fancy do. Thankee, lass," Porson seconded. "I'll be paying ye a Christmas visit." Another speech to make the heart plummet. There was no lower place for it to go without leaving my body. It was already in my shoes. What form would the visit take? Marry me, or else...

At last the stragglers were herded out, with Mrs. Everett bringing up the rear, with a last pointed look at my chair beneath the window. Commoner! Andrew was herded off to bed with no trouble. One odd thing happened with regard to Andrew, however. He said, before retiring, "Miss Trebar is a pretty girl, ain't she, Mab?" That's all, but coming from Andrew it augured a whole breakthrough into the world of reality, for him to have realized girls existed, and some of them were pretty. Pity it could not have been Miss Simpson who awoke him to the fact.

"Edna, Aiken is back," I said as soon as he was gone, with a mooning look on his face.

"Good God! How did you discover it?"

"Jemmie was here earlier on." I outlined my orders, and Miss Aldridge's intentions.

"It will have to be moved. Is Jemmie coming back?"

In my rush and confusion, I had not thought to tell him to do so, but he did not fail me. He waited, shivering in the cold, till the kitchen girls were gone home, then tapped at the door. It was too much when he told me humbly that a barrel had broken open in the school, and was at that moment seeping into the floorboards, to make the school reek of brandy for several weeks. I felt like bawling.

"Leave it!" I said. "Just leave the broken barrel there. Nothing can be done to cover the traces by morning, but we must move the rest tonight, for Miss Aldridge is going to the school tomorrow. Get it out at once, Jemmie, and bring it here, to the crypt."

"I'll do that, miss. I kept a dozen of the lads around to see what you wanted done about trying to clean it up."

An hour later they came, each carrying that heavy load over his back. I had Jem pay them treble for their work. It took three trips. I would gladly have given them the whole of the profits to be out of my difficulty.

I literally did not close an eye that night. I had gotten myself into an impossible position. I always disliked using the crypt, as it indicated either Andrew or myself was involved in the business, but Jemmie had spread the story among his men that he had got hold of the key, and we knew nothing of it. No, my chief concern was Porson. How was I to make him believe me innocent? Ganner would be in the church porch tomorrow with me, preparing the baskets for the poor. I must discover whether he knew anything of this, whether he had told Porson of my identity. I could see no other manner in which Porson could know. If Porson knew, I was finished. I would take my money and flee to America. I saw no other course open to me.

Chapter Ten

Next morning, the town was buzzing with talk of the brandy keg broken open in the schoolhouse. What gall of Miss Sage to use the school for his criminal work! Miss Aldridge was down on my head, reporting that she had been to Crites with the story and he was at that moment at the school, looking for tracks. Tracks he would never find; the boys knew well how to cover their traces, and there was mercifully no betraying snow to give them away. Lord Aiken came riding into town to be told the story. He stopped by the church porch to slip a guinea into each basket, for though he was not a regular resident, he was a charitable man and did his bit to help us. He then went across the street to Owens' store, looking for gloves.

It was soon clear that Wicklow had put two and two together. Not immediately clear, but within twenty-four hours, Mark reported that Williams was spending time scouting on Aiken's place. He had tumbled to it that this was the spot we had been using, and we could not use it again. Nor the school, of course, and I disliked very much using the crypt. With Porson suspecting me, I meant to keep the brandy well away from the church.

On top of it all, I had Porson to contend with, but not before I invited Elwood Ganner in for tea after issuing the poor baskets. I did not beat about the bush. It was too important to allow of any possible misunderstanding. "Did you tell Porson I am Miss Sage?" I asked baldly.

"Never in the world, Miss Anderson," he assured me.

"He seems to know—suspect. His manner at the party led me to fear it. You're sure he doesn't know?"

Ganner hunched his hulking shoulders and looked sheepish, casting his blue eyes down to his hands. This was such an unusual attitude for the illustrious Sir Elwood to assume that I knew I did not have the whole story. "Did you say anything to him, anything at all? I don't know how else he should suspect, and he suspects."

"The fact is, we had a game of cards t'other night at Holly Hill, just the two of us. My wife, Lady Ann, has no opinion of cards or such frivolous entertainments. A man likes to get away and relax once in a while. During the evening the name of Miss Sage arose. 'A right wily gentleman it is,' Porson said, and I agreed. You handle the business very well, ma'am," he added.

"What else?" I persisted, not deceived by the compliment.

"Oh, he mentioned this one and that—the name of Williams arose, but I said I didn't think it was such a newcomer among us. We were both drinking, you know, a trifle foxed, to tell the truth. He named off a few others, and somehow Andrew's name came up. Well, he mentioned it himself in fact. Said the fellow was smarter than he ever figured, for he'd got the price of the living here up to three hundred by claiming he had such an offer elsewhere."

"He *did* have such an offer!"

"I don't doubt it. I said I could not believe Andrew was so cagey, and he seemed to agree. 'More like the vixen,' he went on, or something of the sort. Meaning, I'm afraid, yourself, ma'am."

"You're quite sure you didn't confirm it, Sir Elwood?"

"I promise you I did not. I was not that deep in my cups. I only laughed at the idea, and we said no more."

"I hope you are not in the habit of becoming drunk when abroad, to let out things you should not," I said, severely annoyed with him.

"No, I learned sobriety well when I was Miss Thyme myself. I was not nearly so foxed as Porson. I very rarely get a night out and when the chance comes...But you need not fear I was indiscreet. He cannot possibly *know* anything. He is a little suspicious, that's all. Give him a good setdown when he comes to you, if he *does* come, and he will think he was mistaken. I'll lead him off in some harmless direction if he ever mentions it to *me* again—tell him the whole town knows it is this Williams fellow, and there will be an end to it. Just hold your nose high, ma'am, and act offended."

You may be sure I took his good advice. Porson came that same evening. What a Christmas Eve it was! At eight he was at the door asking for me. I asked Miss Halka to join us. Porson tried to be rid of her, but I told him bluntly that anything he had to say to me, he could say before my companion.

"I will then, as ye say so, lass," he declared, with a threatening glance to me. "I've come to repeat the offer I made ye after your father's death."

"My answer is the same as it was at that time, sir."

"The circumstances are not the same," he pointed out, glinting his brown eyes at me.

"No, they are considerably more in my favor."

"They won't be once the truth is out, will they?"

"I don't understand you, sir."

"I fancy Miss Sage understands me."

I looked at him, feigning bewilderment. "I think Miss Sage ought to be consulted," he went on, nodding his head.

"If you are aware of the true identity of Miss Sage, by all means ask him," was my answer.

"I've come to the right house in any case."

"Are you *daring* to suggest that *my brother* is engaged in smuggling activities?" I demanded, rising to my feet in a fine rant.

A quizzical look came over his red face. He looked uncertain, while I rattled on to make him dead certain he was wrong. "Miss Halka, call Andrew in at once, and let him tell this *gentleman* that he is mistaken."

Edna arose obediently, looking so eminently shocked and respectable it seemed ludicrous she was party to my whole infamous goings-on. Before she reached the doorway, Porson hollered after her in his uncouth voice, "Eh, no need...I didn't really think young Andrew..." He looked once more to me.

My neck, already as stiff as a board, stiffened a little more. "Well, sir, may I know what you *did* mean? Miss Halka," I went on in a voice of heavy irony, "it is not possible *you* have engaged in leading a vicious ring of smugglers in your spare time, I trust?"

She smiled in derision and said that indeed she had not. Porson looked at the toes of his boots, his fingers, a picture on the wall, then once more at the richly appointed room. "Where did ye get the blunt to fix the place up?" he asked, with just a tiny lingering trace of uncertainty.

"My aunt, Mrs. Harvey, in Devonshire—you recall she took an interest in us at my father's death—has been kind enough to give us a little from time to time, to eke out the pittance Andrew earns, for all his hard work."

This sounded sufficiently like a dun for an increase in Andrew's salary that Porson shuffled to his feet. "I fancy I owe ye an apology then," he said, heading to the door.

He was gone, and Miss Halka and I dissolved in a heap of nervous giggles on our velvet chairs, taking turns imitating him. I never saw Edna behave so giddily before or since. It was pure relief. She had been more terrified than myself, poor thing. "He didn't know which way to look," she tittered, between bursts of laughter. "But he cast many a peep at your ankles for all that."

"I trust this is the last proposal I shall receive from that wretched man."

"I wouldn't count on it," she cautioned.

I felt immeasurably better. The victory gave me strength to go on. With the most exigent of my difficulties overcome, there still remained the matter of finding a new spot for hiding my contraband cargo. Christmas Eve was hardly the time for it, but then it could not be put off much longer.

Christmas is more properly a time for thinking of one's fellow men. This was a subject never far from my mind, though I give it little space. I continued performing what acts of charity I could find the opportunity for. You would be astonished to discover how hard it is to distribute any really worthwhile charity when one has the reputation of being poor herself. Large donations were impossible. A pair of mittens or a warm jacket for one of the students was remarked upon. As to putting good food on a poor man's table or repairing his shack, it was beyond my powers of devising. Miss Halka employed two girls in stringing beads, the majority of which sat in her dresser drawer, but we let on they were more popular than they were, to make an excuse to disburse a little money to the poor.

What I wanted was suddenly to announce myself as more affluent than I was believed to be, and begin to indulge in some really large charity work. Those essays of my students affected me more than I had let on to Williams. They had affected him too, but not to the point where he had let up on his work. I began to wonder if I could not put about that Mrs. Harvey had settled, say, a thousand pounds on me.

"Everyone would think you had run mad to squander your fortune on the parish poor," Edna informed me. So they would too—a sad commentary on mankind. No, I must come into a sum that for one reason or another I had to spend on the poor. Gambling gains might be so dealt with, but the rector's sister could hardly set up a faro table.

One genteel manner of gambling I *did* indulge in, however, and so did Andrew for that matter, which made it seem perfectly respectable to me. The State Lottery was being run at that time. The closest agent locally was Mr. Pebbles at Felixstone. I marvel that Ganner had not got himself the local concession, but perhaps he considered it beneath his new dignity. In common with everyone else who had any reason to go to Felixstone from time to time, I always picked up a ticket when I was there. Money won at gambling might very well be spent on charity, if the winner happened to be a minister's sister. I would coerce Andrew into making me do it. How was I to arrange the win? The true winner was announced in the lottery circulars posted at each sales counter, to ensure the doubting that real people did in fact win the prize. (This was always hotly disputed, but did not seem to interfere with sales.) I could not very well pretend I had come into money by that means. There were also lotteries run, illegally I believe, in London. I would go again to London, pretend to buy myself a ticket and pretend to win. I was anxious to visit the city in any case, during the holiday. Miss Halka and I planned to attend the Christmas comedy at Drury Lane. Miss Halka did not yet know it, but she would also be going to take a look at the mansion inhabited by Lord Hadley and his daughter, if I could discover its address. Some additional ornaments for my tired toilette were also in the offing. One need not be a Lady Mabel to dress herself up a little.

I would donate the majority of my earnings to charity—say seventy percent, and that was sixty-nine percent more than anyone else I knew gave. Surely I deserved something for all my work and worry. My "win" would be a thousand pounds. I felt immeasurably better after taking this decision. I was happy as a grig when Mr. Williams stopped in on Christmas night to wish us merry and drink a cup of mulled wine with us. He too was in good spirits. I thought he would be in the sulks at being deprived of Lady Lucy's company at such a family time.

"You must have done a good business at the shop, Mr. Williams, to be happy away from your family at Christmas," I ventured.

"I am not much accustomed to having the luxury of a

89

family life," he countered, smiling warmly at me. "Friends are an agreeable substitute," he added, with a glance around to include Edna and Andrew.

There was some general talk of the Owenses, still at Bath and with Mrs. Owens still not well. The matter of the spilled brandy at the school arose. "Imagine their using the school!" he exclaimed. "Miss Sage is poorly named. He ought to be called Miss Brass."

"I think Sage is an excellent name," I disagreed. "He has the wisdom of the Seven Sages of Greece to have hit on the school, such an unlikely spot."

"Next we will hear he is using the church," Andrew laughed. Williams' eyes flew to him, questioning.

"Or Owens' shop," I added hastily, to divert him. "Have you checked out your storerooms lately, Mr. Williams?"

"No, by Jove, but I shall do so. The warehouse is half empty, with easy access too, backing on the docks as it does. I don't usually go near them except to take delivery. Ofttimes not for a week at a stretch."

This information was stored up, though the revenueman's own premises were not likely to be used, except in a case of the direst necessity. A titillating thought all the same. I noticed that Williams took three glasses of our mulled wine that evening, a little more than he customarily drank. It seemed to be a good chance to test his feelings on drink, and his attitude toward one who would bring strong drink into the country. "I would offer you another glass of wine, Mr. Williams, but I am afraid that would be leading you astray, as you do not usually drink much."

"Don't let that stop you. I'll have another, please. Delicious. You serve it in the old way with toast, as my mama used to do. I prefer it to the more modern custom of serving biscuits."

"Your mama approved of wine, did she?" I asked, seeing no more subtle way of introducing my point.

"Oh yes, in moderation. We are not Methodists, we Wi—Williams."

It was of course 'Wicklows' that had nearly slipped out. He tensed up just a little, checking himself, and went on. "All things in moderation is a good rule. Wine, or even brandy, is not evil in itself. It is man's lack of controlling his appetites that does the harm. The same with a love of gambling or power or money. In moderation they are normal and even perhaps beneficial. Life would be deuced dull without them in any case," he finished up, which relieved my mind considerably, I can tell you. I was afraid that derelict papa might have turned him into a fanatic, but it was not the case.

"You hear that, Andrew," I said lightly, to ease any impression I had been digging for information. "You must control that lust for the organ."

"I say, Williams, how about playing us a few tunes on the pianoforte?" was Andrew's substitute.

He played Christmas carols for a while, with the rest of us singing. It was the happiest, homiest part of that whole Christmas. A feeling so strong one could almost reach out and touch it pervaded the room—goodwill, fellowship, love. How could it all be based on deception? Williams *liked* us, liked being here, sharing Christmas with us. I could not be wrong about that. At the very height of this warm glow, he suddenly looked up and said he must be leaving. It was like a dash of cold water in the face of a dreamer. It was early too, earlier than he began his patrols, only ten o'clock. Surely on Christmas he could take the night off. We had a nice meal in preparation below, somewhat elaborate, with some roast fowl and a raised pigeon pie. He had taken his Christmas dinner at the inn, I knew, with a party of his own, bachelors and misfits like himself.

"You are not leaving so soon?" I asked, surprised.

"Have some more wine," Edna suggested. He settled in for another half hour. Edna went to the kitchen to hurry on the food, and Andrew suddenly wandered off in a fit of distraction, saying something about Diogenes. It was to his study he went, not the gallery.

There was no mention of Williams leaving this time, or of its being improper for him to be alone with me. Rather, he arose with a pleased smile and joined me on the sofa.

"I am happy to have this chance to talk to you in private," he began.

"What is it you wish to say?" I asked, smiling every encouragement, to see how far he would go.

"Just—Merry Christmas," he answered, and reaching out, he lifted my fingers to his lips. Never was a 'merry Christmas' laden with so much intimacy. I made not a move to repress him. I was curious to see to what lengths he was willing to go, behind Lady Lucy's back.

"A very merry Christmas to *you*, sir," I replied, letting him hold my two hands.

"Would you like to make me very happy?" he asked.

91

"Perhaps. How should I do so?"

"By calling me Stanley when we are alone."

"Only when we are alone? But what is the reason for the secrecy? I dislike underhanded dealings. If you are—if you are interested in forwarding any intimacy with myself, I should think I might call you so before my family," I said, with a shy but fond regard.

"I would be honored."

I smiled my most beguiling smile, full of tenderness and hopefully dimples. "And friends," I said. "Of course I do not wish to compromise you, Stanley, if your mind is not quite made up." Let us see you wiggle out of *that*, Sir Stamford Wicklow!

A nervous laugh erupted from his mouth; my hands were dropped as though they were red-hot coals. He was not willing to go so far as to get himself engaged behind Lady Lucy's back. "No indeed!" he said, in a hearty voice. "Business would fall off in a rush if I turned up an engaged man, for it is only my being a bachelor that keeps the shop full."

"You plan to vacate the shop soon, do you not, and see your patron, Lord Hadley, about that position with the government?"

"Yes. Yes, I do. Very soon. In fact, it is my leaving early tomorrow for London that causes me to leave you early this evening."

So Lady Lucy was not to be entirely deprived of his presence over the holiday season! I sat back and proceeded to put him on the griddle. "You don't mean you go to London tomorrow! But that is marvelous! Miss Halka and I go the next day. We shall all be there together. We must arrange to meet and do something. Go to the comedy at Drury Lane, and out to dinner."

It was a better comedy than I was likely to see at Drury Lane that ensued in the saloon, as I watched him squirm out of it. "Ah—ah, that would be wonderful!" was his first speech, spoken in a hollow voice. Then he began backtracking to safety. "Of course I shall be very busy. That is—Lord Hadley has been kind enough to offer to put me up at his place, you see. Very kind of him really, and I only his steward's son. And he usually entertains in a big way. He plans a ball—I am not sure which evening. How long do you plan to stay?"

"We don't have to be back till New Year's. We can stay a week. How long do you stay?" I would, of course, be back before my next delivery.

"Only three days."

"Surely we can work out a meeting for one evening."

"Maybe afternoon would be better."

"Fine, let us make it for the day after tomorrow, in the afternoon."

"If I am not busy. I have business meetings to attend, with some cronies of Lord Hadley's. Where do you plan to stay?"

We had already made a reservation at Stephen's Hotel in Bond Street, electing for a good central location, but I did not mean to let him off so easily as telling him would do. "My aunt, Mrs. Harvey, has asked us to stay with her. Do you know, she is a very good friend of Lord Hadley," I said, exaggerating the acquaintance to set him trembling. "Neighbors from Devonshire. She mentions him often in her letters. In fact, he has a daughter that my aunt has written of—Julie, I believe it is. No, Lucy, I think. If Lord Hadley is having a ball, you may be sure my aunt is attending, and of course we too shall be invited. Oh, how nice, and *you* will be there, Stanley! Now what shall I wear?" I asked, putting a finger to my cheek in perplexity at this imaginary problem.

He looked like an absolute ghost, his face white and staring. "Why, what is the matter, Stanley?" I asked.

"Nothing," he gulped, then laughed nervously. "Well, well, what a small world it is. You know Lord Hadley and Lucy."

"I have never actually met either of them. Only heard my aunt speak of them. Do *you* know Lady Lucy?"

"No! That is—I have seen her about the house, you know, but have not actually met her." I could see his mind working feverishly behind his blanched cheeks, which were resuming some color. "That is," he went on to contradict himself, "I *did* meet her once, at a different ball. Stood up with her—once. Or twice."

"What is she like? But you are a poor one to ask. I can see she made very little impression on *you*."

"She is pretty. Black-haired, vivacious."

I have always admired black hair of all things. If I could change any feature of my appearance, I would instantly turn my blond curls in for black hair. I had a feeling Lady Lucy would be a brunette. Of course I said none of this. "I suppose she has a dozen beaux. Perhaps she will share one of them with me."

"Actually, I am not at all sure Hadley will invite me to his ball," he said, turning desperately to any avenue of retreat he could lay tongue to. "He does not *always* do so, and with my leg bothering me…"

"Is it bothering you again? What a pity, and I was just noticing this week how it seemed to be completely better. You must have a good surgeon take a look at it while you are in London. Promise me you will, Stanley."

"Yes. About the ball, Mab, I expect he will have a business meeting planned for me that night."

"Surely not the very night of the ball," I pouted.

He was at his wits' end. I would not have been a bit surprised had he called off his whole visit. "Mrs. Lawrence Harvey?" was his distracted question. He was trying to fix in his mind just how likely it was that I should turn up at the ball.

"Who, my aunt? Yes, Mrs. Lawrence Harvey. Have you heard Lord Hadley speak of her?"

"No," he said, but in such a state I doubt he knew what he was saying. "You go the day after tomorrow, you say?"

"Yes, and as you plan to stay three days, we shall both be in the city for two days together."

"Why are you going?" he asked.

"For a little holiday. My time is completely free. We can meet whenever you manage a few hours free. What luck we are all going at the same time. Where does Lord Hadley live? Perhaps he is my aunt's neighbor in the city, as well as in Devonshire."

"Belgrave Square," he replied, looking to hear my aunt's address. "And Mrs. Harvey?"

"Portman Square."

"A pity they are so far apart," was his relieved statement to that.

"You have your whisky, Stanley. They are not *that* far apart. I shall be looking for you."

"I will certainly be there, if I can find a single minute free."

"Now *don't* tell me Lord Hadley is such a dragon he won't allow you a minute to call on your—your very special friends. I shall put a bee in his ear if he doesn't let you come," I promised playfully. "My aunt will direct you to an excellent man to see about your leg. She is invalidish, and knows all the best doctors."

He rubbed his leg, as though it bothered him that very minute, but in his confusion he rubbed the wrong one. He looked so worried, so downright woebegone that for a moment

94

I was tempted to take pity on him, till he said, "Lady Lucy has already recommended a good doctor."

That remark took care of my pity in a hurry. He left before the food arrived from the kitchen. I could not keep him in the house, he was too anxious to get home and begin working out plans to avoid us. How sorry I was that my aunt was in fact in Devonshire, and not Portman Square. I suppose it was the first thing he discovered when he got to London. And a great relief it must have been to him too. It brought me resoundingly to my senses, to see how his *real* intentions were riveted on Lady Lucy. If I needed such bringing to my senses, that is to say. Truth to tell, I was finding him dangerously attractive since he had removed the wadding from his shoulders and stopped calling me "ye". I had begun to entertain some hopes his match with Lady Lucy might have foundered on the shoals of a longish separation.

Chapter Eleven

I have mentioned in passing a place called the Eyrie. It sits high on a cliff overlooking the ocean. Much too high, with its sheer rock cliff pitching down to the sea, to be used as a good landing spot. It would take a creature with the leaping ability of a mountain goat and the stamina of an elephant to get the kegs of brandy up that incline, though from the top the tranter's wagons would have easy enough access along a gently winding path up from the main road. Its isolation made it a tempting spot for me. It was connected by legend with the most renowned smuggler ever to land a barrel in England, Miss Marjoram. But then a whole host of exploits bedazzled that gentleman's name, at least three quarters of which are imaginary. With Williams nipping off to London a day before me, I decided to go for a drive up to the Eyrie. It is uninhabited, of course, except for ghosts. These are hangers-on from the days of Miss Marjoram, which inclined me to think he *had* used the house for smuggling. A ghost was a wonderful incentive for keeping the curious away, especially on a dark night, and more especially in those old days when the world was more simpleminded.

The tale of ghosts had not kept Williams away. He had looked into it earlier on in his visit, but had not returned more than twice. Due to its inaccessibility, I imagine, he had decided it was innocent. Busybody that he was, he would not be long in discovering what was afoot if the men used it regularly at all. Unless he could be made to believe any activities there had another motive, and what would any sane person be doing late at night at the Eyrie? No *sane* person would be doing anything, but a lunatic...I juggled various village simpletons about in my head as I drove along, with Mrs. Kiley in the forefront. But no, she would not do. My accomplice at the Eyrie must have more wits than that about her—or him.

This was no more than woolgathering as I wended my way in the gig up the winding path to the summit, mental meanderings to put from my mind the image of Sir Stamford Wicklow simpering and smirking at Lady Lucy. I was determined not to moon about like a lovesick calf. It was chilly on the cliff top, thus ensuring me plenty of discomfort as well as the required solitude. I approached the old house with definite misgivings. It was like a fairy castle designed by an astigmatic demon—all minarets and gables, slightly tipping this way and that. The whole structure was held together so precariously a good gale might topple it over. The once brown wooden shingles had dulled to gray, with an occasional darker spot showing beneath where a shingle had fallen off, exposing protected wood. The windows were of irregular shapes, and stuck into the walls at odd places. There was an octagonal window high up at the front, giving the place the air of a misbegotten Cyclops. From that window, one would have a view for miles across the sea. There were other windows, uncommonly long and narrow, set in at uneven heights. All were smudged with several decades of dirt, dust and mementos of seagulls.

Gathering up my courage, I tackled the sagging stairs of the verandah (which was quite simply in peril of falling off) and reached the front door. It was locked. Back down and away to the rear, where a stone stoop was still in good repair. The back door was on the latch. It opened without a key, making me wonder whether it was not inhabited by someone, a traveling tramp or an illegal squatter. I opened the door and peered in. There were no footmarks on the floor, and it was dusty enough that any traffic the last year would have left traces. I went in, finding myself in a stone-floored kitchen, with an ancient black monster of a stove standing guard over a long table, on which rested some few rusty vessels and utensils. I scuttled quickly through this room to the chambers above. They were nearly empty. Anything worth removing had been taken away; what remained was a few dilapidated pieces of furniture, the stuffing hanging out where animals had been into them for nesting or nesting materials. The gothic decor was complete with cobwebs and spiders, a mouse scampering across one corner of the room, squeaks and squawks as I trod lightly on the uncovered floorboards—the works. I was thankful it was broad daylight. I took a quick run upstairs to see more of the same squalor—

ten bedrooms, not one of them fit for human habitation. I returned below, after just taking a peek through that dusty octagonal window. It was so placed, right at the front of the house, looking straight out to sea, that any lugger approaching for miles, or any official vessel chasing it, would be easily visible. A light in that window would similarly be as clear as a lighthouse beacon to men at sea. If Miss Marjoram had used the house for anything other than a lookout post, he had more wits than I. As I entered the main saloon belowstairs, I felt a cooler breeze, and looked, thinking to discover a broken window. What I saw was not a broken window, but a raised one that someone had forgotten to lower after leaving by it. I smiled softly to myself to think Williams had gone to the bother of breaking in, when the back door had stood on the latch.

Back to the kitchen for a last look around. There was a rough door, presumably leading to the cellar, but I had not quite the heart to tackle a cellar, despite the torch I had brought with me. I turned to leave, then turned back to that door. What if the cellar was the answer to the riddle? Where more likely than a cellar in the bowels of the earth, to hold access to the sea? Foolish of me to have wasted time abovestairs. It was here or nowhere. My heart beat faster with combined fear and excitement as I went down the rickety old stairs, holding my torch high, into a deep, dank, dark cellar. I could swear I still smelled brandy down there.

I peered around in the gloom at incredible blackness. Faint outlines of objects began to swim into view as my eyes adjusted to the dark. Big round things, lined against the wall—barrels. Brandy barrels, each with a bunghole in it. Miss Marjoram had done some decanting here, it seemed, emptied the barrels into smaller containers for retail selling. Miss Marjoram was up to anything. I poked around, no longer afraid, for I felt I was in the presence now of friendly spirits. I mean the late Miss Marjoram and company, not the dregs of brandy.

The doorway was not hard to find once I realized it had to be there. It was off in a nice dark corner, locked, but after coming this far I was not about to be stopped by a locked door, when there was a crowbar beside the barrels. I had the lock off in a minute, and was standing at the top of a steep stairway, hewn out of natural stone, with the unmistakable smell of salt air blowing up on me. The stairway must lead right to the sea. So it did, I soon discovered. Light was seen at the bottom of the stairs once I got around a sharp bend in them. Water lapped across the bottom steps—black water beyond—the sea was deep here. The steps ended in the mouth of a cave. The cave was not large enough to allow a lugger to enter, but a smaller boat could be anchored in the cave, for the final leg of the transporting. Miss Marjoram's men must have stood on these very steps, waiting for their load, and carried it up to the cellar.

I was weak with admiration. Here I had been thinking myself well named Sage. I did not hold a candle to Miss Marjoram for ingenuity, but I had at least sense enough to realize I must have this property. Must have easy and legal access to it, without arousing too much interest locally in my own direction. I had plenty to occupy my mind on the way home. The only time Sir Stamford intruded his greasy smiling face was when I thought how much fun it would be to outwit him. I had been born and reared here on the coast, and had no inkling of this house's secret. Sir Elwood Ganner had not known it; I doubted a living soul knew it, even including the place's owner.

I stopped at the Registry Office on my way home, and discovered the property to be in the name of a Mr. Simon, in London. With a visit to London pending, I wondered whether I could not arrange to buy or rent the place there, do it through a London agent, using some other name than my own. Edna was privy to all my news and plans before we sat down to dinner. She was excited, but cast a hundred difficulties in my path.

"How can you possibly buy it or rent it without everyone knowing you have done so? Your name will appear on the records. Besides, it would cost a pretty penny to buy. More than the thousand pounds you speak of giving to charity."

"I doubt it would cost that much. It's falling apart. A down payment and a mortgage…"

"Buy a house in some name other than your own? What if you should die? Who would get it?"

"I would prefer to rent, certainly. It would be so much cheaper."

"I don't see why you don't just use it. Who is to stop you? There's never a soul there from year's end to year's end. I never heard of any Simons living in this area at all. I wonder if they would be kin to the Johnsons—Meggie Johnson married a lad named Simon, did she not?"

"What has that to do with anything?" I asked impatiently.

"Why, if the house is Meggie Johnson's husband's, there could be no harm in using it."

"Why, Edna, that would be trespassing!" I replied laughing.

"Much that would bother *you,* hussy! The least of your problems."

"You overlook the main point. When someone is living in a house, he has the right to keep off trespassers. The likes of Williams would be less likely to be creeping down to the cellar to see what he missed the first time around if the place had an occupant."

"No one in his right mind would live in that ramshackle rabbit warren of a place."

"I have settled on a lunatic as my tenant," I said, to shock her. "Oh, an eccentric is all I mean. A fierce-tempered fellow to keep people away."

"You'd have every youngster in the neighborhood hanging around if that is the sort of tenant you have in mind. They love to provoke folks who give them a strong reaction. The Nortons have every apple on their trees stolen, not because they are any better than anyone else's, but because old Ned is such a fool he goes hollering and chasing after the lads. Choose a duller tenant."

"Not a bad idea. An invalid, for instance."

"I still think you should speak to Meggie Johnson's mother and see if something can't be worked out."

"Don't be foolish, Edna."

"It is you who is foolish. I think you've run mad. You've been acting oddly ever since you found out Mr. Williams is engaged."

"Mr. Williams may marry his sweetheart today for all I care."

"I daresay that's why he went up to London," Edna answered.

My heart gave a terrible lurch in my breast. I felt suddenly giddy, weak-kneed. It was all the commotion of the trip to the Eyrie, of course, and the plan to rent it. It took quite a toll of my nerves, all the planning and bother. "I am only joking, my dear," Edna said at once, being so addlepated as to think my little spasm of nerves was related to Williams' getting married.

"I couldn't care less about that," I said, shaking off her offered help to seat me, as though I were a disabled octogenarian.

If he had married Lucy, we would not have known it till he came to Salford with her hanging on his arm, for we saw not a sign of him all the time we were in London, despite repeated cruises past Belgrave Square in a hired cab. We did not know which mansion belonged to Lord Hadley, of course, and had not the least intention of actually hounding Mr. Williams, but I thought we might catch a sight of the wedding party. Edna assured me such a social occasion would be reported in the journals. "In the normal way it might, but as Wicklow is working under cover, it might be done quietly, secretly."

"My dear, you worry yourself for nothing. He would not get married in the middle of this job he has undertaken. I'm sure all this Lady Lucy business is a misunderstanding. Wicklow is a gentleman; he would not lead you on so shamelessly. And how could he bring a Lady Lucy to live in Salford?"

"What is wrong with Salford? Lady Ann doesn't seem to mind it. I hope he *has* married her and gone off to Devonshire, that we might be rid of him once and for all."

"You could write your aunt another letter."

"We don't have a copy of the *Observer*, Edna. Maybe the account of the wedding is in the *Observer*."

She gave me such a pitying look I longed to crown her with my reticule. "I only want to know for business reasons. If I read they are gone off on a honeymoon to France, for instance, I shall have clear smuggling for a spell."

"I'm sure he'd never do such a thing to you. *I* know when a young fellow is in love."

"And how do you come to be such an authority on the subject?" I asked sharply, then immediately felt very sorry, for a spinster, as I was coming to learn, was tender on that score. "Well, never mind Wicklow, and never mind the *Observer* either. Is not this a lovely room, Edna? I am happy we changed our lodgings to Stephen's. And the mail too is much better for traveling than the coach. We are becoming quite the seasoned travelers. One only learns these things by doing them."

"A pity Andrew would not have come with us. Two ladies alone cannot do all the things that escorted ladies can do."

Two unescorted ladies felt it not too fast to attend the Christmas comedy at Drury Lane. I thought we might catch a glimpse of Wicklow there as I had mentioned specifically we meant to attend, but we did not see him. It was a wretchedly stupid play we saw. The children at the school could have done better. I was amazed that sophisticated city people could be so well entertained at that farce.

I had certainly not gone to London to waste my time chasing after Mr. Williams. I had better things to do. First in priority was to attend to acquiring the Eyrie. For the exorbitant sum of a crown, an attendant at Stephen's Hotel was kind enough to discover for me where to apply for such information. I might just caution you while I am on the subject of tipping that at such a place as Stephen's Hotel, you are expected to distribute more liberal gratuities than obtained good service for us at Reddelstone's. It seemed every time we turned around there was a liveried boy with his hand out, and they were none too happy with a shilling either. At home a hired hand on a fishing boat worked a long day for that sum, and counted himself fortunate to have got the work. The dining room as well at Stephen's was very dear, and the food no better than elsewhere, though a little more daintily served, with more footmen than was quite comfortable hovering about the table like vultures. Another time, I think we shall go back to the Reddelstone, where you are made to feel welcome, and not as though you had gotten out of your depth.

To return to my story—I was directed to a municipal office, where I learned the "Simon estate," as it was grandly labeled, was in the hands of a firm of solicitors *miles* away, but still within the precincts of London. Away on the east side it was, on Cornhill not far from the Tower. The reason for this was that Mr. Simon was attached to the East India Company, and stationed off in India. When he was in the country, the firm of Milne and Linus was convenient for him, no doubt, but it was extremely inconvenient for anyone else. And expensive too. The round trip in a hired cab cost us a guinea flat (plus that ever-menacing gratuity). I had the notion everything in the city was more expensive than formerly, and soon had the added idea that the price of brandy as well was due for an increase. All the wicked expense was worth it. I hired the Eyrie for a year at a hundred pounds. Mr. Linus suggested a sum of two hundred, mentioning the salubrious location by the sea, but neglecting to mention those sea breezes would not stop at the door, but sail right into one's saloon due to the poor condition of the building. He had the audacity to describe the place as "furnished"! I could hardly tell him I had seen those furnishings, but implied that I understood the place had been empty for some time and was not apt to be worth two hundred pounds a year to anyone, least of all me. He settled for one hundred without too much trouble. I signed myself as Miss Jones, and left with the lease in my reticule.

With the minarets of the Tower beckoning us in the distance, we took the opportunity to have a look at it while we were within a shilling of the place. It cost us a good deal more than that before we were let in. The rate was two shillings and ten pence each, and that a special reduced rate for a party of more than one. Edna felt a sight of the crown and regalia was well worth the price (perhaps because it was not herself who was paying). The King's Menagerie was certainly interesting. It is not every day one has a chance to see live wild beasts. The monkeys in particular were very amusing. They reminded me of the girls at Salford, all hanging round in a bunch chattering, pointing and generally making a spectacle of themselves with no concern for what anyone thought. The elephant made quite a determined effort to relieve me of my reticule. It took the hat right from one gentleman's hand and returned it, slightly the worse for wear. I thought this a sufficiently amusing trick that I spoke to the gentleman in a bantering way, congratulating him on getting his headgear back. It set Edna into such a pucker that she dragged me off, chewing my ear for being a "forward creature, making up to every pair of trousers" we met.

I had to remind her I was no longer her charge, and with one thing and another we were hardly speaking by the time we got back to the hotel. There were no messages for us. Of course we had not told anyone we were putting up at a hotel, so this was hardly surprising. Still, I think if anyone had been very eager to see us, he might have tried a few hotels right on the main street.

Chapter Twelve

It was my intention to get not only a lease on the Eyrie, but a tenant for it. My next step was a trifle odd, no doubt. I cannot think it warranted the "insane" or "criminal" Edna took upon herself to bestow on it. Certainly it was unnecessary for her to state so repeatedly it had anything at all to do with Mr. Williams, except that he was the revenueman I had to fool. She would have it it was all spite because of his marrying Lady Lucy, while assuring me between bouts of ill humor that he had no intention of marrying anyone but myself. I had finally to forbid her from mentioning that man's name to me again till we were home.

To avoid making a short story long as I seem to be doing, I shall outline at once what I did. I hired an actress, who was *not* a prostitute, no matter how many times nor in how many euphemistic phrases Edna called her one. She was amazingly uncivil to me throughout the entire trip, Edna. The newspapers were advertising for actresses for a new play opening, and I went along to look them over, which unfortunately had to be done from outside the building. I'm sure no one took the notion I was a lightskirt, standing there with a perfectly respectable middle-aged chaperone with a face like sour vinegar. The gentleman who asked me if I was lost was as elegant as may be, and did not persist in the least when I told him I was waiting for a friend. I thought it rather sweet of him to inquire whether he could not be of help to me if my friend did not turn up, but Edna would have it he was trying to scrape an acquaintance with me for his own vile reasons. Never mind.

Several painted women came complaining out of the theater, refused any role in the forthcoming production. It was this batch of rejects I was interested in. I chose one who was all alone, looking somehow *desperate*. I cannot imagine what role she had applied for. She was no ingenue—had not been for a quarter of a century, and they continue playing ingenue roles well into their thirties, you know. The ancient playing such a part at the Christmas comedy had to caulk her wrinkles before every performance. All painted up and from a distance, the wrinkles don't show, but when she made her bows at the end of the show, she looked a perfect hag, with the light striking her face at just the wrong angle. My actress wore a garish blue outfit, once elegant, now shabby. Her poor hair was tinted a horrid reddish color, with the dye job not lately repeated, so that half an inch of white showed at the roots. She was pitiful. She had a lost look about her, strolling slowly as though she had nowhere to go.

I felt she was destitute enough to accept any sort of a job, but was slow to approach her, as I did not know quite how to put my proposition to her. I followed her for half a block, while she looked in at windows, then pulled out a handkerchief to apply it to her nose. When I saw the finger out of her glove, I had hopes she would not demur too much at my offer. I stepped up, trying not to look either brazen or condescending, and asked in a friendly way if she was one of the actresses I had seen coming out of Covent Garden.

"I didn't see *you* there, did I, dearie?" was her answer, given in a mock-duchess sort of a voice. She looked me over pretty closely, frowning at my clothing, and more so at Edna, who stood by like a disapproving statue that wished itself elsewhere. "What if I was then? Ain't against the law, is it?" she continued, abandoning all attempts at a noble accent.

"No indeed, I should hope not. Ah—positions are hard to come by, I suppose?"

She sniffed, pulling out her handkerchief again. The less said about that article the better. "What sort of parts do you do?" she asked me. I dislike to say her eyes alit on my reticule, but I'm afraid they did. She intended hitting me up for money, which was excellent. I would hit her up in turn to perform for me.

"I'm not an actress actually," I answered, sadly, as though I would like it of all things to be one.

"You're not one of them Methodists?" she asked suspiciously.

"No. No, I am just visiting in the city. I think it so very exciting, your being an actress. I never met one before."

"So it is, a very exciting profession. I have played with the best—Edmund and Sarah. Mrs. Siddons, you know, and Edmund Kean. So charming. But that was a few years ago."

Some several years ago, before these personages had become stars no doubt, but I did not say so. She was being the duchess again. "Rather chilly today, is it not?" she continued, but made no move to hasten on.

"It certainly is. I wonder if there is somewhere we could have a cup of tea and chat a while. I am Miss Hadley, and this is my aunt, Miss Williams," I told her, grasping the first names that came to mind.

"There's a spot around the corner don't charge you an arm and a leg," she offered. We followed her, Edna hanging a step behind to show her disapproval. If they charged a fingernail it was more than the tea was worth, but it forwarded the acquaintance, and that was the thing. She started off by being one of the brightest names in the theatrical world of London. Edmund and Sarah her constant companions, but by subtle degrees I got her to realize I was good for more than a cup of tea if she were in need, and before long we got away from theatrics.

Over the second cup she was already lamenting, "I'm down to my last shilling, and that's a fact, dearie. I don't know what I am to do. They all forget, once your looks begin to go, they've no use for you. Living in a room so small there's not a spot to hang my clippings. I have clippings. I'll show you," she offered.

"What will you do if you don't get a role soon?" I asked.

"Starve," was her forthright answer. "You wouldn't care to try the sausages, dearie? An excellent sausage they give you here. Only a shilling, and you get potatoes with it."

Over sausages I casually mentioned having an old abandoned house belonging to me that she could use free, but then it was a wreck. She would not be interested. Away from London too.

"There'd be no work," she said frowning, but disliking to pass up something for nothing.

"No, I could not pay you much, and besides..."

I don't know whether it was the mention of pay or the hesitant "besides" that set her eyes alight. "Besides what?" was her question.

"The house is a mess. A total wreck. If you wanted to undertake to fix it up, I could pay you a little something."

"I've never played a housekeeper," she answered, considering this new role.

"I should not have mentioned it. It is beneath Kean's acting partner."

"I haven't played with Kean for a while," she allowed. "Maybe I'll give the role a try. What have I got to lose?"

"There's something else I ought to tell you really. It is said in town—just a rumor, you know, but I shan't keep it from you—well, the fact is, Rose Marie [we were now Mabel and Rose Marie but still Edna was Miss Williams], some people say that smugglers use the place. Not that they'd *harm* you, of course, but..."

"It wouldn't bother me in the least. I'd give them a hand. There's my salary!" she said on a bark of laughter, then reaching out she gave my arm a cuff. "My own pa used to work for them when we were living at Dover. Many's the night I've hauled the poor old soul out of his warm bed when the tap came at the door. Oh dear—I daresay a proper lady like yourself wouldn't approve of that."

My plan had been no more than to get her into the house to keep Williams out. My men would be provided with a key to come and go in the cellar without her knowledge, for it was a huge old house, and past midnight she would not be likely to be in the kitchen or cellar. They moved like mice, noiselessly. Eventually, if she proved trustworthy, I would tell her more.

"I do not disapprove of smuggling," I allowed, and went on to explain my reasons. "No, actually I approve," I ended up.

"Clap hands and it's a bargain then," she said, giving me her hand to shake, like a gentleman. We went around to her room—what a pitiful sight it was—dark and small, with her yellowing clippings piled in a heap on her bed. They had been read and thumbed till they were as soft as muslin. I took her back to the hotel with us, her worldly possessions in a straw suitcase—weird, garish gowns and ostrich feathers for the most part.

I judge people quickly. Edna had a dozen warnings to issue me, but I had taken a liking to Rose Marie. The fact of her having puffed her career up a little did not qualify her for "a constitutional liar" in my view, as it did in my companion's. I thought the time would not be long till Rose Marie was a full-fledged member of my gang. If you can't trust a smuggler's daughter to be close, whom can you trust?

We finished out the remainder of our visit in Rose Marie's company. The woman's eyes bulged from her head when she learned where we were putting up. "Stephen's Hotel?" she asked, her mouth open. "My dear, it's for Johnnie Trots. A regular fleecing you get there. If it is a touch of class you're after, try Grillons. And if it's only a clean bed and a decent

107

meal, go to Storms around the corner and stay in comfort for half the price."

Rose Marie was so startlingly at variance with the other patrons of Stephen's that Edna and I checked out and removed to Storms. Another time we would go to Grillons, but with our new friend in tow, we settled for Storms. The rest of that visit was a very different and livelier one than I had ever spent in London before. She dragged us from theater to theater, from shop to shop, and from café to café, often introducing us to persons we would as lief not have met, but doing the whole with such good humor and verve that it was impossible to object. We became quite the bosomest of bows, Rose Marie and myself. Edna remained stiff-faced throughout it all. The closest she came to accepting it was to comment, "Well, at least the actress seems to have got your thoughts off Sir Stamford for two minutes in a row. That is more than the play at Drury Lane accomplished."

On the last evening of our visit, Edna proclaimed herself too beat to go out again. She would have dinner in her room and go to bed early. I took the opportunity to open my budget in full to Rose Marie—true identity, Miss Sage identity, the whole thing.

"I know it, dearie," she told me, patting my knee and nodding her head wisely. "I'm glad you confided in me. I daresay you'd have done it sooner but for the old dragon you have guarding you. Very proper you should have a chaperone, of course, being a lady, but I have often pitied the young ladies who can't budge without some old malkin at their elbow, spoiling their fun. Truth to tell, I didn't quite twig to it you were this Miss Sage you speak of. I figured him for your beau, but I knew you were in on it somehow. Takes one to know one, eh?" she asked, giving my elbow a nudge with her own in the commonest way imaginable.

"So if you would be willing to help out in little ways— convince Mr. Williams, for instance, that you are indeed an invalid [it had been decided she would be invalidish] if he comes snooping around, and just generally keep an eye on things, you know..."

"A light at the window! The gentlemen bringing the stuff in from the sea will require a signal, for the cave will be impossible to find in the dark."

"Yes, little things like that—then I can pay you more than the sum we spoke of."

"How much?" she asked, her eyes alight.

"Same as the gentlemen. Ten shillings a trip, on top of the sum we spoke of before. And of course I shall take care of the running of the house—fuel, a bit of furniture, and so on."

"That's grand of you, dearie. Really generous, and you needn't fear I'd ever say a word, for I'll be in it as deep as any of them, won't I? 'We're all for nubbin cheat together,' my pa used to say. 'If the law don't get you, the gentlemen will,' was the way they put it to anyone that had a thought of squealing."

All the details were settled; then she turned around and threw a spanner at me. She wanted a companion—someone to talk to. A backhouse boy had already been agreed upon to do the heavy work and, more importantly, run errands. This was not what she had in mind. She'd be lonesome all alone in that great hulk of a house. Who would not? She already had her companion in her eye. I feared it would be a man, for her conversation and her wandering eyes made it perfectly clear she was not blind to the attractions of the opposite sex. She was *not* a member of the muslin company, she insisted, but a virtuous woman. Still, I think her virtue had as many lives as a cat. My relief was great to hear it was her sister she wanted. The sister was in service at a fancy home in London—a widow, childless. I heard the whole history but it is irrelevant to us. She brought her around, ignorant of the whole affair, for me to inspect. Pearl's hair was undyed and her outfit was neat and plain, but in other respects the women were somewhat similar. They had lit out from home thirty years ago together and gone their separate ways in London, keeping in touch, but leading very different lives. I could see no moral to be gained in comparing their fates. All Pearl's virtue and hard work ought to have led to some better reward than being every jot as poor as Rose Marie at the end of the thirty years, but it was not the case. Of the two, I think Rose Marie had the more interesting life, but that is perhaps my own prejudice speaking. I would rather taste the dregs and lees along with the top of the bottle than not have a sip at all. The talk was led subtly to smuggling, at which point Pearl abandoned her virtue and stood up for her father. It was good enough. In for a penny, in for a pound. I hired Pearl as well as Rose Marie Mettel, bringing double wrath down on my head from Edna. I really do not know why Pearl agreed to go along with us. Boredom with thirty years of running to answer bells perhaps.

All the way home, we devised a background for the sisters, to account to the villagers for their taking over the Eyrie. Rose Marie was an outgoing woman, and artful enough to make anyone believe anything. She was to be nurse-companion of all work to her pseudo-employer, whom we christened Miss Silver, due to her metallic name. Rose Marie became Miss Lock. Miss Lock was free to jaunter into town whenever she wished. She was to be an ardent churchgoer so she could pop in to see me when she was there, should we have any business to discuss. My greatest regret was that she could not live in the town, for I was infinitely amused by her conversation and manner.

We were not so naïve as to enter town on the same coach as the sisters, Edna and I, nor even on the same day. The women stayed overnight at Colchester, to fill out their wardrobes for their roles, and follow us the next day to Salford. "You'll be lucky if you see a sign of that pair, giving them five pounds. They'll skip back to London, and that will be the end of them. Good riddance too. Unless they take it into their heads to blackmail you," she added as an afterthought.

The next evening, however, the rumor was buzzing around town that an invalid had moved into the Eyrie. She had become, during the day, a sister to the owner, Mr. Simon. Silver was close enough to Simon to have given birth to this invention. I regretted I had not thought of so logical a thing myself, and would inform the sisters of the change of name on the first opportunity.

With my next delivery only three days away—a special delivery too, for I had managed to get a load of cognac, more profitable than cheaper brandy—I had to contact the higgler. When he came to pick up Edna's glass beads, I told him we would require Jed Foster's fishing smack to be tethered at the Eyrie cave. Jemmie was round-eyed with delight at my having discovered Miss Marjoram's secret, and I was stern in making him realize the importance of the gentlemen approaching the spot with the greatest stealth, to prevent Williams from becoming suspicious of it. He hit on the capital idea of providing fresh commodities to the women—milk, butter, eggs and so on—in his role of higgler, thus giving me another line to them. It was logical he pick them up as clients. It had occurred to him even before he knew their real reason for being there. Jemmie always answered the door before opportunity knocked. The new residents settled into Salford without a single embarrassing question arising.

Chapter Thirteen

I was curious in the extreme to discover whether Mr. Williams had brought a wife back to town with him. When no one said a word about such an occurrence, I assumed he had done no more than visit his fiancée. I felt if he had any sensitivity or conscience at all, he would let our romance die a natural death. He proved to be without either one. Our first meeting, which occurred on the second day I was back, was taken up with mutual and insincere repinings at our having failed to find each other in the city. He darted over at noon hour "the *minute* I heard you were back! You might have let me know last night." This was uttered with a wounded countenance, to denote the lover's chagrin.

There was more lover-like scolding for my negligence. "Why did you not send a message to me at Hadley's? You knew I was there. How was I to know to which of the dozens of hotels you went when your aunt fell ill, and was unable to make the trip?"

I had to give him some excuse for Mrs. Harvey's not being at Portman Square, and had given her a bad case of flu. "Was it not wretched timing on her part?" I asked.

"Wretched cruelty on yours, not to notify me of the change of plans. I had half a dozen outings planned for us."

"What of all your business meetings?"

"They were not so long as I feared. I sat through that demmed farce at Drury Lane two times, hoping to see you. Had you been anxious for my escort, you might have sent a note around to me," he complained, in jealous, offended accents.

"I thought we might bump into each other somewhere or other," I replied, dismissing it as a mere detail.

"I went to six hotels looking for you. Where the devil did you stay?"

"Stephen's," I answered, not naming Storms, which was not quite grand enough to boast of.

"I was sure you would be at Grillons. It's a nice spot. Try it next time. I kept hoping you might be at Hadley's ball—that your aunt might have arranged it in some manner."

"How was the ball? Did you stand up with Lady Lucy?"

"Of course," he answered, without so much as a blush or a batting of the lashes. "Well—a guest in the house, naturally I must."

He did not realize it, I think, but there was a defensive note in that last speech. "It must have been a pleasure as well as a duty, Mr. Williams. You described her as a vivacious, pretty girl, if I recall. Why, if you look sharp, you might make a match with her," I said archly.

"I am not at all interested in making a match with *her*," he told me, bold as brass, while he grabbed my two hands and gazed into my eyes with a meaningful look. "And I remember—or did I dream it—that you were to call me Stanley when we are alone."

"It was no dream, Stanley. I remember very well that it was only when we were alone you wished for the intimacy. I wonder why that should be?"

"I thought you understood why. Until I have established myself in a respectable line of employment, I do not wish the gossip-mongers saying Miss Anderson has lowered herself to make an alliance with a drapery merchant. I would like to put a ring on your finger, and announce our engagement today. I would like it very much, Mab," he said in a soft voice. His head inclined a little toward mine. I thought he was going to kiss me, right there in the saloon in the middle of the day with all the doors open, and Edna and Andrew somewhere about.

"How did the business talks with Lord Hadley go? Will it be much longer you must remain so far beneath my touch?" I asked, with a fond look to indicate I had no aversion even to a draper.

"Excellent. We had very fruitful talks. As soon as the Owenses return, I am to go to him in London."

"There is no talk of the Owenses returning?"

"Not just yet," he replied, frowning. "Her recovery is slower than we had hoped. By the way, Mab, I have been wanting to ask you about that Porson fellow who was making those very annoying statements at your party. He behaves as though he owns you."

112

Get Your
Coventry Romances
Home Subscription NOW

And Get These
4 Best-Selling Novels
FREE!

You give a lot of love in your life. Let Coventry give you a little old-fashioned romance.

HELENE Discovers true adventure, friendship, love, and intrigue after turning her back on her refined upbringing and a flurry of society men she couldn't respect...

LUCY War and scandal make two brothers the objects of her love and hate. But, shockingly, not the way she expected...

LUCIA Loves one man but marries another to escape a spiteful stepsister...

LACEY Beautiful, spirited, and wealthy, she runs away and hides her identity to find true love...

Lacey, Lucia, Helene, Lucy...these are some of the memorable women who come alive in the pages of Coventry Romances. Historical love stories that, month after month, make you feel the elegance and grandeur of another time and place. And now, without leaving your home, you can share in this special kind of romance!

The Coventry home subscription plan is the easiest and most convenient way to get every one of the exciting Coventry Romances! You'll be sure not to miss any of these great historical romances, and you won't even have to go out looking for them.

Get Your *Coventry Romances*

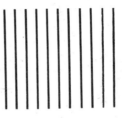

"I don't think he will any more. I gave him a sharp set-down."

"I didn't like the cut of him above half. Low-minded type. Oh, we have some newcomers here in Salford. Have you met them?"

"I heard the Eyrie is rented. Two women, I understand."

"A lady and her nurse-companion. The latter was in the shop. She seems a lively soul, vulgar as can be. I liked her." Then he laughed, quite a natural-sounding laugh. "That would be my low origins showing. *You* would think her beyond anything."

"I'm surprised the Eyrie is fit to live in."

"It's a total shambles," he said, letting slip he had been there. He realized it at once, and rattled on, "Or so the woman said in any case. Good business for me. She will have to do a deal of shopping to get it set to rights. Did you ever hear the Eyrie used to be a smugglers' den?" he asked, in a casual way.

"It used to have the reputation of it long ago. Legend from the days of Miss Marjoram," I corroborated, as he already knew.

"If that is the spot they're using now, they'll have to move their base," he remarked idly.

"What is this interest in smugglers?"

"A notion of Hadley's. The customs fellows in London are all in the boughs about the quantity of brandy coming in here at Salford. Hadley feels if I could do something to discover the ring, it would stand me in good stead with the party. He is a friend of the president of the Board of Trade. Just an idea, you know, as I happen to be here."

"A wretched idea! You must know my views on smuggling, Stanley," I pouted. "If you lift a finger to help them, I shall disown you. Buy all my ribbons in Felixstone." I was shocked to see this brought an uncomfortable look to his face. He had maintained his pose through all my taunts about Lucy, but this one hit the quick.

"I hope you are not *unalterably* on the side of crime." he ventured.

"Oh no, I am quite opposed to taxation and the crimes of the government. *I* am on the side of the righteous poor."

"Ah good, then you are on my side. I am as poor and as righteous as they come." This was mere persiflage to divert the course of our conversation. He did not wish to discuss his real work with me, and I must own I was happy enough to drop the matter.

"I hope you got that leg of yours looked at by a good man while you were in London."

"No, it didn't seem to be bothering me at all. I wonder if it would be the sea air here that is hard on it."

"Perhaps it requires the regular exercise of waltzing."

"A pity my favorite waltzing partner will not lower herself to attend the assemblies. It would be such an excellent excuse to get her in my arms."

I had a vision of him waltzing with a vivacious Lady Lucy. It proved a good cure to his insidious charm. Yes, inveterate idiot that I was, I felt myself softening toward him again. Neither in London nor in Salford had I seen any gentleman I liked better, nor half so well, but I would not give way to my weakness. I wished to do a little planting of the idea I was soon to win a thousand pounds in a London lottery, to make it less startling when it was announced. My chance arose very soon, when we began to discuss my trip to the city, with my telling him of its highlights (those of them that were for his ears). "And of course I bought lottery tickets," I said.

"I usually buy mine at Felixstone."

"So do I, but there was one in London with a thousand pounds prize. Only fancy if I should win it."

"Not much chance, I'm afraid. I imagine they are all fixed, but that doesn't stop anyone from taking a chance."

"Much good it would do me if I did win. Andrew is opposed to gambling. He would make me give the whole to charity."

"He isn't that big a gudgeon."

"Oh yes, stuffed full of rectitude."

"Hardly worth your while buying a ticket then."

I dismissed it with a hunch of my shoulders. The matter was not to be belabored, only mentioned. Williams still had to go to the inn for luncheon, so he left then, asking if he might drop in that evening. Setting himself up as quite an established suitor, you see. Curious to discover how far he would go, I gave him permission.

He proved, when he arrived at the front door no later than eight o'clock, to be ready to go to most any lengths to secure a second girl friend. To get me alone for some serious flirtation, he had brought a catalogue with him, and sat in a corner with me perusing its pages, while I selected those items I wished to see on the shelves of Owens' shop. The other few hundred customers were nothing to him. It was an eye-opening experience to see how much excuse for dalliance a determined flirt could discover in a catalogue. Eye-opening too to see Owens' markup on his merchandise—one hundred percent, and *more* on some items! He was robbing us blind. As bad as the government.

We looked at the muslin lists first—he was preparing orders for spring. As I favored blue, he ran his finger down the list, stopping only at blue selections. "Blue checked on white ground," he read. "No, we don't want *squares* on you, interfering with nature's curves. Sprigged muslin—now I wonder if it would be the right shade of blue for you." A glance into the eyes—deep, meaningful. "Cornflower blue it should be, with just a hint of sapphire in this evening light. Funny how your eyes seem to get darker as the sun goes down."

"You consign me to muslin, do you Stanley? It will surprise you to hear I am planning on a silk gown for spring."

"Excellent—an evening gown, you mean. I trust this means you are to make your debut at the local assembly rooms, and I shall get to—waltz with you yet. You remember I mentioned my reason for liking the waltz."

"Yes, it gives you a chance to get your arms around all the girls."

"Only you. You are the only one I shall waltz with."

"Miss Trebar may have something to say about that."

Andrew, who sat across the room working on his Sunday sermon, cocked up his head at the name. "Did you say something about Miss Trebar, Mab?"

"Only that she likes waltzing, Andrew."

"Miracles never cease!" Williams said in a soft aside, with a very amused smile on his face. "Now who would have thunk it, that Andrew would take to that bold chit."

"Does she indeed?" Andrew asked, continuing his interest in the matter for two whole statements, which, for Andrew, indicated a keen interest. "You must teach me to waltz sometime, Williams," he went on, but that was the extent of it. He never mentioned it again.

"We shall have to look lively to beat him to the altar, if Sally has her claws into him," Williams said, then went on with more compliments, heaping praise on my charms at every new page of the catalogue, while I egged him on, smiling and smirking like a Bath miss.

The visit to London was soon forgotten. It was good to be back among old friends and familiar places. Good too not to have to hand out a tip every time you turned around, and to be able to drive one's gig without feeling like a Johnnie Trot, as Rose Marie described us provincial types. I even enjoyed going back to the schoolroom. I need hardly say I took an exquisite pleasure in my Eyrie. We used it twice with good success (more than paying the year's rent) and had no trouble from Williams. He was desperate to catch Miss Sage, so he could get back to Lady Lucy. This led him to take a rather unwise step. I heard of it Saturday when Rose Marie, who was now a frequent visitor to the town and an occasional one to the rectory, called on me.

"I've a bit of a problem, dearie," she began, with a face that said she had a large problem. "It's Williams, you see. He wants to call on me."

This I had not foreseen. She was too old, and her charms too tired, for this to be a courting call. "What was his excuse?"

"He wants to see if he can find how the brandy is getting in. He plain out and confessed it. Not the whole thing, but he hinted how some gent in London would welcome a spot of help, and it would do him some good. How can I put him off without looking suspicious?"

"What did you say?"

"I said yes, but made it for Monday to give us a couple of days to think up an excuse to be rid of him."

"We dare not let him go. I think Miss Simon must take a turn for the worse, and you send him a note tomorrow canceling."

"The plague!" she exclaimed at once, indulging in her propensity for the dramatic. "That will keep him a mile away. The gentlemen used it once at Dover."

"Too obvious. Besides, it would prevent your visits to town, Rose Marie, and you wouldn't like that."

"To be sure I would not. It's quiet enough without losing my trips to town. Pearl is not lively company. She is not that happy here. I think she would like to return to service in London. But I can always jolly her into staying."

"Please do, for the time being at least. What we'll do is this," I decided rapidly. "Stay away from church tomorrow—that will prepare Williams in advance for some trouble, then Monday morning send him a note by the higgler that Miss Simon is very ill. You'd better send for the doctor as well, for the looks of it. You are an actress—can you make her look ill with powder or chalk?"

"She doesn't need much help," was the answer. This was

116

a reference to her sister's refusal to paint, dye, curl or wear bright clothing.

"And Rose Marie—you had better keep that kitchen door well locked. I don't want him slipping in unseen by you."

"One of the lads got me a dog. He's better company than Pearl."

"Who, the lad?" I quizzed her. Rose Marie had set up a circle of beaux who called on her at the Eyrie, to lighten the tedium of her hours. I daresay Pearl was put out with this.

"No, the dog."

On Sunday morning Rose Marie was not at church. Monday on my way to school I met Jem on his way to Owens' shop with the note for Williams. He waved at me with a broad wink. "Poor Miss Simon is feeling poorly," he said. After school, I stopped at the shop to confirm that Williams was not at the Eyrie. When I saw him flirting with Miss Simpson, come all the way down from Felixstone for the purpose, I knew we were safe for the time being. Williams was of course a wicked flirt, but I assumed the majority of it was done in the spirit of gathering information for his work. I thought it was only myself he courted for enjoyment. He must have enjoyed it, or why did he come? I never told him a thing. It was despicable of him to carry on behind Lucy's back— that goes without saying. Suddenly it seemed much worse for him to be carrying on with *two* other ladies. Really this was the outside of enough. There was nothing to be gained from Miss Simpson, a foreigner (in the Salford sense) who knew nothing about smuggling here.

When I saw the tape measure dangling from his fingers, and realized he had been measuring her up, I could contain my ire no longer. He looked surprised at the anger in my eyes. I made no effort to conceal it, but did think of an excellent manner to hide its cause.

"Miss Anderson," he said, with a guilty look toward Miss Simpson, who nodded at me, then looked quickly away.

"Take your time, Mr. Williams. I am in no hurry, though I fear if Miss Simpson is looking for a belt, she is come to the wrong shop. Mr. Williams has none tiny enough to fit your waist, Miss Simpson," I complimented her.

She laughed happily and confirmed the fact. Sally Trebar seemed suddenly less horrid as a potential sister-in-law. As though she wanted a belt! No lady ever wore such an item, and she could have got any length of ribbon she wanted cut off. She continued talking to him a little longer, not letting

117

my impatience hurry her in the least. When at last she was gone, Williams came toward me, a little embarrassment lingering on his face.

"What's the matter, Mab?" he asked. "I cannot be rude to the customers, you know."

"Customers? You cannot think *that* is what I am angry about!" I exclaimed, displaying every element of well-simulated shock.

"What is it then?"

"You are going on with this business of trying to help that man in London—the man from the Board of Trade. Don't bother to deny it. I had a note from Miss Lock and she told me you had asked her help."

"I told her not to tell!" he said quickly, angrily. "How did you come to be in communication with her?"

"She had planned to come to the rectory Sunday afternoon and help me with some ordering for the parish poor, but wrote to put it off. She mentioned having to cancel a visit with *you* as well. Now I know perfectly well why you wanted to go there. Don't deny it."

"She didn't *tell* you so."

"She didn't have to spell it out. In this one isolated case, I know it was not the woman's personal charms that instigated the call. You know my feelings about smuggling. If you mean to catch the smugglers and have every second father in Salford put into irons, I want nothing more to do with you, Stanley."

I could see the consternation on his face, could read as well as though he had written it what was in his mind. Frustration was there. I think he wanted again to tell me the truth, but as the truth was so much worse in my eyes than his lie, he could not do that. Nor did he seem to be much of a mind to deny his efforts to stop the smugglers. I really wondered that he stuck at disclaiming any intentions along those lines. To a consummate liar like himself, it could hardly matter. "I'm doing it for us, he said. "It will help me to a good position in London, so we can get married."

It was the first time the word "marriage" had been used between us. There had been inferences and strong hints, of course, but not an outright statement before now. The timing of it, following his visit to Lucy, seemed so very inappropriate too. "I don't seem to recall saying I would marry you, sir!" Oh, but how my heart beat at his words.

118

"You have led me to believe... Well, you did use the word 'compromise' at least."

"I am using it again. Your going on with this scheme compromises any chance of ever marrying me, Mr. Williams. I won't see you again if you don't stop this."

"Mab, I *can't* stop! I need the boost this will give my career. I have debts, obligations you know nothing of. I have worked very hard for this chance. I can't give it up. I *know* now it is the Eyrie Miss Sage is using. It must be. I was out in a boat and discovered a cave right below it, with a boat anchored! The boat hasn't been there ten years either; it's newish. The stuff is brought right into the cellar of that house. I can catch the whole gang and be made anything I want in London."

"What about the people here? You'd throw all those innocent men into jail, or see them hanged?" It was hard to get this speech out. He *knew,* knew the whole. How lucky it was he had told me!

"No, I don't plan to do it that way at all. I have been thinking about all you and Andrew told me—and those writings from your schoolchildren. How could you think I meant to punish those poor people? I am not a monster. It is only Miss Sage himself I mean to capture. It is all set in London— I have made the deal with Borden, the top dog with customs. He's not interested in the small fish. It is only Miss Sage I want."

"How will you do it?" I asked, exerting every effort to keep my voice steady.

He looked suddenly wary. I don't think he had meant to tell me a single thing, but had stumbled into it somehow. "I don't know exactly, but he has to be in contact with his men. I'll ferret him out somehow."

"You don't know who it might be, Stanley. It might be some perfectly honorable and respectable person, doing it to help the poor."

"Fat chance! It's a bloated businessman lining his pockets. If it were all charity, that would be different. It is only Miss Sage I mean to capture. The others may go free with my good wishes."

"They won't carry on without Miss Sage. Even if he does line his own pockets, so does he line the pockets of the poor."

"Not to any considerable extent. I mean to work in the city for some *lawful* scheme to help the poor. I don't see why the government can't loan money, for instance, to set up a proper fishing fleet. If a bunch of the men formed a group it could be done. There never seems to be as much fish as they want at Billingsgate. This much I do know, if men are allowed to flout the law with impunity, they lose all respect for it. 'Wherever law ends, tyranny begins.' Those are the words of an *English* philosopher, amply proven in France not so long ago."

"The law does not have to *end* for tyranny to begin—bad laws are tyrants. If you mean to go on with this, we are through." This was desperation speaking. I *must* divert him from discovering the truth.

"Don't deliver that ultimatum unless you mean it, Mab."

"I do mean it!"

"Don't try to lead me. I don't have the ring in my nose yet."

"You have the limited mind and stubbornness of a bull for all that."

His stormy eyes were glaring. "I find it odd you are so determined to be against me, when I understand you have often helped Crites in the past."

"Very true, but then Officer Crites has such a gentlemanly, persuasive way about him that none of the girls can resist him," I answered foolishly, and turned to leave the store.

He did not try to stop me.

Chapter Fourteen

It was far and away the best thing that could happen to me, to be cut off from frequent visits with Williams. Best from a personal point of view, but for business reasons, it would be better to keep in touch. His having discovered my cave, for instance, was a vital piece of information, and only stumbled onto because of our relationship. And how annoying it was to have to abandon my perfect Eyrie so early in the game. I had hoped to get at least a year's service out of it—use up my lease. My mind was all in a whirl when I went home. I would keep firmly and constantly in mind that we were enemies, and not let my heart run away with my head, as it kept wanting to do.

It was war between us, no more, no less. My enemy was suspicious, and I must direct his suspicions from the Eyrie. Make him think some other spot was used. I scanned my mind, and found it going back to Aiken's place. Lord Aiken had not remained long, just for a Christmas holiday. Williams had already been investigating there. He must be led back to it. There is a nice stretch of shingle beach just below Lord Aiken's estate, actually a part of the estate, I believe, but not built on at all. We had used the dock, but that nice quiet length of beach, so open to prying eyes, beckoned me. I trifled with various ideas—landing a batch of empty barrels and making Williams look a perfect fool when he went dashing in to rescue barrels of air. But he would not do that. He would hang back in the dark, waiting to follow Jemmie to me. It was only Miss Sage he was after.

Still, for the next shipment fast approaching, he might be lured to that beach for a diversion, while we got the stuff up the stairs of the Eyrie. Yes, definitely that would be an amusing exercise. I would arrange through Jem, who had a dozen rascally gentlemen he met during the length of his higgling route, to pass along plans to have empty barrels landed at the beach, to distract Williams. Jemmie disliked my idea. Too many men involved—a crew at the beach, and another at the Eyrie. And what if Williams did not fall for it? The lugger could be burned off from the Eyrie, of course, but unless we had another landing spot, which we did not, it would mean losing the cargo.

"One coffin would take a deal less work and men than all them barrels," Jem suggested with a cagey look.

"Williams would hardly be interested in a coffin," I thought.

"He'd be interested enough if we tried to keep him away, wouldn't he then?"

"It was not my intention to try to keep him away," I pointed out.

"Aye, but the best way to get him there is to make him think it."

It is lowering to have to confess Jemmie's crooked mind had outpaced my own in this case. I inquired politely how this could be done, to humor Jemmie, though I had a fair idea of the answer.

It was a reworking of the old plague victim stunt he had in mind. In the bygone days when people were more gullible and more afraid of pox and plague, one had only to claim a victim was situated anywhere to ensure complete privacy at that spot. An announcement that a plagued corpse was to be buried at the beach would get rid of any unwanted onlookers, including revenuemen, who were no more anxious to fall sick and die than anyone else. Such an announcement might still keep Crites at a distance; I did not think it would deter Williams. Nor did I think he would fall for that old chestnut of a stunt. He would recognize it for a red herring, know we were trying to lure him to the spot and look elsewhere. Some new element was needed to obfuscate the issue. We would let him learn, quite by accident—no public announcement—and at the very last possible moment, that a French ship was to land a victim at the beach. He would think he had discovered something we wished to conceal, and, hopefully, leap to the conclusion he had outwitted us. He would go expecting to see a hundred barrels landing behind the coffin, only to find that what was landing was exactly one coffin.

"We'll require *two* French ships in that case, Jem, one for the brandy, another for the coffin."

"The *Orléans* is at Ipswich now. It'll be coming down tomorrow. I'll arrange to have that special item put aboard en route. You can attend to Williams' hearing it at the last minute?"

"Leave it to me."

"We're a good team, miss. This will keep Williams glued behind his tree, or I ain't Jem Hessler."

"There's one more point. I don't want you coming to me after the runs to report unless there is trouble. Only if it is urgent. He might follow you, and it is Miss Sage he is after."

"But if there should be trouble, miss, that's the very time I shouldn't go to you. It could mean he's on to me, and be dangerous for you."

"That's true. We must have some signal, some way you can let me know there is trouble. What could we use?"

"The church bell maybe, but that would alert the whole village."

"That is as well as coming right to me, sitting on our doorstep as it is. Something else. How about Mark? No, he would be followed as easily as yourself."

"How about Lady?" he asked. "She's as clever as any of the gentlemen."

"Could you train her to come to me, with a note stuck under her collar?"

"She knows you well enough that if I gave her a glove or whatnot belonging to you and told her to deliver it, she'd be at your door in a flash. Mind she'd have to bark a bit to let you know she's there. She's a right clever girl, but she hasn't learned to knock on a door yet."

We tried an experiment with Lady and my old tan kid glove that same evening. It worked like a charm. That clever Jem had fashioned a new collar for her, a wide leather one split at the back to hold a note safely.

I was nervous and tense after our little talk, worrying about my cargo and my ruse, and figuring the best way for Williams to "discover" about the plague victim. Everyone is so frightened of the plague that it is no easy thing to get permission to land a victim at all. If the victim is deceased, it is the understanding that the coffin will be burned to ashes instantly it is landed. For this a certificate is required from the officer of health. You might be forgiven for thinking the parish officer of health would be a medical man, but it is not the case. When there are certificates required (which might be hastened, you understand, by a little under-the-table largesse) Sir Elwood Ganner, Bart., is your man. The philosophy which got him this job is that our health is too important to leave in the hands of doctors. It requires the deft and skillful fingers of a politician. I must add in Ganner's defense, however, that he *did* make vaccination against the smallpox compulsory, with Jenner's wonderful vaccine. He had a clinic set up in the church porch (where else?) with myself in charge of helping the doctor, and Sir Elwood Ganner in charge of talking to the press. I am not sure, but I think that might have been the cause of his being knighted, and was said locally to be also the cause of his new black carriage, though I cannot swear he made any money on the purchase of vaccine and the hiring of people to administer it.

I knew from Jem that this certificate was to be requested at five-thirty by the captain of the *Orléans,* or his deputy. It was my duty to drop in at the same hour, to interfere lest the certificate be denied. When I spotted the stranger, dressed in rough sailor's garb, enter the Parish Office at the appointed hour, I nipped smartly down the street, taking care not to let my eyes stray to the left, where an outline at the doorway of Owens' shop suggested the form of Mr. Williams. We were not speaking since the altercation in the shop. Nodding, each being careful to make the nod shorter than the other, but not uttering a word.

Ganner was just stuffing a folded bill into his pocket and some loose change into the parish coffer when I entered. The matter had already been arranged to the satisfaction of both parties. The sailor took his certificate and left, whistling.

"Plague victim to be buried," he told me. "Must be burned first for safety's sake, of course. No need to tell it around town. It will only cause talk and worry." He patted his pocket happily, while the setting sun glinted from his shining scalp.

"I wouldn't mind if a certain party heard it," I said, giving him a measured look to indicate this was not whimsy, but business.

He looked at me with a leap of understanding in his eyes. "That is an old humbug trick, Miss Sage. I doubt it will work. I was obliged to use it on Daggar once in the old days."

"The stuff is not coming in on that ship. The person I would like to hear about it is Mr. Williams."

"I thought as much," he nodded. "Read about Wicklow being sent down, and thought it a bit odd Miss Anderson was allowing a draper to run tame at her home. You are awake on all suits, sly puss. Shall I stop by Owens' shop and let it slip out in a casual fashion? I'll caution him not to mention it to anyone, to make him think it a great secret. Yes, and I shall also ask about the wool Miss Anderson is always pestering me for. He might wonder at your being here, if he happened to see you enter. We would not want him to think you are involved in the other business in any way."

"I would appreciate it, Sir Elwood," I told him, and went home by the back way, for I was not sure I could keep from grinning if Williams nodded at me. I had no worry about Ganner. Miss Thyme was quite adept in his dealings.

That evening I was on a bed of nails wanting to know what was going forth. It was all I could do to keep from donning Andrew's trousers and slipping down to Aiken's place myself. The cargo was to come at one o'clock, a little later than usual. The hour was chosen to coincide with the burial, one being considered late enough that the streets and beach would be empty. As one slowly ticked toward two, I waited at the front door, looking for a dog that did not come. I lost several hours of sleep, and slept in the next morning to make up for it. I regretted not being able to talk to Jemmie, and thought if I went into the streets I might see him. A simple nod and his crooked grin would tell me all was right. Surely I would have heard had anything gone amiss.

I dressed up and went out immediately after lunch. I did not see Jemmie, but Rose Marie was doing her weekly shopping. At the butcher's door we hove to to exchange greetings.

"How is Miss Simon?" I asked. She must have been sick to death of the question. Everyone asked the same thing, though no one except myself had ever seen her.

"Recovering nicely, dear. Had a nice quiet night and all," she added with a meaningful smile. It had gone off well then. "Mind the higgler, when he brought our milk and eggs this morning, said things were less quiet at Aiken's place. There was a plague victim buried, did you hear?" This last was asked in a noisy voice for Mrs. Marson's benefit, as she was coming out of the butcher's with a wet brown bundle in her arms. The tale of the plague victim was now out in the open.

I expressed suitable amazement, then Rose Marie went on in a lower voice, "Yes, dear, a great commotion there was. Now they're saying there's an exhumation order to dig up the coffin. Well, the ashes, you know, and make sure there's a body buried at all. I cannot think who did it, got the order."

I did not have to think. I knew it was Williams. So he must have told the constable his true identity. He was becoming more daring, more determined to catch me. And when he found the stones in that pile of ashes, he would know that while he stood watching the blaze, the stuff had been landed elsewhere. He would know, or strongly suspect the Eyrie. I was well satisfied that he had not only been outwitted, but would *know* he had been made a game of.

"I'm just about to duck into Owens'," Rose Marie added, with a questioning look to see if I had any orders.

"Good. Tell him Miss Simon is much better, and invite him cordially to take tea with you tomorrow."

"He wants to search the house—the cellar!" she reminded me.

"Let him search. He won't find anything but the empty barrels left over from Miss Marjoram's days, will he? The tranter is moving the stuff out at four on Sunday morning."

"He doesn't know for sure about the cellar and the secret stairs."

"He knows. I must find a new spot for the time being."

"If you say so, dearie."

"Act perfectly innocent, Rose Marie. Express every horror at the discovery, and claim you mean to put locks two inches thick on the door. I don't have to tell Kean's acting partner how to convince him."

"It'll be a real pleasure! Mind you I like the rascal for all he's on the wrong side of the law for us. It's such fun to see him trying to act like a commoner. I could give him a few lessons."

She delayed her meat buying till she had performed for Williams. Later, she stopped in at the rectory and told me Williams had accepted her offer. He meant to go ahead with his investigation, of course. My threat and its two-day execution meant nothing to him. How should it, when he was engaged to Lady Lucy? As he was flagrantly flying in my face, you may imagine the icy reception he received in the choir on Sunday. He hung around after the service to help me with my pelisse. I accepted his help with a cold "Thank you" and not so much as a glance at him. I heard his footsteps coming down the stairs after me, but kept a step ahead that I not require his help with the door.

His next move was to try to strike up a chat with Andrew, with what success I know not, as I walked immediately home at a swift pace, without looking over my shoulder. Nor did I see him in the church yard later through the curtains. Going straight to the tavern for his lunch, as he had his afternoon's work cut out searching the Eyrie. He did not come to us in the evening, nor on Monday or Tuesday, but on Wednesday he went to the choir practice. I looked at everyone but him as I led them in song, and made sure I kept my pelisse beside me so that I could get it onto my own back afterward without his help. He hung back as the others galloped down the stairs, picking up a few songbooks from the back chairs. I accepted them with a nod and tied up my bonnet, glancing down into the church to see if Andrew was there.

"I am walking you home," he said. "I told Andrew this afternoon I would see to it."

"That is not necessary, Mr. Williams. It is only a step."

I turned and went downstairs, with him behind me, reaching over my shoulder for the door, which I got open just as he put his hand on it, so that he fell forward on my back.

I twitched and made a tsk of annoyance, as any old maid would.

"Sorry," he said, in accents that held no sorrow whatsoever, but a great deal of angry vexation.

The gallery stairs terminate in the church porch, where the calico is given out, and on Christmas, the baskets and blankets. This small anteroom is pitch-black when the door is closed, as it was on this occasion. It is as much these four steps as anything that make me welcome Andrew's company for getting home. Not that anyone was likely to skulk about and bash me over the head, but one could if he wanted to, and it is rather frightening. I stepped quickly across the little porch, fumbling for the door handle in the darkness. I felt Mr. Williams' hand there, also on the latch. His other hand fell on my elbow, where it tightened to a hard grip.

"We're not leaving till we've had a little talk, Mab," he said.

I was not in the least frightened, though he tried to put a menacing tone into his voice. "Stay and talk to yourself," I advised, pulling at the handle. His fingers tightened over mine, pushing the door closed.

"No, I am going to talk to *you,* and you are going to talk to me. This is nonsense, fighting about a band of outlaw smugglers. What do they mean to either of us, that we should become enemies over them?"

"If they mean nothing to you, then stop trying to catch them."

"They *do* mean something to me. They mean I can marry you. Get a good job in London, and become respectable—a gentleman."

All this was said in the perfect darkness so that I could not see the sly smile he wore. He had his voice under good

127

enough control too that I could find no dissembling tone in it. Oh, the dark plays strange tricks on us. It was so easy to think, there where I could not see him, that he was serious, that he did indeed want to marry me.

"Mab," he went on, in a coaxing, wheedling way, while his hand squeezed my arm. "They are criminals. They break the law every day. I've told you I'll not tattle on any of the men—just let me catch Miss Sage. Now I *know* it is none of those poor out-of-work devils that are behind this. It's Porson, or someone like him. He deserves to be caught." I held my breath, then relaxed to hear it was Porson he suspected. He went on talking. "I know the Eyrie is used, know where the stuff comes in. I know which of the boys is the scout and I suspect he is also Miss Sage's contact. I have only to discover where it is he darts off to after each shipment, and I have the whole thing sewed up, with a really good position in London secured, so that we can get married."

My heart was hammering in my chest, not with delight at his double-dealing tale of eagerness to marry me, but to hear he knew all the wheres and hows, that it remained only for him to follow Jemmie to me. Good God, I had come within a sliver of being caught. "If you catch Miss Sage, Stanley, you lose me, *forever*," I told him, my voice shaking with fear at the full truth of this.

"No!" I was suddenly and unexpectedly locked in his arms, there in the darkness. "No, don't say that. You know you don't mean it. I promise you I won't harm any innocent villagers. I have compromised half my mission, and you must compromise a little too. For *us*, darling," he added in a whisper, just before he kissed me. It was such a beautiful kiss, long, tender in the beginning, as a first kiss should be. Just a light touching of the lips, but then some spark seemed to fly between us, it had almost a sensation of electricity, that charge that flew through my body and his. I felt a convulsive jerk as his arms tightened around me, holding me till we seemed fused into one being. When I recovered my senses—no, rationality; every sense was alive during that brief interval—I found I was clinging to him with all my strength.

"Whatever—*whatever* happens, Mab," he said, his voice breathless in my ear, "you are marrying me. Now I'll take you home."

We walked the few steps hand in hand, with not another word spoken between us.

Chapter Fifteen

Williams did not come into the rectory that evening. I don't remember whether I asked him to. Nothing had been settled between us. I had not talked him out of his investigations, and I had not said I would marry him if he succeeded. What was of a good deal more interest to me was why he had done what he did. Why did he persist in this game of loving me, when it had become so vexatious for him, for us both? I was of no help in his work—he was not coming for that reason. I began to feel that despite Lady Lucy, Wicklow was coming to entertain a real regard for me. Either that, or I am no judge of a kiss. Things were different between us after that night. There was no more teasing, flirting or lovemaking. Neither was there any announcement of a betrothal, but there was a calm assumption on Wicklow's part that I was his. He looked at me in a different way—more softly, proprietary—I don't know. He just looked as though he loved me, and I knew it. I also liked it, but was very much unsettled in my mind.

I wrote to my aunt, mentioning in the most casual way possible whether Lady Lucy had yet married Sir Stamford, hoping she would write back that the engagement was off. She did not answer me for an age.

Rose Marie called and told me Wicklow had been through the cellar, without saying a single word of any importance, the sly thing. The next event that occurred was that a large sign appeared on the wall of the post office, offering a reward of one thousand pounds for the capture of Miss Sage. Words fail me to describe the sensations that went through me when I saw it. It seemed so odd, to think my offering the Hessler brothers shelter from Crites had led to this. Impossible not to project a little into the future, and wonder what my ultimate fate would be. But this was too dismal a prospect.

Like everyone else in the village, I made a special trek down to stare at the announcement. The wording of it intrigued me, a schoolteacher with her mind glued on grammar. One thousand pounds reward for information leading to the arrest of the smuggler known as Miss Sage, his band or contraband cargo. First I was a little angry at that "his" band, as though it were beyond a female to be Miss Sage. Then I read it again. What the Board of Trade meant surely was only to offer such a reward for my capture, but that was not what they had printed, in black and white. They had added "*or* contraband cargo," italics my own. Even after paying the Frenchies, that left more than I ever made. Why not turn one load over to the Board of Trade, and pick up the thousand pounds instead of eight hundred pounds from Pettigrew in London? It delighted me, to think of outwitting the government on a technicality. By hook or by crook, I would figure a way to let Wicklow (or Crites) catch a cargo, but there would not be one of my gentlemen within a country mile of the cargo when it was taken.

I went home, locked the study door to pretend I was marking papers and sat with my chin in my hands, figuring as I had not figured since first taking the reins of my position. Wicklow already knew of the Eyrie. Very well, a load would be found there, but first we had to land it at the cave without his knowledge. He suspected the Eyrie so strongly that it would be hard to lead him off that track.

While I still sat thinking, there was a tap at the door. The higgler had come to pick up Edna's beads, and he was shown in to me as Andrew was nowhere about. I had much to discuss with him. "How are the men taking that sign the government posted?" I asked. "You don't think they might report you, or try to discover from you who I am?"

"Devil a bit of it, miss. Two hundred pounds split between us all *once* ain't likely to be a temptation. Besides, we're all in it together. Our guilt would keep us in line if our honor did not. But the honor is enough. The word of a gentleman has a special sort of meaning here on the coast. Old Frank Higgot went to the gibbet without telling on a single soul some few years ago. My pa used to speak of him. I'd credit any of our lads to do the same. I know I would myself, and so would you, wouldn't you, miss?"

"I would, Jem. Word of a gentleman," I told him unhesitatingly, and meant it. I can't tell you how his integrity affected me. I felt proud to be associated with him, and the rest of my gentlemen.

This settled, I outlined the plan I had mulled over to claim the reward without putting any of us in danger. The money would be split evenly among the men. He was tickled pink with it. A lusty shout of laughter sent Edna dashing to the door to warn us to silence. "The problem is to get the next load landed at the Eyrie without Wicklow seeing us," I finished up.

"He's got his head so full of that notion, we'd have easy work landing it almost anywhere else," he said with a meaningful little smile.

"Clever lad! If I ever retire, Jem, you shall be the next Miss Sage, and that I promise you."

"I always figured to take the name Miss Parsley," he said, laughing. "My ma grows it in her kitchen garden. Right pretty stuff it is. Tasty too."

"Planning to replace me, are you?" I quizzed lightly.

"Only when you're ready to step down, miss. You *did* say, at the beginning, you'd give us a hand for a while. Ganner said so at least, and I think you said something the same to me once."

"If only you were a little older."

"I'm nineteen, miss. Older than I look. It's my being smallish that leads folks to think me younger than I am. You were about the same age, I think, when you began. But I wouldn't want you to get the idea I'm trying to elbow you aside, for it's not so."

"I know. Now about this load coming in a week from Friday. There's none this week, with the moon at the full. Dare we land it at Aiken's place again, after pulling the old coffin stunt?"

"Hmm, happen it was a good idea we put a real carcass in the box after all," he said, stroking his chin. "Made it look like a real plague victim and all, to lead suspicion away from us."

"Jemmie—you never told me! You mean there was a real body in that coffin?"

"Oh, aye, but a dead one, of course. I didn't like to speak of it to you. It's a mite unsavory to talk of to a lady. The lads dug up a corpse lately buried in the parish field, where no one would be apt to miss it. The skull never quite goes in the burning, nor the organs. There's always traces enough to tell. I was glad we took the trouble, when I heard it was to be dug up, for it makes it look as if it was nothing to do with us at all. So I reckon we can use Aiken's place right enough."

"There is that jut in the coast that hides it from the Eyrie. We'll land it at Aiken's, but it must be removed to the Eyrie later that same night. We'll hide it in the stable as we did before, and when Mark gives us the signal Wicklow has given up for the night, we'll transfer it to the Eyrie."

"If Crites don't get to interfering. *He* don't suspect the Eyrie at all, and might have an eye on Aiken's, unless..."

"Unless some helpful schoolteacher mentions the Eyrie to him," I said, smiling. A new idea darted into my head, so fiendish it would shame Satan. Crites half suspected Williams. If I not only mentioned the Eyrie, but went on to say Williams had been seen hanging about there...Was it possible he would be induced to arrest Williams for us?

You will be thinking me a strange sort of a creature, to do this to a man I half loved, and half believed loved me. It is that miserable four-letter word "half" that accounts for it. I knew he was, or had been, engaged to Lady Lucy, and at that time he was still making up to me so there was not sufficient reason to believe him serious now. In my deepest heart of hearts, my feeling was this: that he loved both of us at once. Half loved the two of us—that wretched word "half" again! It was not enough for me. All or nothing at all. I am a fine one to talk, being in such a position I could not marry him if he were serious about his offer. He was lost to me in advance, so why not get on with the more serious business of the enterprise?

I owed him a little payment for the London visit too, when he had put off seeing us. And through all his declarations he kept insisting he wished to become a "gentleman" for my sake, when he was already a baronet. This was patent lying, and if Crites bothered him a little, it would clear the slate. Miss Sage, you will notice, was a pretty careful bookkeeper. The next step was to arrange an accidental meeting with Officer Crites. The sign on the post office door was the likeliest spot to find him. I dashed off another note to Mrs. Harvey, expressing the hope she was not ill, as she had not replied to my last. I had to wait half an hour to get Crites alone, fifteen for him to arrive, and fifteen for the other stragglers to leave. I would be late for my dinner, and Edna would be quite convinced I had been captured. She prophesied this catastrophe regularly, doing my nerves a great deal of good.

"Officer Crites, here is a help to you in your work," I began, indicating the sign. "I expect you have been besieged with people all day long, dropping you hints about Miss Sage. Tell me," I said, lowering my voice to a conspiratorial whisper, "who is he?"

He tried to put a clever expression on his rabbit's face,

with very indifferent success. The teeth defeated him. "Afraid I'm not allowed to discuss it," he said, with a superior air.

"It's Mr. Williams, isn't it?" I urged, still in my secret voice. "Oh, you are so clever, you had it all figured out ages ago, even before Mr. Williams started using the Eyrie for his dealings. But I shan't tell a soul."

Poor Crites, his eyes nearly left his head, while his teeth bounced out from under their concealing lip. "The Eyrie! When did you—what do you..."

"Why else would he be visiting Miss Lock, paying her calls? She is not his type, would you say, Officer Crites?"

He was not about to let on I had just told him several things he was unaware of. He swallowed a couple of times and sought to discover more, without revealing his ignorance. I was eager to give him every help. He was full of delight and schemes when he took off down the road, with a wink and a nod over his shoulder, and even a reminder that I might soon be sharing a thousand pounds.

I went on into the post office to mail my letter, just taking a casual glance at the letters on the table beyond the cage that had not yet been picked up. When the name of Mr. Williams stared up at me, I felt a strong urge to get a closer look at it. It was franked, with a name that looked very much like Hadley. "Mr. Williams asked me if I would inquire whether there are any letters for him," I told Joe Parsons, who is the clerk. My reputation was sufficiently glossy that Joe handed it over with no more than a leering smirk.

I resisted the impulse to rip it open. I could not believe it was a business letter. The scent of violet emanating from the envelope would have told me it was from a lady, if the spidery handwriting, in purple ink, had not. As the frank proved on close inspection to be Hadley's, the identity of the lady could be in little doubt.

Wicklow's worried, guilty countenance when I handed the missive to him was a good corroboration of the identity of the sender. He looked as culpable as a man caught with his fingers in the cash box. "Oh, from Lady Hadley," he said, quickly laying it aside. "I am vastly relieved to hear from her. I came away from London leaving one of my best jackets behind. She will be asking what I want done with it."

"I haven't heard you mention Lady Hadley before," was all I said. I had certainly heard my aunt mention her funeral, however. I felt not a single qualm at my treatment of Mr. Williams as I strode briskly home.

Chapter Sixteen

The hours dragged by on leaden feet over the next several days, as I waited for my load to come in. The evenings, with Wicklow smiling at me in the parlor, were as bad as the rest, for I tried to keep a civil tongue in my head to him. I inquired solicitously for the safety of his jacket, and the health of Lady Hadley, keeping my wayward tongue between my teeth when he had the effrontery to tell me not only that Lady Hadley was fine, but that she was busy trying to arrange a match for her daughter. When the Friday night that was to see the load landed *finally* arrived, I was on nettles, wanting to join my men. From ten o'clock onward I paced the room anxiously, though there would be no news for hours yet. I was with my gentlemen in my mind, while my body was forced to remain anchored at the rectory. It was ideal smuggling weather, in the winter, at the dark of the moon. My men must be cold on such a night as this. Stanley too would be cold, lurking in the shadows at the Eyrie, and Crites, creeping up behind him. At two, I had heard nothing from Jemmie and received no visit from Lady, so I assumed the plan had succeeded, and went to bed.

In the morning, I had several callers. The first was Officer Crites, in a high state of perturbation. He ought not to have told anyone his story by rights, but such news as he thought he had discovered really must be shared and discussed with someone. It is impossible to keep a huge, palpitating grievance totally to oneself, and the unfortunate man had not what you could call a friend in the whole village. I put on my most civil face to greet him.

"Officer, come in," I invited cheerily, and took him inside to hear his tale of woe. "What happened last night? Did you catch Miss Sage and the smugglers?"

"No, they got away," he confessed sheepishly. "They did not land it at the Eyrie, as you thought."

"When I heard in the village that Mr. Williams had been there, looking through the cellar, I made sure..." I let my voice dwindle off, hoping he would pick up and elaborate on the name mentioned.

"He was there," he informed me, bloated with news. "Miss Anderson, he is not a smuggler at all. He is a special agent sent down from London by the Board of Trade, and not telling me!"

"What a shabby trick!" I answered at once, in a manner that (I hoped) combined ire and sympathy. "And what a strange way to set about things. Why, how should he hope to catch the gentlemen, without your help?"

"Exactly what I asked him myself. Why did he not make himself known to me? He was kind enough to say he wished to work in complete secrecy. He did not say so, but there is surely an imputation in that remark that he does not trust me."

"This is beyond anything! If he cannot trust a customs man, whom can he trust? You, who know all their tricks, could have been an inestimable help to him."

"He trusts no one, that fellow. Going behind my back to get that reward posted. They never would agree to a reward when *I* was in charge. Anyone could catch them with a huge reward to send all the townsfolk trotting to give you clues. But one of their own, you see. They all stick together. He is a baronet, Miss Anderson, and a colonel—was a colonel, but has sold out. It is all a great secret, I hardly need tell you, but I can always trust your discretion."

"You may be sure you can. I shan't tell a soul. But what happened? How did you discover all this?" I prodded gently, while my body felt like bursting out of its skin with curiosity.

"The most disastrous evening, Miss Anderson. I writhe to remember it. I went to the Eyrie at eleven, and after slipping about a bit through the trees and bushes, spotted him there. He had a hand telescope. They never issued *me* a telescope, and he was training it on the sea. When a lugger was spotted coming along, he moved up close to the house, and I thought he was getting set to signal it—thought he was Miss Sage, you see, telling it where to land. It was all as dark as could be, and the lugger hadn't any lights burning at all, which is a good sign it was a smuggling vessel, you know, for in the general way you would see a light or two moving about on board. So I crept up softly behind him, and knocked him out.

135

I hit him a stout blow on the back of the head. He was out for ten minutes, and I had got him all bound up by the time he came to. Such a string of oaths as he swore off at me, I never heard the likes! Barracks talk, it does not bear repeating. Then he asked what had happened to the ship. How should I be able to watch the ship and himself at the same time? By the time I went down to the shore and had a look, there wasn't a sign of it, but it certainly did not land at the Eyrie. That I *do* know, and would swear an affidavit on it. So in effect he didn't know a thing more than I knew myself, in spite of his thousand pounds reward, and his fancy telescope. A dandy one it was, with silver mountings. You can see a mile with it. He says he bought it himself with his own money, but if he did, he is making a good deal more than *I* make, for I could not afford anything of the sort."

I surmised Wicklow had already called him to account for letting the ship get out of view while he concerned himself with one man, and said not a word of remonstrance in that regard, but only urged him on with his story by an encouraging nod and suitable feminine cluckings. "Then he told me the cock-and-bull story—that is, I did not believe a tenth of it at the time as to who he is, and what he is doing here. It sounded like a ruse to get away from me, and I refused to untie him. Well, the upshot of it is that I took him into town, still tied, and we went along to Owens' shop and he showed me documents and letters proving beyond a doubt that he is a special agent sent down from the Board of Trade to put a stop to Miss Sage. He had a report there on myself as well which I tried to get a look at, but he shuffled it under some other papers. He is giving me a bad character, of course, or he would not have been at pains to hide it from me. There will doubtlessly be inspectors down here asking questions about me. I hope I may count on you to put in a good word, ma'am, for you at least know how hard I have always worked at my job. The townsfolk all hate me, but *you* have been kind enough in the past to give me a hand upon occasion. A minister's sister and local schoolteacher must have a good deal of influence."

I assured him of my wholehearted support, then slipped in a question as to what had come of the ship. "We lost sight of it entirely while riding into town and looking over his documents. He lays it all in my dish, but if I believed that every stranger who told me he was an inspector *was* an inspector, where would we be? I'd never make a catch." He never made one anyway, but this point was of course not raised.

It was time to proceed to point two. "You think the load that was aboard that lugger was landed, do you?" I asked.

"I expect it was, but it was not landed at the Eyrie."

"No, unless they went past it to fool the revenuemen, then doubled back. It would be strange, would it not, if it was landed there after all?"

"I cannot think it at all likely. I would suspect Lord Aiken's place, if it were not for the fact that the coffin landed there a while back did in fact have a plague victim in it. It was exhumed, you know. Williams' work again. He thinks himself so clever, but the coffin did contain a corpse, for there is a skull and some remains which prove it. We will be lucky if we're not all infected, with having a plague victim's coffin opened and the remains probed. Who is to say a fire will kill all the germs? Much a city baronet and colonel cares if we are all killed with the black plague."

"It would certainly be a feather in your cap if you could find that load that landed last night," I said, having some little difficulty keeping him on the track.

"I wish I could do it. It didn't land at the Eyrie. I'll have a look at Aiken's place, just in case, and run down to the school as well. I'll look into all the old regular spots. As sure as I'm sitting here, there are a hundred barrels of the stuff within walking distance. How I'd love to lay my hands on it. Williams has no more idea where it is than I have myself. Only his name is not Williams at all, actually. It is Wicklow. No one from the Board ever suggested I should change my name, use an alias."

"As you are a local man..." I said, keeping every jot of mirth out of my voice. I had decided on no firm plan for informing him (or Wicklow) of the load resting in Rose Marie's cellar. If they could not be led to it by indirection, Rose Marie could always "discover" it herself and tell them. She was to come to me that same morning to see if her services were required. I decided Crites would be the one to discover it. It would do his ego some good, and really I felt badly that he had fallen into such a muddle after I put him on to Williams. We went on to discuss the matter for some time, till Rose Marie arrived. When I heard the knocker sound, I went to have a few words with her privately in the hallway.

"I have decided. Crites is here. Tell him."

"How will I say I found it?"

"Say you heard some ruckus in the cellar late last night, and were too frightened to investigate till daylight. He'll be so overjoyed he won't ask many questions."

She trailed into the room, acting her chore with relish and a certain expertise. The performance that ensued was worthy of Siddons. "Officer Crites! The very person I was looking for!" she exclaimed, then ran forward and latched onto his sleeve in excitement. A nice, professional touch, that. "I have found it! I have won the reward!"

"What? Miss Lock, tell me at once!" Crites replied, grabbing her hands and giving a genuine show of rapture. "Where is it?"

"In my cellar at the Eyrie."

"No, it can't be."

"It is, I assure you. Dozens and dozens of barrels."

It took a deal of assuring, but after five minutes, Crites was confirmed in his belief that by some impossible means, the gentlemen had landed the stuff under his nose, without being seen. That was his interpretation. It did not occur to him for a moment that it had landed elsewhere and been moved. He had a one-track mind.

"We'll go at once and put it under guard," he announced, with his old confidence restored.

"Who will you trust to watch it?" I asked, thinking he would include Williams in the victory.

It was soon clear that his plan was to conceal the find from Williams. He meant to get the senior officer down from Felixstone and put the matter in his charge, but first he had to go to the Eyrie and actually ascertain that the stuff was there. Then he would send a messenger to Felixstone and guard the load himself, with his life if necessary, till it could be carted off safely to the customs house at Felixstone. We had only an office here, not large enough to hold all the barrels. "I wonder Wicklow didn't think to order up a customs house from London while he was about it. I'm sure they would have been happy to oblige him. I'll not say a word till it is in Felixstone or he'll take the whole credit for himself, and *I'm* the one found it. He never confided in *me*, now he shall have a taste of his own medicine, and see how he likes it."

"Serves him right," I agreed.

Crites had entered the house a broken man; he left it triumphant, his chest swollen, his step light and his eyes beaming at Rose Marie. I was pressed to say nothing to Williams, and kept the faith. I did not go into Owens' shop till

is sufficient to turn me against you," I finished up sharply. "All these months you have been deceiving me, when you know how I feel about the smugglers."

"We have been through all that," he said impatiently. "I have given you my word I mean to capture only Miss Sage, and not persecute any of the smaller fish. You agreed to it."

"I did not agree!"

"You haven't said a word of objection since the night I— I told you what I meant to do." He meant "the night I kissed you."

"The matter has not arisen since then. I thought you had abandoned the idea of this work."

"You knew Rose Marie showed me through her cellar. You knew why I went," he reminded me.

This was not easy to explain away, so I ignored it. "Next you will be telling me you mean to diddle Miss Lock out of her thousand pounds," I said, to change the direction of his thoughts.

"There will certainly not be a reward of one thousand pounds paid for the cargo. They might give her a hundred, as a token."

"They will pay her a thousand, if I—she has to go to the highest court in the land! Oh, such a shabby trick! The poster said 'or' cargo." I was still holding the paper, and pointed it out again as I handed it back to him.

"You seem mighty familiar with the poster," he said.

"Who is not, by this time? I have been reading it carefully, thinking there was not a doubt in the world that Miss Lock would win the reward. There can be no other logical interpretation put on the wording of it."

"We'll see," he said, and shoved the thing into his pocket. "Never mind Rose Marie. I want to talk about us."

"There is no *us* to talk about, Sir Stamford. There is only you, a customs officer, and me a confirmed enemy of the customs men."

"You don't seem to be such an inveterate foe of Crites," he said, looking at me with a calculating eye. "It was you who hinted him to the Eyrie, if I am not mistaken."

This nearly knocked the breath out of me. How could I go on proclaiming myself a staunch foe of revenuemen, after that piece of chicanery? I think, as I look back upon it, that was the first moment Wicklow began to suspect me. Our eyes met, and for a fraction of a second so short it hardly happened at all, there was accusation in his regard, and an acknowledging guilt in mine. A fleeting thing, no more, but very powerful. A seed is a tiny thing, but may grow to any size. In a heartbeat I recovered and answered in a light, dismissing way. "Oh, Crites—you could tell him the time and place of a shipment and he would not catch them. I had not an idea in the world the Eyrie was actually used. With Miss Simon in residence, how should anyone think of it? Merely I was sending him on a wild-goose chase, teasing him, if you like."

The flash of accusation was long gone from his eyes, but my weakness of heart continued till I saw how he accepted my excuse. There was no suspicion left when he asked, "I wonder if *she* could be in on it, Miss Lock?"

"She would hardly have reported finding the stuff in her cellar in that case," I laughed gaily. With relief really, that I had shimmied my way out of a tight corner. "She wouldn't dare risk their vengeance, if she were working with them."

"The reward might have been inducement enough."

"As you are on terms with the woman, why don't you ask her, next time you are looking about her cellar?" I asked sweetly.

"I'll do that, but meanwhile, let us get back to us."

"Don't you think we have discussed enough grammar for one night, Sir Stamford? We have been through the meaning of 'or,' and the lack of any meaning in 'us,' as it relates to you and me. While you go on with this business, I will not see you. As a suitor I mean," I added, as literally not seeing him at all in the town was of course impossible.

"Don't put me in a corner, Mabel. I was sent here to do a job. As an officer, it is my custom to finish what I start."

"You should be more careful of what you start."

"So I should. I admit I have not the relish for the job I had when first I came. When feelings enter into it—I refer to my sympathy for the poor people hereabouts—it is difficult to be objective. Still, Miss Sage is none of these poor, simple people. He is exploiting them, as surely as the government is mismanaging the matter. It is not Porson, as I first thought. I managed to get him drunk one night and he hasn't a notion who it might be. And it isn't Elwood Ganner, though I shouldn't be surprised to learn he used to have a hand in it. He has certainly got a very fine houseful of valuables, and a bigger bank account than even his municipal bribery can account for, but there have been no large deposits regularly for some time. He has been replaced by someone artful enough to do his banking elsewhere. It is not Lord Aiken, for

he isn't here often enough to see to the details. But it's someone of that sort. Some greedy, clever scoundrel, lining his
pockets while the poor take the risks and do the work. I'll
find Miss Sage, and when I do, you will feel differently. You'll
see what sort of a person it is you're defending so staunchly."

"You won't give it up, in other words?" I asked, cutting
through all his rodomontade, and disliking his description
of myself as a greedy scoundrel very much. The "clever" did
not sit so poorly.

"I won't. And I won't give you up either. You'll see. You'll
see I'm right."

What a pusillanimous creature is woman! Why didn't I
lay it on the line. Give it up, or else. Then he would have
had to give up laying siege to me, in at least one of my
incarnations; either Miss Sage or Miss Anderson. I sat with
my lips closed, pouting. I was afraid to push him to the extreme, afraid he'd give up Miss Anderson. "And that, my girl,
is that!" he concluded, in a very firm, masculine and possessive way.

"I am sick to death of this tiresome business," he proceeded
in quite a different tone. "Of more importance to *us* is a new
shipment of muslin that I have got in at the shop. I have set
aside a couple of ells for you. I want you to start preparing
your trousseau."

This was carrying dalliance too far, to be actually urging
me to set up a hope chest, and he engaged to Lady Lucy. He
frowned, and went on, "Why are you looking at me in such
a way?"

I realized then that some of my shock was showing, that
I had my lower lip hanging in amazement. "Surely it is the
custom for an engaged lady to prepare her linens against the
day she finally marries. I hope it won't be too long," he went
on. "Is it that the groom does not usually concern himself so
closely in the amassing of the domestic wares? But as a sometime draper, you know, I have become interested in such
matters. And really we will need an awful lot of things. Oakvale, my ancestral home, is pretty well stripped of goods and
chattels. Anything that could be carried away was sold to
settle the mortgage when my father died. It was the only way
I could hold onto the land and home. We'll build it up again.
You are an excellent manager, and I am a hard worker.
Please don't exclude me from all the shopping. I have already
picked out a tea set and bought it from the traveler last time
he was around. I have it packed in my apartment this minute.

145

I pictured us having tea in the morning from it. A white ground it is, with blue flowers that just match your eyes. Shall I bring it over next time I come?"

"That—that would be lovely," I managed to get out.

"It will, won't it, Mabel? I can hardly wait. Ah, here is Miss Halka with *her* tea tray," he added, then said not another word about trousseaus or tea sets, or Miss Sage either. He stayed for three quarters of an hour, had tea, with a warm, secret smile over the cup at me, took a polite leave and left me totally confused.

Chapter Eighteen

The next days were such extremely busy ones, I hardly know where to begin reciting them. First, and most gratifying to me, there was the matter of Rose Marie's reward, which, as I believe I said, was to be split even-steven among all the gentlemen. A circular came down from London that there was no reward for the capture of the cargo sans Miss Sage. The cargo, at this point, sat in the stableyard at the inn. If they meant to withhold the reward, Miss Sage meant to redeem her cargo. *Ça va sans dire.* Plans were in the process of formation, of which you shall hear more anon. But first we meant to try for the reward. With a little help in composition from myself, Rose Marie posted off a reply, not only to the president of the Board of Trade, who would have filed it in a wastebasket, but with copies to the more prominent newspapers in the city—the *Gazette,* the *Post,* the *Morning Herald,* the *Chronicle,* as well as the *Pilot,* the *Star* and the local news sheet, the Salford *Sun,* which only comes out once a week. This name is supposed to contain a jocose reference to our weather, which leads me to conclude the weather has changed since the paper was named, for we get plenty of sun nowadays. I learned something I had not known before. Newspapers, like people, have politics. It was possible to judge their politics (the papers', I mean) by the coverage they gave Rose Marie's case. The Tory sheets (the *Post* and *Herald*) consigned us to page three or ignored us entirely. The Tories were in office at the time (aren't they always?) and did not wish to embarrass themselves. The Whigs, most especially the *Chronicle,* granted us a central position on page one. As to the Salford *Sun,* there was very little news of any other sort carried that week. Not that it is Whiggish; Ganner is a Tory, but he does not actually *own* the paper, and did not feel the matter reflected on himself at all, so let Sandy Blair print it up in a manner to entertain the local population.

The *Chronicle* even went so far as to send a reporter down to Salford to get the details. Rose Marie, worrying (unnecessarily, I think) that she would be recognized, claimed illness and sent Mr. Hunter to me. He was a very nice sort of a gentleman, well bred and very interested. It was he who informed me as to newspapers having politics. I played up to him a little to ensure good coverage for our case, and had more success than I ever thought. Unfortunately, when the story subsequently appeared on page one of the *Chronicle,* it featured my name in large black letters: SCHOOLMISTRESS ANDERSON TEACHES PRESIDENT A LESSON was the banner, with the next line saying Miss Anderson in Battle with Board of Trade. They carried on this campaign for four days, till the Board was forced to relent and give Rose Marie her money. Quite a *cause célèbre* it was, till a couple of M.P.'s became involved in a duel and pushed us back to page three. Aunt Harvey wrote me the stiffest note you ever saw, calling me to task for my forwardness and mentioning not a word about Sir Stamford Wicklow and Lady Lucy. The note came from London, which explained her seeing the journals so quickly, and perhaps also explained the lack of an answer to my earlier letters, which had been directed to Devonshire.

Meanwhile, before we knew Rose Marie was to get the money, Merrill finally got up off his haunches and arranged for the cargo to be shipped up to the Felixstone customs house. If it were to be necessary for us to reclaim it, the reclaiming would be accomplished much more easily here at Salford, with all my men at hand. Anyone in the town who was not a smuggler was as angry as a hornet to see Felixstone carts and drivers being hired for the trip, while our own men stood by idle. Carts being used by the Customs Department were always marked in chalk with broad arrows commonly called pitchforks, to identify them as being on official business. It was an appropriate symbol, for they had a devilish time getting their cargo on the road. They had the poor sense to commence the operation at a fairly late hour in the afternoon—after three it was. When I drove past on my way home from school (well after four) they had not yet proceeded a yard. We had been busy to ensure there was not a horse or a mule fully shod. While the haulers took their meal at the inn, Jemmie and company attended to it. The blacksmith, whose broad back has been known to carry three barrels upon occasion, was laid low with a bellyache. He did not wish to have a cold, that would require more than one afternoon away from his forge. They would no sooner get a cart loaded than the linchpins would fall out of the arms, and the wheels roll by the wayside. Harnesses snapped, nags (their mash liberally laced with laudanum) keeled over in the middle of the road. It was better than a circus, to observe the revenuemen in disarray. Crites was running around like a chicken with its head off, making notes of it all for future revenge; Merrill blamed it on Crites, and Wicklow just stood there, looking all around, wondering from where the attack would come, and wishing he had his army behind him, I bet. At last he had the brandy put back in the stables for safe-keeping before darkness fell, just as we hoped he would.

We waited till night had fallen before we went after our cargo. With so much confusion in the middle of the main street of the town, Phillips' wagons rolled right along the old sheepwalk, which runs parallel with the main road, a couple of hundred yards behind it. His wagons held empty barrels, which were toted in the concealing darkness to the back of the inn stable, there to replace the full ones. Jem had arranged to loosen the slats of the back wall of the stable, so that it could be done from the outside, at least till the guards had imbibed enough liquor to be sleepy. Jemmie told me later that night that Wicklow came to the stable door twice a minute, to look over the barrels, count them, then return nervously into the street, scanning the darkness for trouble. It was like taking candy from a baby. We left them the front row of barrels—ten—and made off with ninety.

When the reward came through the next day, our captured load proved the most profitable one ever brought in. The government appeared so ridiculous by this time that they managed to suppress the story entirely in their own press. Mr. Hunter ran a couple of articles in the *Chronicle,* writing the whole thing up as a farce, and so it was too. He did it as an analogy of the wedding feast at Cana, where the water was turned to wine. I thought it was very clever, but Andrew said he should be excommunicated for comparing Miss Sage to Jesus Christ.

There were new advertisements pasted up at the post office, removing that expensive "or" and substituting "and." Wicklow was in the boughs about the whole affair. He didn't come to play the organ for a week. He also missed a choir recital to show me a lesson, but as it was the night Mr. Hunter from the *Chronicle* was down from London, his presence was not missed in the least.

My moment of glory was somewhat marred by the worry that I had to find another spot for landing my cargo next trip. To abandon it at the height of the season was unthinkable. I had already been way off schedule with the last cargo, and heard about it from Mr. Pettigrew. He would be looking for another supplier if our supply became too erratic. It was desirable to move our landing spot either up or down the inlet, but we were severely restricted. The Felixstone boys would not like it if we invaded their territory, and there was another group hemming us in at the other side. Like flower-mongers, we gentlemen each have a territory, and invade another's at risk of reprisals.

The third lively happening of that busy period involved my imaginary win of the London lottery, and it also involved to a small extent the solution to my problem of a new landing spot. I deemed the time judicious for announcing my win while the town was alive with the story of Rose Marie's reward, to lessen the questions that might arise. Holding in my hands a letter I had written myself and Pettigrew's envelope from London, I said to Andrew over breakfast, "Andrew, you'll never guess what!"

"Mmmm?" he mumbled, his mouth full of toast.

"I have won a lottery in London."

"Mmmm?", slightly louder and more interested. He drew his eyes from Vergil long enough to pose a mute question by raising his brows.

I explained the history I had composed to account for this windfall, and awaited chastisement from him. What must the gudgeon do but say, "That will make a nice dowry for you, Mab."

"Dowry? Andrew—you cannot think it proper for me to *keep* the money!"

"Why not?" he asked.

"Why—gambling! It would not do for me to keep it."

"Papa lost such a lot in the same fashion, it seems like Fate to me," he replied. I really feared Andrew's morality was slipping. Had I led him on to these erring ways with my sophistry on smuggling?

"No harm done," he insisted, weighing in his mind the pros and cons. "I don't think there is any vice in it. It might be better if you not indulge again, but as you have won, I shan't suggest you refuse the prize."

"Refuse it! I don't intend to. I thought I would use it for charity."

"Charity begins at home," he pointed out, in a rare fit of practicality.

I had to awaken him as to what he wanted me to do with it, and spoke on in a modest voice as to the richness prevailing in *our* home as opposed to that of certain non-smuggling families in the town.

"We are not half so fashionable as the Trebars," he said, then turned as pink as a rose, and hastened on to explain he had only been speaking to Mr. Trebar about some official parish business. Mr. Trebar was not the reason for that blush, however. Sally had certainly got her hands on him, succeeded far enough to have lured him into her parlor. "It would be magnanimous of you to give it to the poor. Very magnanimous. I am proud of you, Mabel, but I think you'd do better to keep it for a dowry."

If Sally had not been hinting to move into the rectory, it was more than I counted on. She wanted me out, and apparently considered I would require a fat dowry to win a husband. I was so annoyed I did not notice for a moment that I had got approval from Andrew to dissipate my fortune on the poor. When the story was issued to our first caller for repetition in the streets, it was to the effect that Andrew was displeased with me, and like a dutiful sister, I had agreed to give the sum up to charity. I had various ends already in mind—an outright gift to the poor, to help them shore up their homes, wardrobes or diets as they saw fit. It was ironic that Sir Stamford Wicklow should be the one to show me a more useful way to spend the money. Like Andrew, he thought if I had a brain at all I would keep it. "A thousand pounds is not an easy sum to come by," he said, a little wistfully, which called to mind his home, Oakvale, denuded of furnishings.

In the end, he was complimentary of my decision to give it all up. "If you are determined to give it away, why not invest it in something that will bring in a regular income for the poor?" he asked.

"I would be happy to, but the funds pay only five percent, and fifty pounds a year is not much to help so many families."

"No, no, I did not mean the funds. Invest it in a fishing boat, and let the poor work it."

The non-fishing uses to which a good stout boat could be put were not long in occurring to me. "What an excellent idea! It will give work to a dozen men—provide a half-decent income for years to come." And provide a very useful tool for Miss Sage when it is not being used for fishing!

I had determined to be very aloof with Wicklow, to keep him at arm's length, but as he was better educated and sharper than the local men, he was the natural one to drive a good bargain in the acquisition of our ship.

"I'll get you into my whisky at last," he congratulated himself. "Felixstone is the place to look. I'll go up myself first and scout out something, then we shall drive up together, for you to make the final decision."

Wicklow had as well as given up being a shopkeeper since his secret was out. He was seen everywhere but at Owens' establishment, where he had hired a clerk for the occasional customer that still went in. The men were determined not to give any business to a customs man, and the girls could not feel Chubby Monk, the new clerk, worth the trip. Wicklow roamed the roads on his mount, with a paper in his pocket allowing him entry wherever he wished to go. He was busily and futilely searching barns, hayricks, stables, woods, everywhere for traces of contraband cargo, or a clue to the identity of Miss Sage. On Thursday he went to Felixstone to look for a ship. On Friday after school he waited for me at home in the saloon.

"I have found a tidy little vessel that the owner is willing to let go for a thousand even. She is worth a good two hundred more, I think, but he is eager to sell, and I knocked him down to a thousand, as it is a charity venture. She is called *Seamew*."

"Very good. When can I see her?"

"You don't work tomorrow. Let us go then."

I tried to vary the day of shipment as much as possible, but the French who delivered it had something to say in the matter. I was stuck with Friday again, a day whose significance was surely known to Wicklow. He would not accept Edna's invitation to remain to dinner, but hotfooted it down to the inn, to see if anyone might be in his cups and utter an indiscreet word. This was about the only way he was likely to hear anything of interest, for no man would help him if he could avoid it. An earlier colloquy with Jemmie had seen arise the decision to dump the load tonight, at a distance not too far from shore. It was to be done just at twilight, before our revenuemen began their patrols. The barrels would be let over the side of the lugger at a predetermined point, all of them attached to a line. They would take bearings as well, of course, but I rather think that so far as my men were concerned, it was Tobin's big red barn up on the hill that told them precisely where to go looking. This meant Williams and Crites (still active) would spend an uncomfortable and fruitless night scouting the coast, while my men slept soundly. In the early hours of the dawn, when our weary revenuers gave up and went home, the barrels would be retrieved. This is accomplished by a process known as "going to creep for them." Men go out in a boat that need not be large (Mr. Morrisey's old fishing smack-cum-barge is the common vessel used in these parts), but it is used for so many other things as well that it does not fall under great suspicion. A weighted grapnel is dragged along the sea's bottom till it catches the line, and the load is hauled in, very carefully and slowly, by a bunch of men ostensibly wading for seafood or floating logs (which can be dried and burned for fuel). When Mark determines the coast is clear, the barrels are rolled ashore and concealed in any spot available. Strung over a stretch of a couple of miles, with each pair of men in charge of a set number of barrels, it is not at all easy to find the load. Our tranter, Phillips, dislikes having to make so many stops, but likes well enough that he gets an extra sum for doing it.

The proceedings went off without a hitch. While Sir Stamford and myself enjoyed a rather cool drive up to Felixstone, my boys secreted the stuff in various caves, holes and hollow trees known to them as intimately as the nooks and crannies of their own homes.

Though I was raised on the coast, I have no great familiarity with ships. A few cruises on Lord Aiken's vessel were about the extent of my nautical life. I took Sir Stamford's word for it the ship we went to examine was a snug little vessel, seaworthy and all such terms, with which he seemed very much at home, for an Army man. It is an odd fact that men seem to know either everything, or nothing. Those who are sharp in business, like Ganner, are the same ones who can discern the points of a good animal, or ship or carriage, or a good dinner for that matter. I have heard Sir Elwood give a fair analysis of *King Lear,* then turn around and speak fluent French to a relative of his wife who was visiting.

I wrote out a check for the thousand pounds, and the owner agreed he would sail her down to Salford for us the next day—Sunday. Unlike land travel, sea travel is permitted on the Sabbath. Indeed it is about the busiest day for pleasure sailing in these parts. It was an enjoyable day, the peak of it not the purchase of *Seamew,* but a meeting with Miss Simpson, outside the draper shop in Felixstone, where I make

153

no doubt she had been having her waist measured up. She came frisking up to Sir Stamford in that playful way she has, like an ill-bred puppy, then stopped short when she saw me at his side. "Oh, Miss Anderson, I did not see you," she exclaimed. As if I didn't know it! It was my escort she had dashed across the road to meet, endangering life and limb in a near-collision with a cartload of pipes. "Congratulations on your fame."

"I was very fortunate, was I not?" I asked.

"Why, it was Miss Lock who was fortunate." I saw it was not to the lottery business she referred, but to the newspaper fight for Rose Marie's reward.

"Very true, but good fortune to a friend is shared."

"How much is she giving you?" the rude creature asked.

"I was not referring to money, Miss Simpson," I answered, on my high ropes. "It is the satisfaction that is my reward. I thought you referred to my winning the lottery ticket when you congratulated me."

"No, I had not intended mentioning *that* to you. I thought a minister's sister would not care to have it discussed that she indulged in gambling." There was a sly shot of her black eyes in my escort's direction at this taunt. "I suppose you are here to spend up the prize. You would not want them to see in Salford how quickly you are bent on dispersing it."

"They will see soon enough," Stamford replied, his words hot in my defense. "Tomorrow her purchase will be on display. Miss Anderson has just bought a ship, which she is donating to the poor fishermen of the parish."

"Is it *you* who bought *Seamew*, Miss Anderson?" she asked, privy to every shred of gossip about the town, you see. "I had heard it was Mr. Williams."

"I am acting as Miss Anderson's agent in the matter," he replied quite stiffly.

"How clever of her to have chosen you for her agent," was the pert answer to this civility.

"Who more appropriate than her fiancé?" he asked.

It was worth every penny of the thousand pounds to see her sharp little face curl up in chagrin. "You don't mean it!" she exclaimed. I expected her to use some vulgar phrase such as my having "nabbed" him, but her commonness did not extend quite so low. "When is the wedding to be?"

"Very soon," Stamford answered for me, and was treated to a dozen congratulations, while I received one long, silent, envious look that expressed most of her malice. She did come

154

up with one parting piece of insolence. "You have known all along then that Mr. Williams was working for the government. A baronet, we hear—is it true?"

"I'm afraid so!" I said, smiling as she turned tail and darted off to spread her news. "That was rather an abrupt and premature announcement," I said when she was gone.

"What a hussy! Nothing better to do all day long than run the streets, looking for men and gossip. I used to be sorry to see *you* working so hard, Mab. I used to watch you set out for school in your little gig each day, and come home in the late afternoon, looking so tired. I wished I could take you out of such a hard life, but when I see what a strong character it has made of you, I begin to think it is wrong that ladies in the general way have so little to do with themselves. I don't know anyone else of either sex, and I include myself there too, who would so selflessly have given up that thousand pounds. And it is *you*, the only working lady in the village outside of Mrs. Aldridge, who handles all of Andrew's charity work for him. You lead the choir and still run Andrew's home. I won't be popular in Salford when it is learned I mean to steal you away from them. They'll have to import half a dozen ladies to replace you." This lengthy encomium was delivered in a strong tone of approval, and with a glowing eye. Then he took my elbow and we resumed our walk.

I was much gratified at such a powerful account of my life, and wondered what he would think if he knew the nights of this paragon were given over to leading a band of smugglers. But when I spoke, it was not of this. "The announcement was still premature." I could not but wonder at his having gone to this ultimate length, when there was still a Lady Lucy in his background. "The news won't be long in reaching Salford either."

"I should have spoken to Andrew first. I suppose you are wondering that I have not taken you to meet my family either. The fact is, there is no one but an aunt who keeps house for me. My parents are dead, my mother several years ago, and my father just after I joined the Army. I was a long time hearing of his death, for I was sent first to Portugal, and I was no sooner home from there than Boney escaped from Elba, and I was off to Belgium, to pick up a bullet in my leg. But it comes on nicely. I shall be able to dance at our wedding."

That's all. Not a mention of any impediment to the match in the way of a previous attachment. Was it possible he had

155

detached himself from Lady Lucy? It seemed wonderfully like it when he went on to suggest we look about the shops for things to add to our hope chest. My mind ran back over our courtship, if that is the proper word for such a bizarre relationship as we had. It had been Christmas night when he first stepped up his flirtations—and how he had backed off at that time when I took him up on it. Frightened to death. Then when he returned from that visit to London, and I half thought he would be a married man, he had begun pursuing me harder than ever. It began to seem he had indeed managed to beg off from his entanglement with Lady Lucy. But what of her letter? A lady did not keep correspondence with a man she had just jilted, or who had jilted her, however politely it had been accomplished. Maybe he *had* left a jacket behind. And maybe (here we were getting into murky maybe's) Lord Hadley had remarried, to explain away Lady Hadley.

I was distracted from these ruminations by my fiancé's pointing out to me a tea set, not nearly so pretty as ours, did I think? "Ours" had been delivered two days ago, and sat in state, still wrapped in paper in my bedroom, where I had the fortitude to do no more that undo the teapot, to see what the shape and pattern were. Certainly they were much prettier than the one being pointed to in the window. On that we agreed completely in the fond and foolish way of true lovers, who compliment themselves by complimenting each other on their taste and refinement. A tour of the drapery shop was de rigueur, to ascertain the wares at Salford were superior and the prices lower, with quite as much earnestness as if we owned the shop. And I, as if I were any normal fiancée, entered into all the window shopping and price comparing, agreeing loudly that nine shillings was too much for the muslin.

"I want to buy something to commemorate this day," Stamford said.

"Buy me some luncheon then. I am famished."

We had a nice dinner of roast beef and raised pigeon pie at the inn, taking a private parlor for the occasion. A wicked extravagance, and done without even thinking about it by my escort, which led me to wonder what sort of poverty he was accustomed to, if this was considered normal. It was very cozy and intimate in our private saloon, with red brocade hangings at the windows, and a fire crackling in the grate, to warm us after having been blown to bits at the wharf. We dined in style, taking claret with our dinner. I could not tackle a dessert, and it looked very good too, a compote of preserved pears and spiced muffins. Stamford had three of them, while I warned him he would turn to fat, in the way of so many husbands, if he ate so much. Really it was very much like a meal shared by newlyweds that day, with no constraint between us. At one point he even put a piece of muffin into my mouth, which is surely the mark of commonness, but it didn't seem like it. I only refrained from returning the compliment by remembering seeing Miss Simpson play that stunt at my Christmas party, while all the old quizzes clucked.

We spoke first of the *Seamew* and its operation, which men would be asked to fish it, etc. Stamford had given it some thought, and told me it would be for the men to maintain it and pay for its operation. When he could reel off those men who were in real poverty as well as I could myself, I realized what a sharp idea he had of which of the men in the village indulged in smuggling, but I managed to include a few of my own boys as well, for there was no saying that I would not have need of the *Seamew* from time to time. I had already decided she would be docked at Jed Oxton's cottage. As well as having a dredged dock able to take it, he was employed when he could get the work on ship repairing, and his wife mended sails. This lent an appearance of legitimacy to my decision, though of course the fact that Jed was also a gentleman was the real reason.

I had noticed Stamford whispering something to the waiter early on, and when the dessert plates were cleared away, I saw the result of this private discussion being brought in. We were confronted with a bottle of champagne, then the waiter backed out of the room, bowing and smiling.

"You are extravagant!" I scolded, still playing the housewife.

"I don't get engaged every day, and I hope you don't either," he replied, handing me a glass. It was the first time I ever tasted champagne. I liked it at once. There was no getting used to it necessary. It went down as easily as water, but more enjoyably, of course. After a second glass, there were still several left to go in the bottle. When Stamford glanced over his shoulder a couple of times toward the closed door, I thought he was making sure we were not to be disturbed, and wondered if he had some other surprise in store for me. A public inn did not seem quite the place for what I thought he had in mind, namely a repeat of the interlude

157

in the darkened vestry of the church. An engagement party seemed the proper time, however. I confess (as this is a confession) that I was not entirely averse. Just as these thoughts were flitting through my giddy head, there was a tap at the door.

I had never seen the man who stood there before. He looked like a merchant, and so he turned out to be. He passed something to Stamford, which he looked at carefully and lifted up in his fingers; then he put it back and took up something else. This went on three or four times, then Stamford drew out his pen, signed something, and the man left.

"What was all that about? I asked, alive with curiosity.

"Of what use is an engagement without a ring?" he said, lifting my left hand. Then he slid onto my finger a little golden ring, with five stones, emeralds and diamonds alternating in a band across the top of the circle. "You see how well I have sized you up—a perfect fit!" he congratulated himself. "I hope you like it?"

It was impossible not to like such a beautiful thing. A deep green fire danced in the three emeralds—they were large enough for that, not just chips. Large enough, but not too large and gaudy. Recalling his frequent references to poverty, I feared he had spent more than he could afford, but disliked even to hint at it, for fear of embarrassing him. "Yes, I can afford it, sweetheart," he said, and laughed. "I have taken up mind reading, so you had better clear your mind of anything you don't want me to know. I am not quite in the basket. Colonels receive a little more than a living wage, and this colonel banked every penny he didn't require. You'd be surprised how little opportunity there was to spend money in Portugal. And we high-class revenuemen, you know, have only to crook a finger and the government pours gold into our pockets. Just ask Crites."

Having reasoned away Lady Lucy, this financial report lifted another load from my mind, which left on it only the burden of my career of crime, which was not quite sufficient to ruin the day. I felt as happy as any lucky girl when she has nabbed (to borrow the word Miss Simpson was too high to use) the man she wants. I knew then how very much I wanted this one. He was all I had dreamed of, all those dull months, years, of tending house for my father, and those wretched months of trotting to the school, of lying in my bed worrying about my cargoes and my gentlemen. I wanted to pull free from all that, and become Lady Wicklow. I wouldn't have minded a bit had it been plain Mrs. Wicklow either.

"Do you like it?" he asked eagerly, just a little worried.

I felt tears stinging my eyes, tears of regret, and joy. "It's perfect," I said, and was as surprised as my fiancé to hear a sob intrude itself into this tender scene.

"Mab—darling, what's the matter?" he asked, taking my hands and drawing me up from my chair.

"Nothing. It's just..." A handkerchief was lifted to my eyes, to wipe away the tear. "It's perfect," I repeated more firmly.

"Not yet," he objected, drawing me into his arms. With this detail taken care of he said, "*Now* it is perfect." He lowered his head and kissed me. Then it was perfect. Perfect swelling bliss for about two minutes. Or longer, or shorter. Such matters are not measured in minutes, but in satisfaction. It was a perfectly satisfying kiss.

It was followed by about the most unsatisfying words he could possibly have spoken. "I will catch Miss Sage, and I will do it very soon. Then we will get married," he announced. You never heard such conviction.

Oh, he would catch me surely, but having caught Miss Sage, he would never in the world marry Miss Anderson.

Chapter Nineteen

Dumping a load and going to creep for it was not the preferred method of importing brandy, as you may well imagine. I disliked to have to use it again so soon, but as the time of arrival for the next load drew near, I was visited with no alternative inspiration. The Eyrie was watched, Aiken's place was suspect, the school likewise. At the back of my mind the crypt kept beckoning, but I did not want the brandy to be there, incriminating Andrew and of course myself. I had the *Seamew* to help me, but wished to let it settle first into a routine, for it was much discussed and watched when it first made its bows at Salford. A nubile heiress could hardly have evoked more interest. Miss Anderson, by the by, was considered next thing to a saint by the poor villagers. I felt like the greatest hypocrite who had ever drawn breath. Really I was extremely unhappy for a lady who was in charge of a highly successful enterprise, doing at last some real charity, and engaged to the man she loved.

About our engagement, no announcement whatever was made or even mentioned once we got home. In fact, Wicklow suggested I might prefer to wear the ring on a chain round my neck for the time being, "till things are settled," as he vaguely put it. I had no real desire to announce it, when it was so uncertain whether a wedding would ever take place. If I was miserable, Wicklow was only slightly less so. I heard from Jemmie that he now ate his meals alone at the inn, whereas he used to be joined by the local men. He was also eyed askance when he walked out, though the girls still smirked at him. His chances of hearing anything about the smuggling were virtually nil.

To return to my cargo, still left without a hiding place! Actually the foregoing is fairly typical of my thoughts at that time. I could not concentrate on one thing without another's intruding itself. Despite the difficulty of thinking straight,

I finally had an inspiration. I chanced to be speaking one day to Mrs. Everett, the purchaser of Fern Bank. She was always hailing me up on the street to complain of a leak or a draft, a spot of mildew or wood rot—always a complaint. Her threnody reached its zenith that day.

"Well, it's finally happened," she proclaimed in a loud, injured, accusing and withal thoroughly satisfied voice. "The roof has fallen in on our heads. It only missed suffocating Jerome and myself in our beds by the good quality of the new canopy I had put on a month ago. 'Thank God,' says I to Jerome, 'I replaced that old frayed rag Miss Anderson had on, or we'd not be alive this day to tell the tale.' Not a square inch of plaster remains on the ceiling—and half the hallway the same. The attics all awash and two bats nesting in them. Jerome is having a new roof put on. It is costing us a fortune, to say nothing of the expense of putting up at the inn while it is being done, for I will *not* tolerate the noise and racket of the infernal hammering all day long. But that is what happens when you buy an old wreck of a place."

"You only get what you pay for," I pointed out. I alit on the news that Fern Bank was untenanted, and inquired to see whether the servants remained. "They are given a holiday. Jerome's valet and my dresser are at the inn with us. I could not do without my dresser."

She had done without one till about two months ago. "Yes, you are dressing very elegantly lately, Mrs. Everett."

She took this for a compliment. "The girls are all gone home for a week," she went on, "but that butler you left behind is still there, to keep an eye on things during the day."

"He stays at night as well, does he?"

"To be sure he does."

One butler was not likely to be out patrolling the grounds at night, and in the worst case, I could confess to Hackley. He would never turn in Magistrate Anderson's daughter, whom he still called Miss Mabel, from having known me from the cradle. My intention, of course, was to have the brandy landed at Fern Bank. The secret hut in the woods, the poachers' hut where Andrew and I used to play smugglers and revenuemen, was ideal for it. There was good landing too at the cove, and Fern Bank was far enough removed from all the regular landing spots that I did not believe it was included on Wicklow's route.

Jem confirmed this. One small difficulty arose in that Jem did not know the hut I spoke of. Fern Bank was never part of his higgling rounds, and poaching there was poor as my father allowed his friends to hunt the place naked. The hut was well concealed too, so that I was by no means sure Jemmie could find it, and there must be no uncertainties at this crucial time. I would have to go with him and show him the spot, but could not do so in broad daylight. It was set up we would go together after dark, a few hours before the shipment came in.

As darkness came on that night, I sat uneasily waiting for nine bells to chime, our hour of departure. Who must take into their heads to come and plant themselves in our saloon that night but the Everetts. Putting up at the inn brought them too close for her to resist coming to lodge more complaints. This turned out to be a mixed blessing, for while it made my departure impossible, I learned one item of importance. After a long dissertation on the evils of buying an old barn of a place—"no saving in the long run—quite the contrary"—the news came forth. "We had to have the stone drywall restacked, six yards of it tumbled down, what a mess! And then there was that old hut in the spinney inviting tramps or smugglers to come in and make themselves at home. *That* is torn down, and a nice little walkway made through the spinney by chopping down half the trees, so I can see from the window what is afoot. With this Miss Sage character running the town, no one is safe."

She was lucky Miss Sage did not brain her on the spot. My eyes flew to Edna. Andrew, it is hardly necessary to say, had slipped over to the church to play the organ as soon as the front knocker sounded. I arose and made an excuse to leave the room. I scribbled off a note for Jemmie telling him to wait for me—Important—and left it at the back door. It was close to eleven before that pest of a woman and her husband finally left us, with the hour so far advanced there was nothing for it but to don my disguise and go with Jemmie to find an alternative storage spot for our cargo.

The night was dark and cold, the wind piercing, but I hardly noticed. Between looking over my shoulder for a follower and trying to set on some hiding place, I was not much bothered by the other minor discomforts. I dickered between stables and icehouse, summer pavilion and fuel house, rejecting each for one reason or another—too small, too open, etc. We arrived half an hour before the lugger, time enough for Jemmie to stay at the prearranged spot to meet them while I scouted and set on the pinery as our spot. Our pinery at Fern Bank was an elaborate affair, Grecian in design, and every bit as elegant as the main home. When Mrs. Everett spoke of tearing it down, she was showing me how little impressed she was with it, but she had of course not touched a single stone in it. She had let the orange trees and pine-apples wilt away, just as she said she had. They stood like desiccated corpses still in their planting boxes, the leaves of the trees rustling in the draft when I opened the door. Those lovely tropical scents that had used to greet one here were all gone, with only a dusty, unpleasant odor from a few fruits not removed before the place was abandoned. There was am-ple storage room, and good concealment from the dead foli-age. The landing went well enough. I caught a glimpse of the lugger as it hoisted sails to depart. Jemmie and I remained behind and breached a barrel together, then he saw me home. Wicklow was just coming out of the school, to hop astride his mount. I could not suppress a smile to think how frustrated he must feel.

I was smiling on the other side of my face Monday morning when I received a summons to the rear door to meet the higgler at the ungodly hour of six-thirty. It was fortunate it was myself who heard his knocking.

"An accident, miss. Don't tell me I should not have come, for I know it, but I wasn't followed. A barrel fell off the tranter's wagon just at the gateway to Fern Bank. The smell is something awful. We tried to lower it with water, but daylight was coming on, and we dared not linger."

"Get a load of manure up there at once, Jem, and drop it. We don't want to draw attention to our new spot. Thank God it's Saturday. If I had to go to work today I could not do it."

"It's too late, miss. The milk carrier was not far behind us. He'll have spread the tale around town as sure as God made apples."

"Very likely. Well, Fern Bank was never meant to be a regular spot, and so long as Phillips is safely on his way to London, we'll not complain. It leaves us without a single safe spot for landing. I'm afraid we must take a holiday for a few weeks."

"Pettigrew won't like it. And it's the good stuff too, from Cognac. Our gentlemen won't like missing out on that."

"They wouldn't like hanging either. We're not far from it."

The accident brought another call from Mrs. Everett down on my head, for some general complaining, the nature of it being that if the roof had not fallen, she would not have been obliged to vacate her home, and the smugglers would not have used her property. It took some sophistry for her to lay the blame on my shoulders, but as that was precisely where it belonged, I did not give her her customary argument.

Throughout this entire interval, Wicklow kept calling, making as much love as usual. "Miss Sage becomes desperate," he crowed on this occasion. "I have driven him as far north as Fern Bank—your old home, Mab. Half a mile farther and he is backed into Felixstone territory. If a couple of the smuggling rings can be put at each other's necks, we revenuemen can retire. It is the fact of the Everetts not being home that caused it, of course. I thought my hinting to Mrs. Everett she should rip down the poachers' hut and thin out her spinney would be sufficient to keep Miss Sage away. They used the pinery, I fancy."

"You'll drive him out of business entirely," I answered, trying to control my rising anger, but noticing too how accurate his guess was. His mind worked so much like my own.

"I hope not. It would be a shame to do that, and miss out on catching him, after all my work. He will only set up business again as soon as I am gone. But he won't stop. He is too bold, too conceited to think I'll catch him. I'll drive him to the wall yet. Oh, by the way—did I tell you I must take a run to London?"

London was irrevocably linked in my mind with Lady Lucy. Would he go to see her? So precarious was our relationship that I never revealed to him any knowledge of his affair with Lucy, though I could have claimed my aunt as the source of it easily enough. "Will you go to see Lord Hadley?" was the closest I came to it.

"Yes, it is a business trip," he answered. Yet surely a baronet did not require to dance attendance on his patron. "Don't mention to anyone when I return. I'll be gone from Wednesday through Saturday, but have not said so or Miss Sage will land a load at the main dock in town during my absence. He becomes brazen enough for anything. Still, I am gaining ground. He had to dump the second last load. If another comes in by *that* method he won't like it. It is troublesome for him. And me. It would require the dragoons to catch them at that stunt."

His mind was all on business. There was no teasing, no
164

flattery, but only a peck on the cheek as he left. This despite the fact we were alone together for half an hour in the saloon. I thought over what he had said, after he left, and had to agree he had run me to a standstill. Ganner, when he dropped by one evening, said as much. "No point taking unnecessary chances. He'll be gone soon enough, and you can resume operations."

Dumping was the only means left. Miss Sage would retire, and let Miss Parsley take over eventually. But for the sake of the men, Miss Sage might as well make use of Wicklow's absence and bring in that profitable load of cognac that fetched such a good price in London.

Chapter Twenty

I have had reason to wonder since if Wicklow was testing me, telling me and no one else he would be gone till Saturday. At the time, my only doubt regarding that gentleman was whether he was going to see Lord Hadley, or his daughter. On Friday night, Crites, ever a load behind in his knowledge, was seen to be centering all his attention on Fern Bank, so it was the Eyrie chosen as our landing spot. I foresaw no likelihood of trouble. I sat in the saloon with Edna, doing some embroidery, when the door knocker sounded at ten o'clock.

Ten is a rather late hour for a social call, yet too early for Jemmie, nor would he come so publicly. The only person I could imagine it to be was Wicklow. My first surge of pleasure had soon turned to fear. He could not be back! He said Saturday!

It was only Ganner, but with such news! "I just thought you might be interested to hear Sir Stamford is back in town. I was on my way home from taking dinner with the Everetts at the inn, and happened to recognize him jogging down the road toward the Eyrie. He told *me* he would not be back till Saturday."

"That's odd. He told *me* he had put out the story he would be back on Friday, and told *only myself* he would be here on Saturday. What is he up to, Sir Elwood?"

"A good question. I don't like the looks of this at all. Why go out of his way to tell the two of us, and no one else, a lie? I believe he has tumbled to it I was involved in the business in the past. Is it possible he knows you have replaced me? I know he has been snooping around at my bank, asking questions that are none of his business. He can prove nothing against me; what we must do is see to protecting you. I suggest very strongly you draw a halt to your work at once. Do you have a load coming in tonight?"

"Yes."

"I was afraid of that. He hoped you would do it—that's why he told you he would be away. Is there anything I can do to help you, ma'am? Where is it coming in? It must be burned off."

"At the Eyrie. If you would be kind enough to drop a note off at the Hesslers', Sir Elwood..."

"Never mind the note. The Hesslers know all about me. The only ones who do, outside of yourself. Have you another spot in mind, or will you dump it?"

"We'll have to dump it. Unfortunate, but as Wicklow himself said, it would require the dragoons to catch us when it is being rolled ashore at all hours and in all different places."

Imagine my chagrin to discover next day the dragoons had been sent down to Salford to trap me! The Prince of Wales' own regiment, the 10th Light Dragoons, were shipped to Salford for the specific purpose of catching me. The *Sun* brought out a special edition to welcome them, for the *Sun* always printed what was proper and never mind whether they meant it. I daresay Sir Elwood saw some prestige to be gained from their presence. I don't know in what manner he made his presence felt vis-à-vis the *Sun,* for the proprietor and editor (all the same person) is a Mr. Sandy Blair, who has no known connection with Ganner. The soldiers were reported to be "on maneuvers,", but for an Army outfit to be executing their maneuvers on the coast in pairs with telescopes lent a very nautical air to the goings-on. No one was fooled, least of all Miss Sage. The only other soul in town who took exception to their presence was Officer Crites. He had not been consulted in the matter. No one ever offered *him* the help of an entire regiment of dragoons to catch the smugglers. And each of them with one of the prized telescopes! Really I think Wicklow might have got one for Crites while he was about it.

So there we were, with one hundred barrels of the best brandy made in France under salt water, in danger of going bleachy and becoming worthless. It would cost me a fortune, to pay for it and get no return, for of course the French must be paid whether I got my money or not. The only thing I could think of to do was to have Jem notify Phillips there would be no load for London, which is rather like killing a midge when a tiger is about to eat you.

As I drove to school Monday morning, my eyes were scanning the spots known to house my gentlemen. It could not be coincidence that each house was guarded by a brace of red-jacketed soldiers. Wicklow knew all my boys, and was taking no chances. They were still there, their postures very little altered, when I returned home in the afternoon. They were very gallant—it is an honor to be in the Prince's own regiment, you understand. One could not complain of their manners. Tuesday and Wednesday this farce continued, while nerves stretched taut. The dragoons worked on shifts; night and day the coast was guarded. I sent out word via Jemmie to my men that nothing was to be done about grappling. Then on Thursday a letter arrived that changed everything.

At last my Aunt Harvey got around to answering my letter. It had been forwarded to her from Devonshire. While I read her brief missive, I saw red—quite literally a red curtain seemed to fall over my eyes, inciting me to a sort of madness. I understand how the bulls feel when they are so aggravated. After a hopeful mention that she would not be reading my name again in the journals linked with smugglers, she got down to the gist of what interested *me*. She had accompanied Lady Lucy to London to meet her fiancé, to arrange final details for her wedding, which was to take place in two weeks. The fact of Lady Lucy's being motherless led her to have pity on the girl. This might also be read as the fact of Lord Hadley's being wifeless and my aunt husbandless, but to me of more importance was that Wicklow had been claiming to receive a letter from the ghost of Lucy's mama. His "business" in London was now explained—wedding business. His sudden eagerness to trap Miss Sage was all of a piece with the rest. He wanted it done in time for the wedding, successfully done, to put him in line for his promotion. It was at this time that I finally realized the full depths of his depravity. Some little glimmerings of it had surfaced earlier, the night of his return from London, when Ganner and myself spoke of his telling lies to the two of us. He knew Ganner had been Miss Thyme; he also knew I had replaced him. There could be no other explanation. He wanted me to bring in that load, and get caught. As well as completing the job he had come to do, it would exonerate him from any moral culpability in jilting me as well. Clearly he would not be expected to honor an engagement to a smuggler. He had suspected me all along, for months. All those long seatings in my saloon, when I thought he had come for romance—it was all business. He did not care a straw for me, never had. I believed the matter of pushing forward even to the point of giving me an engagement ring was to repay me for having so often outwitted him in our business dealings. The matter of the reward for Rose Marie, for instance, and having set Crites onto him. Yes, he knew that—had taunted me about it. He had the effrontery to sit in my saloon, throwing in my face that he had run Miss Sage to a standstill. We would see about that! For about thirty minutes I was too agitated to do a thing but relive the past months, confirming various details in my mind that supported my hypothesis. I could not fathom how I had become such a fool. While I wrestled with my conscience over letting him love me, he had been snickering up his sleeve. He had managed to follow Jemmie to me, obviously. He knew all my men—why should he not know about me? And as if I needed any further aggravation, my aunt's last playful sentence was that she would tell Wicklow, at the wedding, how often I asked for him!

It would have been woefully easy to go into a decline after all this lugubrious thinking. I am proud to say I did nothing of the sort. I was so ashamed of my folly, my weakness, I determined I would not give another thought to Sir Stamford, except to outwitting him. How lacking in pride and determination I had been, only because he claimed he would catch Miss Sage. Well, she had outwitted him more than once, and would do it again, with the dragoons thrown into the bargain.

Instead of sleeping that night, I devised a method of rescuing our dumped cognac before it should be quite worthless. The *Seamew* would have a little mechanical difficulty that prevented her from going out to fish at sea as she customarily did. She would be tentatively repaired, but spend a day cruising close to shore, to ensure she was sound. A leak sounded the likeliest thing. Some caulking must be pulled out, just enough to allow a slow leak, in case Wicklow or the dragoons checked, as I was sure they would do. The day's close cruising would see the grapples pulling the barrels to within wading distance for recovering by my gentlemen. The actual rolling ashore would be done in the dead of night. There weren't *that* many dragoons to thwart us. The entire regiment had not been sent down, but only one company, under the command of Captain Lawson, who reported directly to Wicklow. Wicklow was being called colonel these days, a habit picked up by the locals from the soldiers.

I was not the only person in Salford who was minutely

aware of the dragoons' every movement. They were manna from heaven to the Turner twins and the likes of Sally Trebar, who let off rolling her eyes at Andrew altogether. Did I think to mention Miss Simpson came dashing over from Felixstone the morning after their arrival? You may guess what brought her at this time to billet herself on the Trebars. Awake on all suits, that one. The pair of them kept the roads warm, trotting from one end of town to the other, then down the shore road in Sally's brother's gig, to stop and flirt with each pair of red jackets. Shameless hussies. You wonder what Mrs. Simpson was about, letting her daughter make such a cake of herself.

With Miss Simpson in town, the great secret of my engagement to Sir Stamford was soon public knowledge. He still dropped by to visit me quite frequently, and was greeted with an affability in no way diminished from formerly. I didn't intend to let him know I was on to him. It would be difficult to judge which of us was the better actor. The very evening of the day Miss Simpson came to Salford to join the dragoons he dropped by. Edna, the gudgeon, got up and walked out of the saloon the minute he entered, with a coy mention that we would have things to talk about. I had told her all about his duplicity, for I could not keep it to myself. I believe the brain of an unmarried female develops a soft spot where men are concerned, at about age thirty-five or forty. There is no other way to account for her stubborn insistence that it was all some misunderstanding, for Stamford would not be so low as to hurt me.

"I'm afraid our secret is out, Mab," he began, with an arch smile, as he threw his greatcoat on a chair. He ran quite tame with us by this time, all formality abandoned. "I have received half a dozen congratulations. It is Miss Simpson's doing, of course. I knew as soon as I saw her it would not be long."

"Wretched timing on her part, to proclaim me taken, when the town is full of so many handsome men!"

"Too late for second thoughts, my girl. You're mine now," he declared in a fine fit of passion, and seized me in his arms for an embrace which only a true engagement could excuse. It left me breathless. I suddenly realized which of us was the better performer. There was no way I could match this sang froid.

"It did you no good to make me hide my engagement ring, you see! Truth will out," I teased, trying to match his skill
170

I was ready to attempt pouts, sulks, coy smiles, the whole role of the coquette. I would lay it on with a trowel.

"You're right. True love and a cough cannot be hidden. You might as well wear your ring on your finger now. In fact, you must. Captain Lawson was inquiring of me this afternoon who the ravishing lady is who will never smile at him, and took an oath he would bring you round his finger before he left. I had to pull rank on him, and my rank is only borrowed at the moment. He might take into his head to disobey me on non-military matters."

"Ah, Captain Lawson! Isn't he the *terribly* handsome one, with the black hair and sultry eyes?"

"He said you hadn't even looked at him!" Wicklow exclaimed, simulating jealousy.

"Yes, you see how effective playing hard to get is!" I laughed.

"Mabel, I want that ring on your finger this instant!" he commanded.

"Aye aye, Colonel."

"That's more like it," he said. He lifted the little gold chain I wore round my neck, pulling it up from my collar to look at the ring. "No one has bothered you about the engagement?" he asked.

"No, the excitement of the dragoons, you know..."

He was fumbling with the catch, undoing it, sliding the ring into the palm of his hand. As he put it on my finger, he asked, "How soon can we add a golden band to go with it?"

Some madness compounded of anger, jealousy and spite goaded me to suggest his own wedding date. "How about two weeks from now?"

All my fears that did not really need confirming were confirmed by his reaction. First he laughed nervously, then a strange, amused look danced into his eyes. "Let us make it three weeks, darling. I happen to be very busy *two* weeks from now."

"Another trip to London to dance attendance on the Hadleys, I suppose?"

"Just so. An event of great importance is taking place. I cannot miss it, but it will not interfere with *our* plans. Name any other date you like. Shall I speak to Andrew, by the way? Just for the looks of it. He will not want to hear in the streets his sister is being married, without first hearing it from us."

"Let us wait a little," I parried, not wishing to disturb Andrew with this nonsense. Not that he would care much.

171

"You do not seriously wish to be married so soon, do you?" was his next telling speech.

"I see no point in waiting. I don't think you are very eager to be getting on with it," I pouted, which nudged him into a reassuring peck on the cheek.

"You know better than that. I was only thinking of your job. I assumed you would carry on till the Easter holiday at least. Truth to tell, I was afraid you'd be wanting to go on till summer. I am happy to see you are not quite so conscientious as that." Playing the lover to the hilt, he put an arm around my waist and walked me to the settee. "Now, let us set a date," he said in a firm, commanding manner. "How about the week after Easter? If you give Mrs. Aldridge your notice immediately, you can leave then. I don't think you should leave her with less notice. You will not be easy to replace." He squeezed my fingers, with just a little possessive peep down at the ring.

I was quite simply staggered to see how far he was willing to go. Did he actually mean to have the banns read in church? "You are quite sure you will have caught Miss Sage by then, are you?" I asked in what I hoped was a fairly nonchalant voice.

"Quite sure," was his cocky answer.

"You and the dragoons, that is," I pointed out.

"Lawson tells me they are on maneuvers only."

"Hmm, but when they arrive hard on the heels of your last trip to London, and do their maneuvering on the shore road, one wonders.... But never mind, they are as welcome as the rain here at Salford. Such a goodly number of eligible men."

"Out of bounds to *you*, every one of them," he said.

I did not mention his having returned a day early, and he made some remark about having come Saturday morning, so I said nothing to tell him I knew better. He obviously knew there was a load of brandy dumped, and was at no pains to hide his knowledge. He was playing at cat and mouse, to see if I would let fall any additional information. To prevent that possibility, I discussed a likely spot for our honeymoon. London, I thought. Then he went on to speak of Oakvale. It was all very tentative, however. Nothing was firmly settled, nor did he mention any communication, even by correspondence with his aunt who kept house for him, which was a clear corroboration he had no intention of marrying me. He got nothing out of me about my plans, and told me nothing of his schemes for the dragoons.

The soldiers were a real nuisance to my gentlemen. They got their barrels grappled in close enough to shore to wade for them, but were afraid to bring them in the rest of the way. It could be done under cover of darkness well enough, but the matter of storing them till the tranter could pick them up proved more difficult. Those dragoons were like bees in a flower garden, buzzing here, there, everywhere, looking for the goods. Edna suggested bribing a few of them, but quite apart from disliking to corrupt the King's officers, I did not feel it was at all safe. They would have orders to report any such attempt to Wicklow, perhaps even to be rewarded.

When they were on duty, they were martinets, but on their off-duty hours they were about as accomplished a company of flirts as you ever laid an eye on. They were "walking out" with the local belles within twenty-four hours of their arrival. In fact, Sally Trebar had one of them carrying her parcels home within fifteen minutes of his first step onto the main street. A sudden period of social gaiety descended on us. Families who had never entertained anyone but their own relatives and in-laws were suddenly tossing tea parties and routs for the youngsters, in an effort to unburden themselves of their daughters. Mrs. Trebar ran an unofficial gambling den about twelve hours a day, to get as many red jackets as her saloon could hold. The *real* gamesters among them were not long in finding their way to Holy Hell. When it was learned the officers numbered a couple of noble sons in their ranks (younger sons), Lady Ann, Ganner's wife, invited a couple of nieces down, and held one very dull drum. Salford does not usually bother much with assemblies in the bleak winter months, but spring was declared a few weeks early to maximize opportunities for commingling. The first spring assembly was set for March 5, a Saturday.

As I was quite publicly an engaged lady, even to the extent of Andrew's having mentioned he heard I was going to marry William, and he was very happy about it, I suggested to my temporary fiancé that I would enjoy attending the dance.

His hesitation could not be due to wishing to hide the engagement. I surmised then that it was a reluctance to abandon the coast to Miss Sage's gentlemen. It certainly had occured to me that some decrease of dragoons might be on duty that night, making it a good time for the tranter to take

173

a run down the road to pick up the barrels. I learned to my great surprise that the young ladies of Salford were to be sorely disappointed at the assembly. "I'm afraid I can't take you, Mab," he said.

"You danced in London at Christmas. Your leg is all healed."

"It is not my leg I am speaking of. The fact is, I have forbidden the men, the dragoons, permission to attend, and don't think I ought to go myself in that case. I ought to set an example to them."

My disappointment at the news was double—not to be attending the assembly, and not to get the brandy moved. This double blow kept me, for about ten seconds, from finding it odd he had told me. It was a lie, a trick, was my involuntary reaction. I must hear more, and see if I could discern the truth masquerading beneath the lies.

"I don't want you to mention it to anyone, that goes without saying," he went on, readily enough. "But I know I can trust you. The fact is, there is a load of brandy dumped in the ocean, and my best chance to catch my old friend Miss Sage is when he tries to get it in."

Certainly there was no news in this speech. "Wouldn't he be more likely to try it if you took a few of the men off duty?" I asked, puckering my brow, as though this were really all too deep for my poor faculties.

"He might try it, but with the way it is coming in this time, each hauler responsible for a few barrels, I fancy I might just turn out that I caught all the Indians, and let the chief escape. It is only the chief I am interested in, according to our bargain."

"But if you keep the dragoons on guard, nothing will happen," I pointed out.

"Something will happen. Miss Sage will not let the stuff go bad by remaining too long underwater. He'll try something. Something desperate, I hope. I wonder what it will be."

This was so clearly a bid for information I could only sneer (inwardly of course) at his thinking me such a fool. "What do *you* think he'll do, Mab? You are as clever as anyone in town. What would *you* do, if you were in his boots?"

"I would put it on a ship and float it down to London," I answered, after the requisite period of consideration. I knew this course to be impossible, and deeply regretted too by me. London docks were carefully regulated, and to land it else-

174

where would require a great deal of organization. One's whole crew could not be moved for miles only to land a load.

My fiancé explained all this to me, most patiently. "But it's a good idea," he congratulated. "Tell me another. How else could it be done?"

I confessed myself to be at a loss. "He'll think of something," Wicklow said. "I must admit a grudging admiration for the rascal. He is my nearest and dearest enemy. I know he won't sit back and accept defeat at my hands, without one last effort to beat me. I should be sorely disappointed in him if he did so. But he won't; he is not a coward."

Having failed to pump my brain for information, he was issuing a challenge, I mentally picked up the gauntlet, and verbally closed the subject by diversion. "The girls will be very disappointed. That you aren't letting the soldiers attend the assembly, I mean."

"It can't be done. The move will be made at night. Every hand is needed. And there will be squabbling in the ranks if a few are selected to attend. These noble boys are the very devil to handle. As emotional as a parcel of prima donnas."

"If that is the case, it seems to me you should let folks now, so they can change their plans and make it an afternoon do."

"Not a bad idea," he replied, but with a deprecatory look, as though we both knew this was too farouche an idea to take seriously.

Chapter Twenty-One

I don't really know how it came about that the hour of the assembly was advanced to 3 P.M. It may be that the dragoons themselves prevailed on Sir Stamford to do it when they learned they were not to be let off for an evening frolic. Or it could be—this is more likely, I think—that Wickford told everyone, and not only myself, his plans. Letting on he was confessing to me alone was to con me he didn't know I was Miss Sage. In that case, the advancing of the hour of the party could be laid in Miss Trebar's and Miss Simpson's dish. In any event, the change was known by March 3. It was known as well that only a very small number of guards were to be left on duty, as Miss Sage would never move his ware in broad daylight. "He is like a bat, and only comes out at night," was one of several remarks made during Wicklow' most recent spate of calls.

I sometimes took the notion he was trying to get a rise out of me, for he spoke so often of Miss Sage, usually in an extremely derogatory way. "A parasite preying on these poor, simple people," "an avaricious scoundrel"—such were the terms of opprobrium I had to listen to, while I longed to defend myself. My old arguments were occasionally trotted out to defend Miss Sage, but they were like the cuckoo in June, unheeded. In my uncertainty and depression, I once sank so low as to believe him. I *was* a parasite, a scoundrel, a criminal, sitting at home in comfort while Jemmie and the gentlemen did the dirty work. Then Rose Marie dropped by for a chat.

"As you'll not be using the Eyrie, dear, I think I'll be leaving you. I've got a bit of cash put by, and I see by the London papers a troupe of my old friends has got together to tour the provinces. The Parkham Players, the outfit is called. You'd have heard of it?"

I never had, but raised my eyebrows to denote surprise

176

and delight at her association with the troupe all the same. She rambled on, "The thing is, Pearl talks of nothing but going back to London. She's dull company, I can tell you, but still it would be worse without her. I mean, I wouldn't want to be all alone, with only the backhouse boy for company. And it would look odd, me staying on when my mistress has left and all."

To canvass the possibilities of requiring her services, I asked a few questions about the Parkham Players and life "on the road," as touring was called. "It's jolly. All like one big happy family, laughing and working and fighting together. Of course you're cut off from things. No one knows just where you are, but I'll give you a few addresses in case of an emergency coming up back here."

I could see no reason for her to remain behind, and mentioned I would probably be giving up the business myself.

"That's a pity then. I've enjoyed the run, but there's no point staying around when the show is closed. The lads will miss their bit of extra money, won't they? You don't find many willing to risk themselves to help the poor. It's been a real honor knowing you, dear. Does your heart good to see a body think of someone besides herself for a change. It's just grand the way you've put yourself out for the lads. They were never half so well treated when Miss Thyme was in charge they say. Paid a lot less, and made to take plenty of risks. But there, you've done your share and more, and no one can expect you to turn down a parti like a baronet, I'm sure. Mind he don't go finding out the truth now!" she added with a waggish finger under my nose. With a hearty laugh she was off, promising she would stop in again and say goodbye on her way to join the troupe. Exit Rose Marie. I would miss her.

But as she always could, she had raised my spirits, made me feel I was *not* the scum of the earth Wicklow described. If I had skimmed a little of the cream from the top of the profits of crime for myself, I had done more than most for the poor people. In fact, very little remained to me after buying *Seamew*, renting the Eyrie and not yet having made a penny on the cargo dumped at sea. I expect I made a good deal less than Wicklow with his fat government salary, as far as that goes. No, definitely it had not been financially rewarding. I must pull out before I got caught. I had just one more job to do before retiring, and that was to get that load of dumped brandy to London—do it without getting caught. After some judicious consideration, I decided it would be done on March 5, while the dragoons were being entertained by the young women of Salford. Do it in broad daylight, as a final thumbing of my nose in the face of the customs authorities. When the higgler came to give us the money from Edna's beads (all of a shilling), he was shown into the study for a private discussion.

The greatest planning and cunning must be used, every hauler know his role to a T. To roll the barrels in from their current resting place would not be the work of more than fifteen minutes. The guards were at half-mile intervals approximately. As soon as they had passed a cottage, the men would roll the barrel in and hide it on land. The tranter must not use the regular road by the sea that was under patrol. The old sheepwalk behind the main road, narrow and rutted, was good enough for one trip. The next detail was to get the barrels from the smugglers' places of concealment near their cottages to the sheepwalk. I could see no other way of doing it but to carry the stuff over their backs. It was about a half-mile haul. They had been known to carry it farther, and they would receive double pay, as my parting gift. There would be no complaints. I felt some self-destructive urge to be rid of any money I had made; it was Wicklow's repetitions regarding Miss Sage's greed that led me to it, I expect.

Very well, the barrels would be rescued from the sea between one set of patrols, and carried to the sheepwalk during the next. Let the dragoons come back and pass the cottage in the interval, and see nothing unusual going forth. They would see old Mrs. Oxton mending her sails, Art Peters fixing his fence, for he kept geese and some poultry. They would be treated to a view of Mrs. Edwards hanging her wash—all just as usual, and of course the customary Saturday traffic, already heavier than on a weekday, would be augmented with families coming in to the assembly. Plenty to divert them.

On Friday evening, Stamford called on me in state, bearing a gift of bonbons, like any proper fiancé. I thanked him demurely, and welcomed him to our saloon. I mentioned Rose Marie's departure, spoke of the assembly, and how odd it would seem, to be dancing in the afternoon.

"You mean to go, do you?" he asked, startled. He thought Miss Sage would be taking advantage of the party, you see. Our great minds seemed to think very much alike.

178

"Why, I thought—I took for granted as the party is to occur in broad daylight, you would be able to take me. Will you not?" I asked, preparing a pout in case of a refusal.

"I have given so many men the afternoon off, I planned to take a few trips down the shore road myself," he confessed. Was this a warning to Miss Sage, or a diversionary remark? I rather thought it was an unintended outcropping of the truth, for he looked very surprised at my announcement I wished to attend the assembly. "Business before pleasure, you know," he added, in a humble, explanatory way.

"That's all right, Stamford. Andrew will take me," I assured him sweetly, just presuming on a fiancée's privilege to sulk a little. "If you find a moment free, drop in. I shall save you a dance." What I really wished to accomplish was to let him know Miss Sage would be there, to make the likelihood of moving the brandy less probable.

He felt obliged to utter a few remarks about my standing up with all the dragoons, but I assured him I meant to stand up with only the most handsome, and then only if Miss Simpson and Miss Trebar could spare them.

My men were notified via the usual channel that they would have Wicklow to contend with as well as the dragoons on Saturday afternoon, but our plan was not changed. Mark was to be our wandering scout, his apparent occupation catching moles, with the help of Lady. Phillips was told to have his three wagons at the ready—with a very good cover. He was moving a bachelor's small establishment that day, which was excellent. The few rooms of furniture would sit neatly on top of the barrels. I was to take no active part in the move. If I were indeed under suspicion, what better way to throw dust in any suspicious person's eyes than by going to the assembly, like all the other girls?

My Christmas gown of blue velvet was aired; I was happy for another chance to wear it before the warmer weather came upon us. One has so few chances to wear really fine feathers in a village. The thought darted into my head that Lady Wicklow would have had a dozen opportunities to have donned it over the past few months, but there was no point in repining about what could not be.

Andrew's arm was twisted to secure his escort for the assembly. At two forty-five we left the rectory together, to join the parade en route to the assembly rooms. There was a gay feeling in the town, which always responds strongly to any irregular behavior, especially of a frolicsome nature.

179

We have one of the best fairs on the coast, and our Christmas pageants too are something a little out of the ordinary.

The assembly began well enough. We soon became accustomed to dancing in daylight, but could none of us (we girls) quite get used to having such an interesting surfeit of gentlemen, actually lining the walls, waiting for us to finish with a partner so that they could claim us. It lent a glow to the proceedings, but for Miss Sage, there was another shade not so rosy. How were my men making out? Wicklow was not to be seen, which worried me considerably. The tranter was to pass down the sheepwalk between four and five, giving the party time to be in full swing. To my infinite relief, at three forty-five, Stamford came through the door. There was some satisfaction as well that he found me in mid-waltz with Captain Lawson, who was the acknowledged Lothario of the Army gentlemen among us, as well as the man in charge of the dragoons. Certain ladies, whose names hardly have to be mentioned to you by now, were green with envy to see him stick to my side like a burr, declaring he was Wicklow's special ambassador, sent to guard me. From the flaming eye the ambassador received upon his superior's entrance, it was clear he had made the story up out of whole cloth.

"I see how it will be," Stamford said, as he quite simply grabbed me away from Lawson. "Off flirting with the officers the minute my back is turned."

"When the cat is away, you know," I answered lightly. "Is everything quiet on the shore road?"

"Yes, too quiet," he answered, frowning.

"Everyone is here, at the assembly," I mentioned, lest he get to thinking about the other road, for of course he was aware of the sheepwalk's existence, though it was but rarely traveled.

"No, the smugglers are all at home, doing the usual things."

"No need to worry about them then."

"Andrew brought you, did he?"

"Yes. I didn't even have to use duress, but only mention Sally Trebar would be here. I must warn you, however, she will not give him the time of day when there are so many scarlet jackets present, and it is not at all sure he will stay the course. Your escort home would be welcome."

"Did he actually tell you he would be leaving early?"

"No, Andrew does not think to mention such details. You know what he is like. He is probably at home this minute
180

playing the organ. I see he is not here, in any case," I added, looking around the room. "Unless he has gone into the card room for a hand of whist. He will sometimes condescend to a hand of cards."

"Shall we have a look?" he asked, and to my surprise, immediately left the dance floor. Andrew was sitting in a corner with Mrs. Aldridge and the Slacks, a couple in their seventies. These were his chosen companions for an afternoon's entertainment.

"Safe and sound, you see, flirting with Mrs. Aldridge. Did you wish to see him about something?"

"No, not particularly." We returned to the hall and finished our one waltz.

Between the plethora of escorts and Sir Stamford's status as an engaged gentleman, he was not in his customary demand that afternoon. I saw him stand at the room's edge for one set, then when Andrew emerged from the card parlor and went home (without a word to me!) I took the idea Stamford *did* wish to speak to him after all, for he followed him very shortly afterward. I assumed he was arranging with Andrew for one or the other of them to take me home. It was impossible for anyone to have a minute to herself at that party. No less than three gentlemen were fighting over me for the next dance. What a party it would have been, if only I had not so many worries on my head. As Wicklow did not return, I knew he was out scouring the roads for my men. It was a dreadfully nerve-racking afternoon. After half an hour, I was wishing myself at home in my saloon. The officers' importunities ceased to amuse, and only annoyed me. But Jemmie knew I was at the assembly; if he had to see me, he would come here. I remained on and on, my eyes flying every two or three minutes to the clock on the wall—four-fifteen, four-thirty, four forty-five—soon it would be five. Phillips would have completed the pickup and be safely on the road to London.

Then it happened. At five o'clock sharp, an ear-piercing whistle rent the air. Looking to its source, I saw Stamford in the doorway, his face wearing an expression that was new to me. It was the face of authority. Crisp commands were uttered in a loud, clear bark. The dragoons leapt to attention, hastened out the door to assemble themselves magically into columns as straight as a ruler. The orders given were not entirely comprehensible to me, but our local gentlemen explained that they were to make a "forced march" to the camp,

181

there to get themselves mounted and go after "the gentlemen." In some manner, Wicklow had found out my plan. The ensuing brouhaha was hardly less than that which must have followed the interruption of the Duchess of Richmond's ball, when the allied forces were called from the floor to go to meet Napoleon. I had the most nauseating apprehension that I had met my own Waterloo.

Chapter Twenty-Two

It has occasionally been whispered of me that I wear the trousers at the rectory. I believe there may be some truth in it. I discovered in myself that afternoon a streak of something that I have always associated with men, in any case. I did not panic as the moment of truth descended upon me. I was distressed, of course. To remain unfazed at such a time must indicate a lack of average intelligence. I was plenty distressed, but not cast into hysterics, nor anything like it. While the ladies gathered around, chirping and oohing and aahing at the soldiers forming into ranks, I looked for Jemmie, who should be somewhere around, looking for me. I spotted him inching his way toward me, and under cover of the confused scene going forth before us, it was easy to slip into the assembly hall for a private talk.

"What happened?" I asked.

"Now don't panic, miss. It ain't a desperate situation."

"Do I look panic-stricken? Just tell me the facts, Jem."

"He was riding up and down the shore road, Wicklow, looking this way and that, almost as though he knew we was up to something, but we had our scouts out, and he didn't see anything he wasn't supposed to. Then he spoke to one of his lads, and first thing ye know, one of the redcoats was riding back to the sheepwalk. He must of seen Phillips—he was bound to. Then he rides back to Wicklow, and Wicklow hotfoots it here, to the assembly."

"And this you call not desperate! It seems to me it is not far from it. You've given Phillips word to abandon the cargo and proceed with his load of furniture? Perhaps some of the men can roll a barrel or two to safety. At least they will not be caught with the stuff on their premises. It is pretty hard to prove anything in that case."

"The lads weren't of a mind to give up their last load."

"You cannot mean—but what have they done with it? What are the dragoons doing all this while?"

"A message was sent down the line for them to start for town, thinking to stop Phillips as he went from the sheepwalk to the shore road, ye see, for they didn't know we were on to them. I'd have got to ye sooner, but I had to wait and see what they meant to do. I've had Phillips turn his rig around and go back the other way."

"What is the point of that? When the tranter does not come out of the sheepwalk at the expected time, they will not be long in overtaking him. They are mounted on some of the fastest horseflesh I have ever seen. Where is Phillips intending to take the loads?"

"To Oxton's."

"The *Seamew*?" I asked.

"Aye. I figured there was time to get it aboard and cast off before the redcoats tumbled to what was afoot. They'll waste a while marching to camp to get their nags."

"We are going in circles. It will be dumped again, and grappled for again, and have to be..."

"Nay, they ain't about to dump it again, miss," he told me. "She's been under water long enough we can't lower her again, or she'd be bleachy."

"We can't sail the load to London. You know the place is crawling with customs men."

"Nay, miss, they's coming here, to Salford. That's all."

"I think you have run mad. Wicklow will claim the right to board and search the *Seamew,* and all this runaround has been for nothing. There isn't time to get it to the crypt, and I won't use it in any case. He already knows I am Miss Sage."

"It's Andrew he suspects. He shadowed him home from the assembly, and he's been keeping a mighty close watch on him of late. But I didn't think ye'd use the crypt this time, miss. Ye'll have to come up with another idea."

My mind was a perfect vacuum. Another idea was nowhere in sight. All the regular places as well known as an old ballad, and not more than half an hour to find our spot and move the load. It was impossible. That Wicklow suspected poor innocent Andrew was bouncing around there too, disconcerting me to no small degree. The *Seamew* would dock in the bay, the stuff could not be carted far enough away to be safe before Wicklow was back, or had a deputy back.

"No, you'll have to burn them off. Don't let them land before dark. In fact, I think you'll have to swim out and board the *Seamew*, Jem. No, better take a rowboat; it is too cold. I don't see any other way. Tell them they are to go fishing till well past dark. We'll bide our time and see where it is safe for them to land, and give the signal. What is Phillips doing after he unloads the brandy? Where does he take the load of furnishings he has?"

"It's only going to Stalkley, three miles inland. He can be back tonight."

"Good. Does he come right back?"

"I thought it best to tell him to, in case we needed him."

"Excellent. Meet him, or have your brother meet him, and direct him to go to the inn and wait word there. We may want him on a moment's notice."

"I'll get word to him. And the *Seamew*, she's to loiter round shore, or what?"

"No, send her out a bit, and come back around eleven, to do her loitering under cover of darkness. We'll have to do some sharp scouting to find a safe spot for her to land. A pity we could not take her farther down the coast, but we don't want a war with the smugglers from Harwich on our hands as well. That's all we need. Where is Crites, by the way?"

"He's gone to Felixstone to buy a telescope, miss," Jem answered with a grin.

"Good God, I wish Wicklow were as easy to fool."

"Ye'll think of something," Jem told me, with a confidence which I own seemed badly placed. Then he dashed off, to do just as he was bid.

The evening of the fifth of March was an evening I would not care to have to relive. As I could be of no use in town, I went home, to sit on pins and needles, running to the front door every two minutes, to look up and down the road, for nothing in particular, then up to the bell tower, to view the *Seamew*'s progress. From the front door I saw considerable darting up and down the road by the dragoons, all looking harried, excited and very determined. From the bell tower I saw the stern of the *Seamew* growing smaller and smaller, and I also saw Jem rowing up to his own dock, carrying a string of fish. He had taken time to pick up the family's supper during his errand!

At eight-thirty we sustained a short visit from Wicklow, who came for no other purpose than to insult us, if his behavior was any indication. He asked for Andrew, not myself, though I remained in the room as a matter of course. He did not outright accuse my brother of being Miss Sage, nor, I believe, did Andrew ever imagine for a moment the point of the questions put to him. To myself and Edna, there could be no doubt of his meaning. There were sly compliments on our elegantly furnished saloon, so well done on a churchman's salary. Three hundred pounds a year, he believed Porson had mentioned. There were innuendos about the oddity of a churchman professing the view that laws were not to be regarded if one did not care for them. Even, at the nadir of the visit, there as an imputation that absentmindedness was a cunning disguise for a criminal. None of this fazed Andrew in the least. He answered in his own hapless fashion, turning the compliment on the saloon to myself, and to the last charge replying that he did not think he was absentminded precisely. When he tried to turn the talk to organ, Wicklow arose brusquely and headed to the door. I took a step after him—pure instinct, as I wanted him to leave more than I wanted anything else in the world at that moment. "I'm sorry, Mab," he said, and looked at me. I think there was pity in his eyes, but there was determination in the set of his jaw.

"Seems to be in the devil of a bad skin tonight," Andrew said. "Daresay it's this business of trying to catch the smugglers. Or have you and he had a falling-out, Mab?"

"A little disagreement is brewing," I answered, which satisfied my brother.

"That is a pity. I know how you feel. I don't suppose you noticed whether Miss Trebar was taken home from the assembly by Officer Milne?"

"I don't think so, Andrew," I answered, sorry to see his passion for the chit continued unabated.

At ten, Jemmie came to the back door, to tell me Wicklow had men posted all along the shore road—every man on duty, from the far side of Fern Bank right to the sea in front of our own house and the church, with added strength at such suspicious points as Aiken's, the Eyrie, the school, etc. All my old haunts. The safest thing would be to dump the load, bring the *Seamew* into dock at Salford and consider the business finished. But such an unsatisfactory conclusion for the illustrious career of Miss Sage! I wished a pinnacle for myself, not a defeat. This was no retaliation for Stamford's fast-approaching marriage to Lady Lucy either. What a waste it would be if we should dump the load, only to land at Salford without a single dragoon there to check us out, for according to Jem, the last man was posted at my own front door, nearly a mile from the dock—well, a good half mile and more. We had never taken a load right into town. No one ever had been so bold, in all the history of the coast, including my old predecessor, Miss Marjoram. It had the daring, reckless, implausible ring of Miss Marjoram to it. I felt a tingle of excitement run right down my spine. Wicklow, awake on all suits, had not thought it necessary to post sentinels in the town proper. The dock was a busy and open spot, but at one or two in the morning—who would be there?

Jem was not due back for half an hour. I could no longer sit still. I put on Andrew's jacket and trousers, tucked my hair under his hat and took a quick dart to the dock to see for myself that even at ten-thirty, there was not a single soul around. I would send word to Phillips to get his wagons down here at once, give the signal to the *Seamew* and get the stuff dispatched to London. This determined, I began scanning the closest buildings for good concealment for the operation. I did not wish to have the carts standing on the open dock the whole time. There was a grain storage depot, the fish market area, the ships repair dock, and there, right next to this, was Owens' warehouse, backing onto the sea. The storefront proper opened on the main street. Between the store and the warehouse was a yard for delivery wagons, but when goods came by ship, they landed their load at the dock. How fitting a thing, if the brandy should be stored in Wicklow's own nesting place. He would not think to look in his own backyard for the contraband cargo. But it would *not* be stored anywhere, if my luck held out; the wagons would wait right in the warehouse itself— a huge building.

My mind was made up in an instant. The only addition to the plan was for a few of my men to cause some diversion up the coast, in the direction of Felixstone. Wardle's fishing boat was the diversion hit upon. Wardle's place had in all probability been searched already, for I had learned from Jem that all the smugglers' homes and premises had been thoroughly ransacked. By now, Wicklow knew the brandy was on the *Seamew,* but he could only know it by induction— suspect it strongly, in other words—so he would still be leery of any untoward move by any of my men. The night was dark and still, oppressively so. The naked eye could not spot the *Seamew,* but I knew she was there, hovering within sight of our signal—a dark lamp, whose cover would be raised three times, to signal a safe landing.

The *Seamew* had orders to return to shore around eleven. She would not be there sooner, for if the gentlemen had a fault, it was a little too strict following of orders, without using quite the ingenuity one could hope for from the likes of Jem. I went home and sat like a spider, hiding in the window crack, waiting for her prey to set foot in her web, except it was Jemmie I awaited. He came, approved my plan and left to follow instructions. Wardle and his son were to take their boat out, or make as if they meant to, which would hopefully occupy several dragoons in preventing him. As the hour of landing drew near, I could not sit at home. This was the crisis, the most outrageous stunt I had tried yet. If my men were to be caught, I would be with them. Back on with the trousers and mask, and off to the dock, after first saying goodnight to Edna and pretending I was about to go to my bed. I personally took the dark lamp from Jem and raised the lid: once, twice, three times, then retired to the shadows to wait.

"Phillips should be here. What can be keeping him?" I asked.

"I'll nip up to the tavern and see."

It was lonely and frightening, standing all alone, waiting, but I was not long alone. When Jem came back, he said, "He can't come. He's being watched. There's a dragoon in the taproom with him. He'd have orders to follow Phillips if he moved an inch. I gave him a sign not to come."

As he spoke, the lapping of the waves hitting a prow was heard, the white sails soon discernible through the misty haze. Jem went forward to tell them they must leave again. Some evil genie urged me to interfere. I called him back. "We'll land it while we can, Jem. Can you break the lock on that warehouse belonging to Owens? We'll store it in there. I've seen by the window it is as well as empty—plenty of room."

"Do ye think we should, miss?" he asked, wide-eyed at my gall.

"I do, and I only hope we will have as clear a coast to get it out again in the near future as we have to put it in."

"We'll manage somehow," he chuckled, shaking his head and crowing a little.

The landing went off quietly, quickly, with not an unnecessary word spoken. When the last barrel was within, Jemmie closed the door, reassembled the lock to an appearance of normalcy, and the men disappeared into the shadows, to go home, leaving the *Seamew* docked at the public wharf overnight.

"Ye don't think ye should have the *Seamew* taken home to Oxton's?" Jem asked as we slithered home in the shadows of the roadside bushes and hedges.

"I have a pretty good notion how Wicklow's mind works. He won't expect to find the brandy anywhere near the ship. The public wharf is the safest place we could leave it."

"Blimey, I hope ye're right, miss."

"So do I. Keep your fingers crossed." I disliked to ask him to pray in such a criminal cause.

Chapter Twenty-Three

The Sabbath dawned bright and cool. Wicklow was in the choir loft in the morning, as was Jemmie, nor was the congregation below us in the seated section noticeably smaller. A sort of unofficial truce was in effect on this day of much-needed rest. Wicklow, knowing Miss Sage would not a second time move in broad daylight, was waiting. We all of us went about our customary activities as though in a trance that day—waiting, watching, hoping, planning. For myself, most of all it was a day of planning. Wicklow would have seen the *Seamew* at the public dock on his way home last night, so I had her moved in the early morning back to Oxton's. He had gone aboard and searched her before he came to church. My scouts told me all this, told me he had detected the lingering trace of brandy, which vexed him even more than *not* detecting it on Wardle's vessel the night before. He was understandably in a wretched mood that morning. He hardly sang a note, but kept looking down into the church, mostly at Andrew, with a pensive look on his face.

When the service was over, he said only, "I must leave at once, Mab. I'll look in on you sometime this afternoon, if I may?"

"I expect to be home all day," I answered, trying for an air of nonchalance. I did not feel calm enough to try for any information.

"Will Andrew be home as well?" he asked.

"As far as I know, he will."

He directed a strange look on me, questioning, uncertain—sorry. He *did* think Andrew was Miss Sage. I had been sure it was myself he suspected. Perhaps he thought me an accomplice. And was Andrew the parasite, the greedy monster he had spoken of earlier? I could not think so. I could almost pity him in his dilemma, except that his wedding was so near. To get his promotion, he would turn Andrew in. My pity was not overwhelming.

I waged a war with my nerves during that day, as I sat glued to the window, watching the traffic go by at a subdued.

190

sabbatical pace. At about three, with my heart nearly distilled to jelly at the sight, Wicklow came into town and went down to the wharf. If he decided to get to his own living quarters through the warehouse, I was done. I breathed a little easier when he came back up from the dock, turned onto the main street and used the front door. He had not noticed the scent of brandy from the warehouse then. There are few odors that permeate so thoroughly and linger so long as brandy. But then there are few breezes so stout as sea breezes, and it seemed he had not sniffed my cargo out.

I thought he might be freshening his toilette for a call on me, but though I sat on for some time, he did not emerge from the front door, nor did he go to the tavern for dinner. His servant was seen to dart from the doorway in the general direction of the school, down the sea road that passes all our old familiar haunts. He could be going anywhere, most probably carrying orders to the dragoons. There was a goodly number of them promenading the main street with the local girls, every one of them trying to see if he could discover anything of interest for Wicklow. As the shadows of evening began to lengthen, Wicklow had still not called on me, nor had he left the building. Of this I am fairly certain, for when I was not there to watch myself, Edna replaced me. She was extremely nervous throughout the whole ordeal. I had the onerous chore of assuring her there was nothing to worry about, while my insides heaved and lurched, like a fishing smack caught in a storm. The sickening thought kept intruding itself too that even if Wicklow had not come out the front door, he might have gone out the back, into the yard, back into the warehouse...

"You are pretty cool," Edna said. "Nothing to worry about indeed, with one hundred barrels of brandy stashed in the revenue officer's own warehouse."

"My name is not inscribed on them, Edna," I reminded her. "Only on Stamford's heart, carved in stone, you see. The worst that can happen is that we lose them—we are not caught red-handed at least."

"You will be when you try to move them. When will you do it?"

"As soon as he budges from that apartment, if he ever does. Only after dark, of course. It must be done in the dark. Phillips went halfway to Ipswich this morning, to have an excuse to be on the road tonight, coming back. He'll hold the

191

wagons outside of town, down the road a bit. The men will have to carry the barrels that far."

"There he goes now!" she exclaimed, grabbing my arm in her excitement. "He is crossing the street! He's coming here! No, he goes toward the tavern. He must be having his mount saddled up. He would not do so only to come here. He must be going out—down the road."

"Thank God for small mercies. Jem's brother will shadow him, and let us know where he goes. I must learn if he has been into the warehouse too."

We were greatly surprised to see him stop off at the little cottage that housed Crites. He could not be asking for help—that was not in character. While we stood watching, Crites came out the door with him, nodding and smiling, and looking mighty pleased about something. They spoke together a few moments, then Wicklow turned his horse down the road, and Crites just stood there in the street, looking after him, but with his chest puffed out in gratification. He held in his fingers what looked very much like a telescope. I wished I had one myself that day. I would not risk any conversation with Wicklow, but Crites was always voluble. I decided Edna and I would take a little walk, to fill our lungs with fresh air, before ostensibly turning in for the night. We threw on our pelisses and bonnets with little regard for appearance, to be sure to waylay him before he disappeared.

"The evenings are still chilly, are they not, Officer?" asked in a friendly way.

"Very chilly indeed," he agreed, with a smile a foot wide. Had I commented on the sudden warmth, I expect he would have agreed with equal relish. A close examination of his smiling countenance told me he had just heard some good news, for the telescope hung loosely at his side, forgotten. No news could be so good to a revenue officer as news of a seizure, unless it would be the capture of the chief smuggler.

As this was my first conversation with him since news of my troublesome engagement had leaked out, he had to congratulate me, and to my surprise, he went on to utter all manner of commendation on Wicklow. "A fine gentleman," he praised. "Wide awake on all suits."

"You have changed your opinion of him since the last time we spoke," I quizzed amiably.

"Ha ha, so I have. So I have indeed. An about-face, you might say, and yourself the same, ma'am, if I may be so bold. But he improves on longer acquaintance. Once it was learned
192

who he was, it was only natural you should try...that is...so very eligible." His comments petered out into silent embarrassment, with his teeth tucked into his lower lip.

"Yes," I agreed. "Now where is that fiancé of mine off to? I saw him speak to you just now." It was clear from Crites' continued friendliness that the word spoken had nothing to do with myself being in any way involved in the business, even through Andrew. "He was to call on me this evening, but he seems to have forgotten."

"Business before pleasure, ma'am. There is big business afoot tonight, as I need hardly tell Sir Stamford's lady."

"Those infernal smugglers!" I nagged, like a jealous woman, peeved at whatever removed her lover from her side.

"It won't be much longer, ma'am," he replied with a knowing nod, almost a smirk, I would call it. "Aye, things will be warmer before this night is over, if we know anything, eh?"

"What do you two dutiful officers know that the rest of us don't?" I asked with an arch smile.

"There can be no harm in telling *you*, Miss Anderson, we shall have Miss Sage under irons before the night is out."

The flesh crept on my scalp. Had I not been wearing a bonnet, I am sure my hair would have stood out six inches from my head. I had to try for a name—try to discover whom they took for Miss Sage. In my distraction, I hit on the one name Stamford had mentioned more than once. "Surely it is not—Porson?" I asked, in a strange, hollow voice.

"I see your fiancé has intimated something of the truth to you. Well, as you know anyway, there can be no harm in confirming it. Yes, it is that villain, Squire Porson. The gall of him, using your boat, the *Seamew,* for his work. The outside of enough. But if he thinks we do not know where he stabled the load, he is mistaken, and so he'll find out when he goes to retrieve it."

A cold dread that Wicklow had been into the warehouse came over me. I could not risk many more questions, but with Crites being a little slow, I must risk this one. "I hope he has not put it in my schoolhouse again!" I charged, hoping he would reply in full.

"Schoolhouse—no indeed! Even worse—a *sacrilege* I'd call it, to use..." Then at the crucial juncture, he stopped. It hardly mattered. It could not be construed as a sacrilege, surely to place it anywhere but on church territory. Stamford had figured out or discovered we sometimes used the crypt, and as he had had no luck in looking elsewhere, he had decided it was in the crypt again.

I had discovered what I had to know. Wicklow knew perfectly well it was not Porson who had put the brandy in the crypt—he knew it was an Anderson who was Miss Sage. What he did not know was which one, and of more importance, he did not know where the load was stored. I complimented Crites on his telescope—I could hardly fail to, when it was being ostentatiously flailed about in a manner to bring it to my attention. Wicklow was the greatest fellow there ever was, for having thought of it, and thought the Board might reimburse him the price if he sent in his bill, explaining for what purpose it had been bought. I finally got away, just peeping over my shoulder to see where Crites went. He had apparently been ordered to take up his guard at a later hour. He went back into his own cottage, using his telescope to look at his door knocker as he went, and fell flat on his face by stumbling over a cobblestone.

"I wonder why Wicklow gave him the name of Porson?" Edna wondered. "It looks as though he means to protect us."

"It looks to *me* as though he were afraid I might talk to Crites, and he did not wish me to discover anything of importance. Now I think of it, who but Porson and us would have access to the crypt?"

"Why would he tell Crites about the crypt if he was afraid he might talk to *you?*"

"He wants him to keep an eye on it. Maybe he even *wants* us to know he knows, to hasten us into moving it. Yes, that is what he is up to. It might have worked too, had the brandy been there."

Jem soon came to report Wicklow had been down the road, stopping to talk to various dragoons, in an excited manner, as though giving them instructions and a pep talk. Those instructions would surely be to surround the crypt in a large circle, and let my men enter, then catch them as they emerged. I gave the order for the men to slip quietly by one's and two's down to Owens' warehouse and hide wherever they could find a dark spot close by, till they received the word to move.

"When will I give them the word? As soon as Phillips has the wagons standing by?" Jem asked.

"Yes, eleven, we told him. I hope he remembers to have a fresh team harnessed up. Those wagons must be well on their way to London before Wicklow figures out what has happened. But we shan't worry much about that. If Miss Sage has slipped through his fingers, he shan't waste much time chasing Phillips."

"That has been a blessing throughout, that he paid so little heed to Phillips. I'll be back to ye later then..."

"No, Jem. I shall be there myself tonight. I'll stay at the rectory—go up to the bell tower and see the dragoons are in place before I go down to the wharf."

"There is no need to expose yourself so, miss. Let me do it," he pleaded. A true gentleman.

"It's our last job. My last chance for excitement. I want to be there."

"I'll take right good care of ye," he promised. "I'll be looking for ye at Owens' warehouse door. If ye don't see me, just meow like a cat, and the boys will pass the word I'm wanted."

"The boys—do they have any inkling who I am, Jem?"

"None in the world. A few of the brighter ones have caught on Andrew is closely watched, and what with the crypt being used and all, they might suspect him, but then they know pretty well how bookish he's always been too, and can't quite believe it. Some of 'em think Porson, but he wouldn't t̲r̲e̲a̲t us so generous as ye've always done. I've been called 'miss' myself a few times for that matter. They don't know what to think, and that's the way we want it, ain't it, miss?"

"Exactly."

By the time I had got up to the bell tower, darkness had fallen. I could see nothing of the men closing in around me, but with some little experience in the business myself, I knew well enough it was easy for a dark-coated person to move unseen on a moonless night. Certainly they were there, lurking behind trees, skulking behind bushes, straining their eyes for a sight of anyone moving, or a sound that hinted at company. They would become cramped, impatient, cold, as their vigil wore on. Was Wicklow there with them? Of course he was. He would no more miss the final act than I meant to do myself. Did he have any regrets, I wondered. I would have a million later, but excitement pushed them to the rear of my mind, in abeyance.

Edna nearly had a heart attack when she saw me in Andrew's trousers and my mask, but I would not be talked out of going. Tonight was too important to me. I left the house by the cellar door, as it is far removed from the crypt, and the shrubbery at its sides offers good concealment. I had made sure all lights were extinguished within. I crouched low, to prevent any shadows against the whitewashed house. A trick I picked up from Jem. I avoided the main street, taking the loop up behind, into the less desirable real estate of Salford. The less desirable was not so much less desirable as it had used to be. The homes of my people in particular sported a few signs of increased affluence, a coat of paint here, new shutters there. Surely it could not be morally *bad* to have helped them? I reached the warehouse, where no meowing was necessary for Jem to find me. He was waiting.

"We're all set," he said. Heartening words! "Phillips is down the road with fresh teams, and there's no sign of the officers."

The warehouse door was opened, the men filed in in pairs, soon to emerge, each with his two barrels of brandy, one in front of him, one on his back, making them resemble some strange, misshapen animals from mythology. We had twenty-five men; each had to make two trips with two barrels. This took some little time, for the tranter's wagons were at the edge of town. The half hour Jem and I waited for their return dragged by on broken wings. We followed them partway down the road, to see they were safely en route, then slipped back to the warehouse, to crouch in the shadows, our ears perked for any sound. We peered up the dock toward the main street, out to sea, in all directions. The cold black air seemed impregnated with danger. Every soughing wind, every tree that snapped its branches, every bit of twig or loose paper stirring in the breeze, every lap and ripple of the ocean held some menace. My own nerves, I confess, were at the breaking point, but through it all, Jem was unperturbed, his main concern being to wonder how long we would have to wait before the enterprise could be reactivated. His guileless chatter was all that kept me sane. After an eternity, the men were back, again easing their way into the warehouse, while I counted them, trying to discern from their outlines which of my men I was looking at. They all looked very much alike, mere shadows in the night. Lady was rather excited by it all, but her muzzle kept her silent. After counting them in, I began counting them out. I was at number nine when a whistle pierced the air.

It struck my heart to ice. I clutched at Jem's sleeve, while the unworthy thought flashed into my head that I should run for home, for I did not believe that we had been seen. It was a fleeting thought only, but an unworthy one. The instinct to survival is more pronounced in women than in men, I

196

believe. Certainly Jem made no move to desert the scene. "A raid," he said, an edge of panic sharpening his usually calm speech. "We're caught dead this time. Make a dash for it, miss. I'll handle things here." His instinct, you see, was not to run, to save himself, but to protect *me*. I began to see I had no right to the trousers I was wearing.

What generosity, what chivalry—I can still not think of a word kind enough to describe that advice that came spontaneously from Jemmie Hessler, a street urchin still in his teens. How many of those who call themselves gentlemen with the more usual connotation of the word would have done the same? It must be for such as Jem the phrase Nature's Gentleman was coined. He made me thoroughly ashamed of myself, I can tell you. But there was no time for philosophizing, with dozens of men flashing out at us, coming from all directions, except from the sea. Every tree, every bush, every corner of fence and it seemed nearly every pebble and stone of the road concealed a dragoon, some of them wearing the rough outfits of laborers or fishermen.

They descended on us like a pack of wolves, to devour my band. There was some scuffling, a few blows exchanged, but as the dragoons carried guns, flight was the saner course for my boys to follow. Those of them who were lucky or swift enough to flee did so. Poor old Jed Foster, who is really too old for the game, but who needs the money, was captured. Jemmie and I recognized him at the same time. Without a word, Jem dashed out from our hiding spot, brandishing a homemade weapon he carries, to wit, a fist-sized stone held in a sock. He knocked the dragoon on the side of the head, urging Jed to run. It was a futile gesture. Another man grabbed Jed, and Jemmie too fell into the clutches of the dragoons. Captain Lawson it was who got his arms behind his back in a cruel grasp. He was half again as big as Jemmie, and I think he was possessed of a hitherto unsuspected streak of cruelty as well, for I heard Jem let out a squeal like a stuck pig. The man was twisting his arms, breaking them for all I knew.

Throwing caution to the winds, I was out with a weapon of my own, a hastily grabbed branch it was, which broke in two pieces as soon as I laid it across Lawson's shoulders. It was rotted clear through, snapped like a straw, without even inflicting any pain on that brute. But it had at least diverted Lawson's attack. Jem slithered out of his clutches and knocked him a blow on the side of the head with his homemade weapon. I nearly giggled, it reminded me so very much of the picture of David and Goliath in my old Sunday school Bible. More dragoons were coming toward us. I looked about for another weapon. I never could understand the fascination of war for men, but in that instant, some inkling of it dawned on me. This was wretched, fearsome, *desperate* work, but it was the most exciting moment of my life. I saw what looked like a whip on the ground, and reached over to pick it up, to find it was no more than a broken branch of a bush, but it had some lash in it. Better than nothing, I decided, whipping it through the air to test it. I just turned around to select my quarry, when I was grabbed from behind in a strong pair of arms. Twisting my head over my shoulder to see who had seized me, I looked into Sir Stamford Wicklow's face, smiling with infinite satisfaction there in the darkness, his white teeth flashing. He looked to me like the devil incarnate. It was a diabolical smile.

"At last we meet, Miss Sage," he said, in a gloating voice. He lifted a hand to pull off my mask. With only one hand holding me, I wrenched free and took a run. I did not get far, just around the corner of the warehouse. He caught me by the coattails and threw me against the wall, pinioning my shoulders against the tin wall with both hands. It gave an inch under the weight, making a hollow thump of a sound. He was breathing hard with the exertion. One would not think huffing and puffing could sound jubilant, but his anticipatory smile lent that hue to the sounds coming from his mouth. His right hand came up and jerked my mask aside.

I watched, breathing very hard myself, gasping in fact, while his face—fell. I always thought that a very strange, unlikely expression, as though one's face slid off his head, but I know the true meaning of it now. His cheeks, his lower lip descended visibly, just seemed to drop, while his eyes swelled in disbelief. "Oh my God!" he exclaimed, then swallowed convulsively, looking about ten years old, and totally bewildered. "What the devil are *you* doing here?"

An answer was beyond me, and surely unnecessary. He didn't know till that minute—had never suspected me at all! His shock at seeing me was too genuine, too great to make it possible. He was swift to piece the clues together, however. I watched as the knowledge descended on him. Shock gave way to rapid considering, to *knowing,* while I stood, pinned to the tin wall of the warehouse by his strong hands, by his accusing eyes. Helpless.

"You! It was you all the time," he said in a voice that was still incredulous, higher-pitched than his normal voice. Not loud, but high.

Still speech was beyond me. I could only look, while my poor world fell apart. My enterprise, my gentlemen and my own particular gentleman—all torn from me at one stroke.

"*Why?*" It was a pained howl, almost an animal sound. "Why did it have to be you?" What a strange way to put it. I had thought he would say why did you do it? It sounded almost as though he were blaming Fate, rather than myself.

"You know why I did it," I said, in a shaking whisper. It was all I could manage.

"Get that mask back on!" he ordered, suddenly jerking to attention. In a state of total confusion, I did as he told me. Then he took my arm, very roughly, and pulled me along to the side door of Owens' store, along through the dark passageway to it, without another word. He thrust me inside, where it was very dark. We were at the shoe department. Without any illumination, he dragged me across the shop, to that section where Miss Simpson used to come to be measured for belts. Fumbling in the darkness, he pulled some rope from a shelf and bound my arms tightly behind my back. I was too overcome to inquire what he was doing, and why. "Sit down," he commanded.

"On the floor?"

"Sit!" he shouted, distracted; I sat, on the floor. My feet were then bound up in the same manner as my hands— tightly, that is, not behind my back. "Don't make any noise. I'll be back later," he ordered. Still without being able to see a thing, to see how he looked, I heard him stalk from the store, setting the lock so that the door clanged with the finality of a cell door behind him. Though of course it was locked from the *inside*, and if I could get out of my ropes...

This was easier thought than done. I wiggled my hands, arms, writhed on the floor like a snake tied in knots till I was exhausted. The man was half a sailor, as well as a soldier. Between his two skills, he had tied me up in a way there was no getting out of.

Chapter Twenty-Four

You can do a lifetime of thinking in about an hour, when you are all alone in the dark. As though I were drowning, my life flashed before my eyes—the happy days at Fern Bank, the troubled days when I was helping Miss Thyme, the first flush of victory as Miss Sage, the advent of Wicklow into my life and my work—and now this. Defeat. I warned you of inconveniences before you began this tale. It seems, upon further consideration, too mild a term. The situation was desperate. I was for the gallows. That was inevitable now, but worse, I had led my men into the same trap. I had done it out of a sense of false pride too, out of a desire to thumb my nose at Wicklow, to show him I was not afraid of him and his dragoons, could outwit them, even when they knew within a few miles' radius where I was. If I had done it only out of false pride, it would be inexcusable, but to have to acknowledge, there in the private darkness, that it was half spite and jealousy of Lady Lucy that was the true goad urging me on to this folly was nearly too much for human heart to bear. I thought of Andrew, his career in tatters when it was known what I had done, of Edna, even of Mrs. Harvey. All my family and friends ashamed of me. I was a monster. I have heard it said that witches cannot cry. It even occurred to me that I might be a witch, for my eyes remained hot and dry throughout my ordeal. There was a thing in my throat that felt roughly like a pineapple for size and hardness and discomfort, but my eyes were dry. If a witch, I was a particularly ineffectual one, for I possessed no witchcraft to spirit me out of this slough.

My arms and shoulders ached, my back and legs were cramped, my head throbbed with misery so that I hardly noticed what went on around me. I heard scuffling sounds and shouts from beyond. There were no gunshots, but eventually the tramp of booted feet as the dragoons hauled my gentlemen off to some makeshift guardhouse. Then there was silence for some incalculable length of time. Disoriented in the darkness, I know only that there was no sign of dawn breaking on the horizon yet. There was a scratching sound which I soon attributed to rats, the only evil missing from my ordeal. Soon I became aware that my rat must be a huge fellow, five feet at least, for he was lifting the little window across the room. A cool blast of air blew over me, the shape of a head, a human head, and shoulders a shade darker than the window hole loomed up. My heart beat faster, as I considered whether it were better to remain silent or call for help. I was so far gone that I did not even know it was one of my men, for Wicklow or any of his minions would use the door. "Miss?" the voice called. My tattered little guardian angel, Jemmie, had come to rescue me. Then I ceased being a witch. A hot tear scalded my eyes, the pineapple in my throat swelled to the size of a flawn cake, then dissipated.

"Jemmie—here on the floor," I called.

He scrabbled into the room, worked his way toward me, feeling in the darkness for my bindings. He had a knife—up to all the rigs. In an instant I was cut free, and trying to stand up, only to find my feet and legs up to the knees were numb. A million needles pierced them, making movement impossible.

"Ye've got to get out, miss," Jemmie urged all the while. "They've got half the lads rounded up and taken to the school, but I escaped."

"How did you do it?"

"I had my trusty knife slid into my belt, and they missed it when they frisked us for weapons. None of the lads know who ye are, and wouldn't tell if they did. The revenuers will be coming for me as soon as they notice I've escaped. I must hide."

"Leave town, Jem," I advised at once. Wicklow knew him to be the second in command of the outfit. He had spotted him long ago for my contact.

"Leave town?" he asked, shocked at the very notion of deserting his tribe. "Nay, they'll be needing me worse than ever now, won't they? Who's to rescue the stuff if *I* go?"

"Rescue the stuff! You're mad. If we can rescue our own skins we may count ourselves lucky."

He laughed. How very odd it sounded, in that room of horror, to hear cocky, youthful, authority-deriding laughter.

"Run along home then, miss, and let Miss Parsley handle it," he suggested. "Not to say ye haven't done a grand job, miss, for ye have. I'll never match ye for pure brains, but where nerve is needed, a man's mettle is called for."

My mantle was being snatched from me by a youngster not yet twenty. I didn't lift a finger to retain it. If he had the brass to tackle Wicklow after this night's work, he deserved to be Miss Parsley. Meanwhile, it was Miss Sage that Wicklow wanted, and I was still Miss Sage. I counted on his integrity to stick to our bargain. He had promised me he would let the men go, and arrest only Miss Sage. I meant to make him stick by that bargain, come hell or high water. I explained this to Jem, who hardly deigned to listen at all.

"There's nought to fear, miss. They're taking a list of names at the school, but the lads are none of 'em simpleminded enough to give their right names, but have called themselves Mr. Mulligan and Mr. Prunder, and all the old gaffers who have a wife to testify they didn't leave their fireside all night long. Those fancy Lunnon soldiers ain't going to be able to *swear* to the face of a man they took half a glance at once in the dark, and every one of the lads pulling his face out of shape and twitching his eyes and squinting till his own woman wouldn't recognize him."

"They won't have to recognize them. They will have them safe under lock and key at the school."

"Nay, miss, they've only got the half of 'em. T'other half is out and ready to rescue their mates."

"It's too dangerous."

"Ye're shook up from the bit of a scuffle. There's some risk in it to make it pleasurable, and it's only what t'other half would do, if their places were changed. We've got to find some way first to get them dragoons moved from the school, then we strike and let our lads escape. An attack on the brandy is the likeliest way to lure 'em off. They've got no case if they lose their evidence. We'll not waste time with a real raid. I'm thinking the best thing would be for ye to write up a right fancy note under Wicklow's seal ordering the lad in charge of the prisoners to leave, say, two men on guard, and the rest of 'em to go at the double into town to the inn, where they've got Phillips' wagons and the brandy. Say the smugglers that wasn't caught are making a raid. Then we'll disarm the two guards, myself and Abbie Keely will do it, with a few of the younger lads. We'll have our whole crew to really rescue the stuff tomorrow night."

"It would never work."

"I'll just see if I can find any sort of paper with an official bit of a seal on it," was his answer. He sprinted across the shop, up into Wicklow's private apartment above. Before you could say Jack Robinson he was back, with a candle, a pen and ink and all, for me to add to my crimes by forging a note under Wicklow's name. I had become an underling in my own enterprise, doing just as Miss Parsley ordered me. Hope had re-emerged into my life. The reckless bravado of Jem, ready to tackle any odds, had rekindled my spirit. I knew Wicklow's handwriting perfectly well. Even had some idea how he might word the note. Having heard one of the men call him colonel during the scuffle, I signed it Colonel Wicklow, to add authority to it.

"Where is Wicklow? You're sure he's not at the school himself?"

"He was there. He went to the inn to see to the brandy. I reckon he's questioning Phillips. Phillips don't know a thing about yourself, miss."

This settled, Miss Parsley ordered me home. On this point, I refused to budge. Whatever about the men, *I* had certainly been recognized, and running would do no good, unless I meant to run a lot farther than to the rectory. This option was hastily considered. I might manage to get clean away. But if Jem's brave trick failed, if my men were after all forced to stand trial.... No, my bargain with Wicklow was Miss Sage in lieu of her men, and if Miss Sage ran like a frightened hare, the bargain would be invalidated. I would stay. I finally convinced Jemmie of this, and with so much to be done, he could not remain longer to argue, much as he wanted to. "If he's half a man at all, he won't turn in a *lady*," was Jem's parting shot. "And if he does, I'll rescue ye, miss. Ye've got Miss Parsley's word on it."

It gave me some comfort during the next interminable wait for Wicklow to return. I heard through the walls the rattle of wheels, the sounds of many men at work. He was moving the brandy from the inn to the warehouse—Owens' warehouse, which would be easier to protect than a public place. It occurred to me a goodly number of men were there, leaving no great number to guard the prisoners at the school, which would make Jem's job easier. Maybe he would not require my note. I felt bad about the note. Maybe I was too scrupulous to be a truly successful criminal. My capabilities were slipping badly. I had not thought to have Jem tie me up again before he left. When Stamford came back, I was sitting on the drapery counter, with a candle lit beside me. Of course he looked surprised.

"Why didn't you leave," he asked, "as you managed to escape your bonds?"

One glance told me he was in a furious temper. Unrelenting, harsh, vengeful. "We have a bargain," I reminded him. "I mean to stick to it, and if you are half the gentleman the lowest of my boys is, you will do the same. You promised me you would arrest no one but Miss Sage. Well, here I am. Arrest me."

He turned on me then with a great fit of wrath, all his ire from the past months issuing forth. The angle of the attack surprised me. "You never meant to marry me at all, did you?" was the first question he hurled at me. "You have been making a May game of me from the moment I arrived in this town. You threw your cap at me, lured me on with smiles and taunts and flirtation, only to find out what I was up to, so you could thwart my every effort to arrest a band of criminals who are robbing the country of millions of pounds a year. And yourself the kingpin of the outfit."

I sensed it was the personal part of my crimes that was uppermost in his mind. Not deficient in self-esteem, he (and his vanity) had been dealt a blow at his addresses being treated so lightly. Oh, and to think, they were honest advances all the time! Of that there was no longer any doubt in my mind. Whatever had become of Lady Lucy, she was no longer my foe. I was my own enemy. I gulped down that pineapple that was rising again in my gorge, and tried to explain. "Stamford, I..."

"No, don't try it again," was his advice, delivered in a sneering way. "You overestimate your charms to think to gull me *now*. And to think, I never once suspected you. I thought it was Porson, even Andrew—my God, I *must* have been mad! I made sure it must be Andrew when I saw the stuff being carted into the crypt, but it never once entered my head *you* might be at the heart of it. You told me to my face you approved of the smuggling, threatened to stop seeing me, and still I was too blind to put two and two together. I thought you were defending your brother, if you knew anything of it at all. And even Andrew I took for Porson's dupe. I was sure of it when I saw Jem Hessler darting to the assembly rooms after the tranter's wagon was spotted on the sheepwalk, and thought how very like Andrew it was to want

204

der off after telling Jem to be in touch with him there. I never could fathom whether his absentmindedness was *all* play-acting, or partially real. Andrew was a good dupe for you, was he not? A brother who asked no questions must have been nearly as good as one who performed more active jobs. And then of course his mantle of respectability was another aid."

"I never *used* Andrew—not in any way."

"You saved that honor for *me,* did you? Flattering, I am sure. I shall pander to your pride by telling you something. I felt like Judas Iscariot when I thought it was Andrew I would have to arrest. I was not at all sure I could go through with it. I spent several hours trying to work out some scheme that would spare him, because of you. And all the time, all the while I worried about wounding your sensitive feelings, you were scheming behind my back to make a laughingstock, an ass of me. You were hobnobbing with the lowest ragtag and bobtail in the community, leading them into crime and considerable danger, while you trotted up to your choir loft to lead the hymns, and to dispense your charity at the church door, the picture of maidenly virtue. God, it's disgusting! I thought I had discovered some ideal woman in you, someone so devout, so much above me she spent every waking moment doing good for the less fortunate." His voice had been rising to a crescendo during this long tirade. It lowered to a more intimate pitch. "I felt fortunate beyond human comprehension that a woman like you could love me. Even my poverty did not turn you off. How should it, when you were busy lining your pockets with your ill-got gains!"

"I was not lining my pockets. I *was* helping the less fortunate."

"Yes, the less fortunate Miss Anderson. I still can't make heads or tails of you. The more I consider it, the less understandable it all becomes. You give away the thousand pounds you won, *more or less legally* at the lottery..."

"I didn't win it! It was smuggling money. Why do you think I do this? For myself? Do you find me decked in silks and satins, except when I am trying to impress *you?* I have one velvet gown to my name, and I bought it after you came here. Three quarters of the money goes to help the poor. Warm coats for the schoolchildren, a guinea sneaked home in their pockets, another into the hand of any of the hundreds who drop around at the rectory, and the *Seamew* was my effort to get rid of the bulk of the money, to try to do some good among the needy. I was only trying to help, and doing it pretty effectively too, till you came barging in, making life difficult for me."

"If I have made your life difficult, you may console yourself with the thought you have made mine impossible. I was a happy man when I came to this town, I thought myself in love with a perfectly fine girl, was half engaged to marry her, in fact, but had soon convinced myself it was no more than a passing fancy, after I met you. I have managed to squeak out of that attachment, only to find myself entangled with a criminal."

"Lady Lucy will not be aware of the attachment. You were at pains to hide it for as long as you could."

"For *your* benefit! I had not realized you were the infamous Miss Sage, you see, and took the foolish notion the smugglers might mistreat you if your engagement to me became known."

"Quite sure you weren't afraid Lady Lucy would hear of it?" I asked sharply.

"How do you come to know it is Lucy we are speaking of? I did not tell you. Have you had me followed, or are yc indebted to your aunt for the information? I am surprised you haven't discovered as well the connection was broken off at Christmas. She is to be married to a fellow officer, a friend of mine, in a week's time. Well, how should you think I could be planning to marry you, if I were still engaged?"

"I didn't think it."

He looked up sharply, a puzzled frown on his face. "What is that supposed to mean? I gave you an engagement ring, spoke to your brother, half the town knows we are betrothed. My aunt is having Oakvale turned inside out to make it ready for you; my man of business is this day readying the marriage settlement..."

My regrets were as deep as the ocean. He had meant it all along; had never flagged in his intentions, never swerved in his love. I had brought this all on my own head. It did not lessen my remorse. Suddenly there was a shattering silence in the room, as we looked at each other uncertainly. "Well what did you think was going on?" he asked, in a softer voice than I had heard that night.

"I thought you were using me, to find out what you could about the smugglers. First I thought so. Then later on, I concluded you suspected me."

"I don't know where you could have got any such idea.

never did find anything out from you. You of all people were as close as—Miss Sage. *After* we were officially engaged seems a strange time for your doubts to have increased. No, I cannot believe you doubted—not when we were at Felixstone. Something must have happened." His tones, his whole attitude had softened. He had not only ceased speaking daggers, he was not far removed from tenderness.

"Yes, two things happened. One of them was your lie to Ganner and myself about coming back on Saturday. You must have suspected me then, or why did you tell me that, when you meant to return the Friday night?"

"No, it was not you the message was meant for. I was fairly sure Ganner was a sort of silent partner, or adviser—something of the sort. He tipped me the clue about the plagued sailor, and I figured if I told him a secret, he would see it got to the right party for me. As there was some possibility Andrew was the party we speak of, I told you the same thing. But that was later. You spoke of two things. What was the other?"

"I had a letter from my aunt, telling me your wedding date was set. Lucy's wedding, that is, and as she did not mention any change of groom, naturally I thought... And you said you had to go to London that very weekend too!"

"That is not very flattering, my girl," he said, with a little smile beginning to form on his lips. "I was only going to stand best man at her wedding. She wrote asking me to. In fact, you delivered the letter yourself."

"And you said it was from Lady Hadley, who is dead!"

"You had given me enough roasting about a match with Lucy that I did not wish to mention her name at that particular point. If you will cast your mind back, you were as jealous as a green cow that day, with Miss Simpson in the store."

He looked quite satisfied with the memory. While he was in this softer mood, I rushed on to strike a bargain that would save my men (and possibly me too). "Stamford, about the smuggling. We agreed..."

I had rushed my fence. He frowned to be recalled to troublesome reality. All my wrongs resurfaced, to dampen the tender atmosphere that had been settling in around us. It was back to hard business. "You knew from the beginning this romance could never amount to anything. It was no more than a game for you," he charged.

"We have a bargain! You are to capture Miss Sage, and let the men go free. You *promised!*"

"How can I turn you in? A woman—a lady even! The minister's sister, my own fiancée—a walking saint in the public's view." He riffled his hair with his fingers, till it looked like windswept straw. "And how can I *not* turn you in? I have been here longer than half a year, sent to capture Miss Sage, to halt the smuggling. My career depends on it. I was to be made special assistant to the president of the Board of Trade, to take his place in a year's time when he retires. My whole future depends on it. You know what my circumstances are. I am not independently wealthy. I have my way to make in the world. I have worked damned hard at it. I was baked, broiled, starved, shot at in the Peninsula, and crippled in Belgium. I didn't *buy* my commission; I earned it in battle. Then I was shipped home to inherit this can of worms that no one else would take. Hadley led me to it, for old times' sake, but since my attachment with Lucy is broken off, he is less eager to help me. This is my chance—there has g_ to be some reward in this for all my years of work and misery. *You're* the saint. I'm not."

"Turn me in. A bargain is a bargain."

He looked at me, such a look. Frustrated, defeated. I knew he wasn't going to arrest me before he knew it himself. "Don't think your skirts and your halo will save you. You're already a thorn in the side of the Tories with your campaign to get Miss Lock's reward money plastered all over the papers, making fools of us all. More treachery behind my back!"

"I am not asking for any special consideration," I told him, wearing a self-righteous face. He was not taken in by it.

"It's what you deserve," he said, through clenched jaws.

"What are you going to do?"

"I don't know. I'll have to think about it. Go on home now. You won't mind if I don't offer to escort you, Miss Sage? I think you are quite accustomed to navigating in the dark by yourself."

I figured it would be well to keep him occupied while Jemmie freed my men, just in case some overly conscientious officer decided to check on the authenticity of a certain note bearing Wicklow's signature. I tucked in my chin and peeped up, wearing a frightened face. "I never actually took any part in the smuggling. I just planned it. I don't mean to say I am not guilty, but I am *not* used to going out in the dark alone

But I know you are busy. I'll go alone," I said, with a frightened look out the black window.

"I have to go back to the school in any case. As I am going in that direction, I might as well take you," he replied, with no enthusiasm, but with no hesitation either.

Taking me meant he walked his horse, which would give Jemmie a few extra minutes. I set no very hot pace as we walked along the dark main street, neither of us finding much to say. We arrived at my door without anything of interest having occurred.

"Have you decided what you're going to do with me?" I asked before entering.

"No."

"Don't hesitate to turn me in just because I am a woman."

"That is not why I'm hesitating."

"A deal is a deal. I understood the risks when I struck the bargain with you."

"I wish to God *I* had!" he declared in frustration.

"I am sorry, Stamford. But you know it all came about by degrees. I was already Miss Sage before you arrived, and I could not desert my men then, when they had come to depend on me. If I had known..."

"You knew who I was the minute I landed, I think—the first day in the shop. How did you figure it out? Did my accent betray me?"

"There were many things. Your uncertain accent served to confirm it."

He nodded, not paying full attention to our conversation, to judge by his distracted expression. "Go on in now. Don't run away, Mab. That would be foolish. I don't want to have to set a guard on you, but if it comes to that..."

"I have had one chance to run away already this evening. You can trust me to keep my word."

"In *some* matters," he answered stiffly. Then he mounted his horse and galloped off.

Chapter Twenty-Five

Andrew was sleeping the sleep of the just when I returned. His innocent soft snores came from his doorway. Edna did not sleep at all, but came out to meet me as I crept up to my room. I gave her a calming assurance that things had gone well. There was no point in robbing her of the night's last few hours' sleep, as her bleary looks told clearly enough she had not closed an eye thus far. I lay down on my bed, but for me sleep was not even thought of. I had some serious scheming to do still. Stamford was not inclined to turn me in, but neither was he of a mind to go to London with his tail tucked between his legs and report a total failure. Some sort of a nominal victory must be worked out for him. The brandy— at least he must be allowed to capture that, and keep it safe. But that was not enough. As he had said, he might have had a load of brandy any time. No, he would never be satisfied with so little, nor was it fair he should be, when he had captured Miss Sage.

I thought about it all night long, just occasionally slipping into happier reveries of what might have been. It was a thorny bookkeeping chore, trying to find the right balance to place opposite Miss Sage. What victory was large enough to counterbalance robbing him of that success? I do not like to imply my value was so great that nothing on earth could match it, but in this one particular case, I could think of nothing. It was his future against mine. As the dawn purpled through my window, slowly bringing into focus my dresser, washstand and pitcher, I was no nearer a solution than when I had lain down some hours before.

There was some good news awaiting me belowstairs, and some bad. The good news was that Jemmie and his friend had succeeded in freeing their henchmen. He had as well a plan to put forward for the rescue of the cargo, but I quickly vetoed this. Miss Parsley was not intransigent when he learned my safety rested on his agreement. The bad news was that Lady had been shot in the melee of escaping from the school. "Captain Lawson it was that shot her, but it was *me* he was aiming at, so I guess I'm lucky," he said, looking very sad. "I do believe Wicklow had set him on to watch me in particular. Remember at the wharf he went for me right off, and it was the same there. He took me for Miss Sage, I believe."

I sympathized, but as all the men had got away unscathed, there was more joy than sorrow in our talk. One point did worry me, though. "Lady's body will lead them right to you, Jem. They won't be long in discovering her dark coat is only mud, and Lady is well known to be your dog."

"They never knew there was a dog there. She fell without a whimper, and I didn't leave her behind. She was hurt real bad, but Mark got her home. She died at home. I buried her just before daylight out back of your school. The soldiers were all gone, and I didn't want a new-dug grave so close to home. I laid that pile of bricks from the old chimney over the spot, to hide it. Ye'll see them moved a few yards when ye go to school this morning, miss. Don't be asking any questions about it."

"What makes you think Lawson took you for Miss Sage, Jem? Wicklow *knew* I was her, before he knew I was Miss Anderson. He said so, and he made a beeline for me at the wharf, as Lawson did for you."

"I reckon he's known I'm more than just one of the haulers for quite a spell. Well, ye said he knew I was your contact. I suppose when I darted out at the wharf to give Jed a hand, Wicklow said something about Miss Sage. In the confusion, I daresay Lawson saw no more than that we were both a mite smaller than t'other lads. At the school when Wicklow arrived, Lawson tore up to him whooping and hollering, 'I got him! I shot Miss Sage! The ringleader, the fellow in charge of them all.' Ye never heard such cawing and crowing. Another went on to say, 'That couldn't be the leader. It was no bigger than a boy, or a woman,' which is a pretty good giveaway it was myself, for I'm the shortest of the lads."

"I tried to keep Wicklow with me as long as I could."

"He wasn't there when we gave Lawson the note. Abbie was the one give it to him, said Wicklow had sent him off with it, and it was very important. They don't know Abbie for one of us, as he's a new recruit. No, I stuck around after

211

we sprung our lads, to see what happened, and it was then that Wicklow arrived. They're to send men around to all our houses today, looking for a man with a clipped wing, but they won't find any. And they won't find Lady either. Ye might just check the pile of bricks, miss, to see it's not been disturbed."

"I'm not going to school this morning, Jem. I couldn't face it—I didn't sleep a wink."

"Me neither."

"It's not easy money, is it?"

"There ain't no such thing as easy money, miss. Fishing ain't easy either, nor mole catching, nor poaching. Sometimes it seems to me the only ones that come by it easy are them that don't need it—like Sir Elwood. I'll tell Dame Aldridge ye ain't going, to save ye sending over a note. Teaching isn't easy either, I wager," he added, with a commiserating smile. "Er—did ye manage to bring Wicklow round your thumb last night? What I mean to say—will he be turning ye in?"

"I don't think so. I don't really know."

"Nay, he'll never do it. But how can we save his face? Who can we give him instead of Miss Sage?"

It was a strange way of putting the question, for of course Jem did not mean we claim one of the other smugglers was myself, the leader. It set me thinking all the same. Could we concoct some imaginary person—but then figments of the imagination cannot very well be led to the authorities in chains. They are not so biddable. Jemmie left, but the phantom Miss Sage remained behind with me, occupying my mind till the post arrived.

I took no particular interest in the mail that day, glanced at a couple of letters, hardly having the interest to bother opening them, after paying the charge. One was from my aunt. Now, when it was too late to do me any good, she gave me a long exposition on the gentleman Lady Lucy was to marry, even including a paragraph on the disruption of her affair with Wicklow, which took place at Christmas. Absence had done its work in both cases, making their hearts grow fonder, of someone else. If only she had told me sooner. The postscript was a gratuitous blow. A sly congratulation on my "approaching nuptials," followed by a question mark, and the initials S.W. How had she heard of it? From Lady Lucy, I assumed, who could only have heard from Stamford himself. So I had been acknowledged, discussed—the whole thing, all the visits to London had been on the up and up. We who are guilty ourselves fall into the habit of suspecting everyone and everything.

'I was curious to discover who the other note could be from—done in an ill-formed hand, posted from a place in Berkshire called Wantage. It was from Rose Marie, outlining some new and probably invented accolades she was receiving for her portrayal of Cordelia in *King Lear*. At fifty or so she had graduated from ingenue roles to playing married (young) ladies. Ever discreet, she asked in a way comprehensible to us but not to outsiders how my "business affairs" were prospering, and expressed the wish that she could be here to help me. Her sister, she informed me, had not gone to London after all, but on a visit to Dover, had been offered the post of housekeeper to a squire, and accepted it.

My head spun, my eyes were heavy, I was worried, nearly sick with grief and futile remorse. I lay down on the sofa in the front room for a moment to collect my wits, and fell into a sound sleep. "God moves in a mysterious way His wonders to perform," the poet Cowper tells us. How very true that is. Frowning Providence revealed a smiling face to me in a dream, just as Joseph—or was it Mary—dreamed Herod was coming to slay the baby Jesus. The twisted skeins of my problem were all tangled up in a jumble when I lay down. There was Wicklow wanting to hand over Miss Sage, but not wanting to punish me; Lawson thinking he had shot the ringleader; the other dragoon's comment that it was small enough to be a boy, or a woman; Lady's being shot; the coffin burned on the beach; Rose Marie at the Eyrie, and now in Wantage; Elwood Ganner an accomplice—all these disparate elements jostled round together to fall into a pattern, as if by magic. I truly believe the Divine hand of Providence was there, arranging them for me. It remained only for me to take a hand at the physical arranging of the details myself, and for that chore I would require the agreement (preferably help) of Stamford. That was the vital question now. Did he care enough for me to help Miss Sage in one last deception, or had I disgusted him with my behavior?

The razor's edge is a perilous place to perch. One can endure the anxiety for only so long before she pitches herself purposely over the edge into the abyss below. If I was to be led to prison, I wanted to know it, and if I was not, then I must be about the business of saving myself. I dispatched a note to Sir Stamford Wicklow, respectfully requesting him to come to me at his earliest convenience on a matter of the

213

greatest importance. I took care that it was not the neat, grammatical note of a schoolteacher, but the worried plea of a lady in distress, signed with a humble "As ever, Mabel."

That he had not chosen to come before now boded ill. It was beginning to look as though he meant to turn me in, even if Edna, peeping her head in at the door at two-minute intervals, could not believe it. If he declined the summons, I would dash out and hire the best lawyer Sir Elwood could recommend —one from London if that was what he felt was required. And Ganner could jolly well help me pay for him too as my pockets were virtually to let. I was not kept long on the anxious seat. Within twenty minutes, there was a rattle at the front door. I went to pull Stamford into the saloon and close the door behind us. With so many real concerns pressing on my spirit, I had not performed a careful toilette that morning. I do not recall having so much as glanced in the mirror at all, or dragging a brush through my hair. Between fatigue, worry and scheming, I expect I looked a perfect fright. My disarray had the wonderful effect of inciting my caller to pity. I could see it softening his expression, resting in his eyes when he looked at me. A man full of pity for a woman he loves is the most malleable creature in God's world. His first words warmed my heart. "What the devil are we to do, Mab?" he asked. Not a lover-like speech, to be sure, but an acknowledgment that we were in this muddle together. It was no longer as adversaries that we met.

A terribly unattractive sort of a hiccoughing sound came out of my throat, not planned to con him either, but an involuntary thing, of pure heartfelt relief. I reached out for him, and was crushed into his arms. They felt so strong, so protective, I wished I could burrow into them like a rabbit in his warren, and hide for the next twenty years. His voice was gentle, loving in my ears as he stroked my head, my shoulders. "It's all right, sweetheart. It's going to be all right. We'll think of something. I've been wrestling with my conscience all night, and know I must protect you. It is the right thing to do."

I lifted my face from his shoulder to proffer some thanks, and was soundly kissed. "And if it weren't right, I would do it anyway," he added gallantly. "I have had very little taste for my work the past months. Andrew's philosophy and my own experience convinced me the smugglers were more to be pitied than censured, and as Miss Sage has turned out not to be a bloated parasite after all..." He stopped and looked

214

at me, with a rueful smile and a shake of his head. "Will I ever be able to handle you? I doubt it, but I expect you will handle me very well. So, let us put that agile mind of yours to work, and see what is to be done."

We sat together on the settee, our knees touching, our fingers intertwined, but I did not blurt out my whole plan at once, as I did not wish to reveal the full depths of my conniving, horrid brain. "What I have been thinking," he began, "is that since I cannot hand over Miss Sage, I shall claim he is dead—killed in this last raid. You must help me, Mab. I know full well that was no plague victim burned at the beach. Where did you get the body? Hire a gravedigger?"

"No, Jemmie did it. I only meant for them to bury stones." I marveled anew at how closely attuned our two minds were. I fully expected he would continue to reveal to me my own plan, complete in all its details, but he did not yet have hold of all the necessary facts.

"How is Jemmie? Was he badly hurt when Lawson winged him? I'll have to pay him a visit and proclaim him whole and unharmed. I see he is able to walk at least—saw him with his higgler's wagon an hour ago but he looked very much out of sorts. There is a good deal of suspicion he is the one that got nicked. Deserves it too, forging that note under my name."

"Ahem—actually, Stamford..."

He looked at me with a sapient eye. "Actually he is next door to an illiterate, I expect, and the note was written by *you!* Right?"

"He did *suggest* it."

"I am glad he didn't suggest putting a bullet through me."

"He is not at all vicious. He is fine, by the way. He wasn't hit at all."

"Was he not? They all swore Lawson had got him. When they began speaking of 'a little fellow' and someone mentioned even that it could be a woman, I was sure..." He looked suddenly at me, his jaw dropping. "Mab—it wasn't *you!* It couldn't be...I had just left you here...." His eyes began darting over me, as though to find the gaping wound.

"No, it was Lady, his collie, that was hit. She is dead, poor thing."

"Thank God for that! The men had orders not to shoot, except in self-defense, but they are so eager to get out of this place they became a little overly enthusiastic. I understand Jemmie cracked one of them over the head, however, so I could not read any severe strictures to the men. My hope was that we might claim Lawson had killed someone, who would instantly become Miss Sage, of course. We can hardly elevate a canine to the post of chief smuggler, can we?"

"No, but we could very well transplant Lady to a coffin and invent someone else to be Miss Sage."

"Yes, that is exactly what I was thinking, but *who?* At the very least, it means hustling one of the fellows out of town, never to be seen again. Jemmie, that go-getter, is the natural choice, but unfortunately he is out peddling his fish and glass beads this very minute, seen by everyone. These provincial people are so closely tied to their little town, I expect they'd as soon be hanged as have to leave."

"There is one person who has already left—Rose Marie," I mentioned, glancing at her letter, which sat on the sofa table before us.

He looked up, his eyes alight with interest. "By God, you're right!" he said, quick to leap to my meaning. "But where is she gone? It wouldn't do for her to come prancing back in six months' time."

"I have had a letter from her this morning," I answered, handing it to him. He looked it over quickly.

"She was an actress, was she? That's one more point for you. I didn't tumble to that, though I should have realized when she made her entrance so soon after your trip to London there was some connection. And Miss Simon was her sister, eh? I presume you trust them implicitly, as they were used at the Eyrie. So, we can write to her at Wantage warning her away from Salford. There is no danger she will ever be picked up, living like a gypsy with a wandering troupe of actors, and it seems utterly unlikely the sister will ever return here. Both used phony names too, to further confuse the matter. Yes, Rose Marie will make a marvelous Miss Sage. The only hitch in it is that we shall have to produce a body— a human body—for purposes of identification. I expect it is that old bleater of a Ganner who gives one the certificate."

"Ganner won't give us any trouble. With yourself and him to swear it is her in the coffin, no one will question it."

"We'll need a death certificate—some doctor must be in your hire, I expect."

"No, but we can get a certificate from the doctor without showing him the body. When it is learned she has been dead for over twelve hours, Dr. Shebley will not insist on an examination."

216

"I rather dislike revealing to Miss Thyme what I am about, but then he is hardly in a position to tell anyone."

"We'll leave you out of it. I'll arrange the death certificate and identification from him myself, and he will never be sure whether you..."

"Whether I am a fool or a scoundrel," he finished for me, not very well pleased with this aspect of the matter. "You can't have everything, I suppose. And as I am getting *you*, I shan't stick at giving Ganner a poor opinion of me."

"Your help in the matter will not lower you in his esteem."

"Who else in this town have you led astray?" he asked.

"Everyone but the Reverend Anderson and Squire Porson. The former is incorruptible, and the latter was already gone astray long before *I* met him."

"I still wish Porson had been Miss Sage."

"He hasn't time. His evenings are all taken up chasing the village wenches, and catching them too."

"I've noticed a lot of redheads in town. Rose Marie and Lady will do well enough. She is an excellent choice—having lived at the Eyrie as she did, and its being so closely associated with the smuggling. It will be assumed she moved there for the purpose, as she *did*, of course. Before many hours are out it will be reported she was seen within a mile of town long after she was supposed to have left. Hiding out in the hills, directing operations from afar. People are always helpful in such evidence. Yes, and it will be sworn she was seen around town long *before* she came and took over the Eyrie too. I wonder whether folks make those things up, or imagine them, and talk themselves into belief."

"Legends take on a life of their own after a bit, based on a bit of fact, and embroidered with a lot of fancy."

"Or twisted fact. Miss Sage will be head and shoulders above Marjoram and Thyme, what with having claimed the thousand pounds reward for that load she turned in herself, then turning around and stealing it again. Quite a neat caper. Congratulations, Miss Sage." I dropped a curtsy to acknowledge the compliment. "Her cleverest trick will never be known, I sincerely hope! That she had the chief revenue inspector covering for her, I mean, and breaking every law in the book to save her skin."

"Ah no! Her cleverest trick is that she caught him for a husband!"

"A joint victory, that. The revenue officer simultaneously rid the coast of her presence, and rescued her from a life of crime. The coast of Salford is now free of smuggling." Then he looked at me, while a slow smile spread across his face. "At least until I have my report handed in. You must really twist Jem's arm on that point, my dear. I will look the greatest fool in the kingdom if Miss Tarragon, or whatever he means to call himself, brings in a load while I present my brief to the president of the Board of Trade."

"Miss Parsley would not dream of behaving so ungentlemanly. I'll make him promise a three months' moratorium at least."

"Good. By then some other poor devil will have the chore of seeing to it. I don't envy him. Oh, but I envy *me!*" he said, laughing boyishly, while he examined his reward.

Under his close scrutiny, I became aware that I was utterly disheveled, with my hair falling down and my gown rumpled from sleeping on the sofa. I began tucking up loose ends and straightening my skirt. He sat patiently till I was done, then immediately took me in his arms to undo all my work with an embrace that rocked me to my core. That old electric charge seared through me. I trembled to think how close I had come to missing out on this.

When he was done, he sat back, smiling with satisfaction, but I had still a few details to speak of. "You mentioned a new revenue officer, Stamford. What will become of Crites? Will he be replaced? He was afraid you had given him a bad report."

"I wrote out a report but have not sent it in. I was feeling some sympathy with the smugglers already, that long ago. It is not *only* saving your pretty neck that leads me from the path of duty. I begin to think Crites an excellent fellow for the post, and shall say so in London. There is no need to expand on my reasons for wanting him to remain here. Jemmie will have easy pickings, won't he?"

"It will be the first easy money he ever made. Before we abandon the subject of Crites, why did you tell him Porson was Miss Sage?"

"I didn't intend to do so. I set him to guard the crypt to keep him out of our hair once I had determined the brandy was in my warehouse. He really is the devil of a nuisance, you know. Knocking me out at the Eyrie! And always nagging about a stupid telescope that is of no use whatsoever at night in any case. I guess Mark didn't realize there is an underground passage from the store to the warehouse. Makes you wonder whether Miss Marjoram hadn't a hand in the

"You'll see to it?"

He nodded, the sun glinting off his shiny pate. I was eager to get out into the street, where that same sun was turning the air warm with the first taste of spring. The streets were less full than formerly, when we had the dragoons for company. The Owenses were back in their shop, trying to regain the goodwill of all the smuggling families with a big spring sale. There was a sign in the window as well offering lottery tickets, a highly salable commodity since Miss Anderson's win. I met Sally Trebar and Miss Simpson, the former flashing a little sliver of a diamond she had got from one of the officers before he left. Whether she ever gets the man to go with it is a moot point, but I'm sure I wish her well, as it will prevent her from marrying Andrew, who was certainly ripe for plucking. Miss Simpson was so sweet to me I could not make head or tails of it, till I caught on she was angling for an invitation for tea, to throw her cap at Andrew. In a benevolent mood, I asked her along, and was amazed to see her having better luck than I would have expected. Once Sally had awakened Andrew to the fact that there were young ladies in the world, whose duty it was to marry young gentlemen, he seemed much of a mind to oblige her. Andrew is the sort who has to be hit over the head with a notion before he catches on, and she was hitting him pretty hard. I won't be surprised to see him measuring up her waist one of these days, as she has extended her visit with the Trebars for another fortnight. They must be wishing the girl at Jericho. Edna suggests we have her to stop at the rectory, and if Andrew agrees to such an imposition, I shall assume him caught, and do it.

Miss Parsley is busy forming plans for the reinstitution of the enterprise at a future date. I have his word it won't be for three months. As summer and spring are not the preferred season for the trade, and he will have to renegotiate a deal in London, I expect it will be late autumn before he recommences operations. The first dark of October, I fancy, will be the time. In return for his cooperation in the matter, he has a key to the school and another to the crypt.

Stamford did not return in time for Miss Sage's funeral. Everyone in town who is not lame, halt or blind was there. Sir Elwood took the opportunity to give a little speech, as there were some reporters present, and he always likes to see his name in the paper. It was Andrew, all unknowing, who blessed the coffin, which really did seem terribly profane, considering its contents. I assuaged my conscience and Edna's complaints that I was a heretic by explaining that in a way it *was* Miss Sage who was being buried. She would roam no more over the coast. I felt saddened as a handful of dirt was sprinkled on the box by Andrew. Ashes to ashes, dust to dust. Miss Sage had come from nowhere, and was now being interred, in spirit. Still, like a phoenix, she would rise up again in legend and live for aeons. I shall miss my coast. Stamford and my aunt assure me Devonshire is lovely, but some corner of my heart will always be here, and occasionally my body will come to visit Andrew and Miss Simpson (who will by then be Mrs. Anderson if I can read the signs). Edna, I think, wishes to remain here with Andrew, though I invited her to come with me. She was born and bred here, and says she is too old to begin a new life. I think all the same she does not consider herself too old to be casting sheep's eyes at Mr. Owens' brother, who came back from Bath with them for a visit.

The Salford *Sun* brought out a special edition, a copy of which I kept to show Stamford when he returned. "You will be surprised to learn how you tumbled to it Rose Marie was Miss Sage," I informed him, pointing out the pertinent paragraph. "Your suspicions were alerted by *Miss Anderson's* relating to you the old legend that the Eyrie was used in the days of Miss Marjoram. They wished to introduce my name so they could go on and bring up my little victory regarding the reward money. You may be a hero in London, but you will always be half a scoundrel here, and we take this opportunity to remind ourselves you lost *that* round."

"You can't win 'em all, and I won a round in London."

"You are to be the assistant to the president of the Board of Trade?"

"No! I wouldn't touch the job with a pair of tongs. I want to get out of that policing type of work and join the common herd. Wellington was at Lucy's wedding. He is as sly as they come about a fellow advancing his career, you know, and he takes a little interest in me from having been with him in the Peninsula, and at Waterloo. What I really want is to be a Member of Parliament, as a start at least. I didn't see how I could afford it, for the job does not pay, of course. He arranged a few sinecures for me. Booty, if you like, delayed booty from my war career."

"You don't mean bribery, do you?"

"Lord no! I'll be working like a slave, and deserve *some* remuneration for all my toil. I am not Miss Sage, after all, to work for nothing. Wellington calls any bloody thing you can lay your hands on and keep hold of booty. That is his formal definition, mind. Hadley put in a good word for me too. He was happy enough to see me refuse the Board of Trade offer, as he has it in his eye for Lucy's husband. I'll stand at the next election—a formality only, as the seats are definitely Hadley's to give. A deplorable way of running the country, isn't it? But we must take things as they are, and I do mean to be a good M.P., and work for the betterment of the poor. It will give us some time at Oakvale before we must go to London, and my little bonus for the job at Salford will help fill up our house. We have a tea set to start with in any case."

"If I weren't such a philanthropist, we would have a thousand pounds besides."

"I have no regrets. Don't you have any either. It was a good job, well done. And thank God it is done."

My story is done too. I hope I accomplished what I set out to—to encourage you to take the reins of your life into your own hands, to take a chance. I wish to each of you good fortune, strong hearts and a marvelous husband. So does Stamford.